OXFORD
MENACE

By Veronica Stallwood

Deathspell
The Rainbow Sign

Kate Ivory Mysteries

Death and The Oxford Box
Oxford Exit
Oxford Mourning
Oxford Fall
Oxford Knot
Oxford Blue
Oxford Shift
Oxford Shadows
Oxford Double
Oxford Proof
Oxford Remains
Oxford Letters
Oxford Menace

OXFORD MENACE

VERONICA STALLWOOD

headline

First published in Great Britain in 2008
by HEADLINE PUBLISHING GROUP

1

Cataloguing in Publication Data is available from the British Library

Hardback ISBN 978 0 7553 2641 9

Typeset in Times by Avon DataSet Ltd,
Bidford-on-Avon, Warwickshire

Printed and bound in Great Britain by
Clays Ltd, St Ives plc

Headline's policy is to use papers that are natural, renewable and
recyclable products and made from wood grown in sustainable forests.
The logging and manufacturing processes are expected to conform
to the environmental regulations of the country of origin.

HEADLINE PUBLISHING GROUP
An Hachette Livre UK Company
338 Euston Road
London NW1 3BH

www.headline.co.uk
www.hachettelivre.co.uk

For Michèle Nayman

With thanks to Doris Taylor for the background information
and to Keith Blount for the brilliant software

1

Kate Ivory closed the front door and walked out into a perfect autumn morning. The sky was a deep blue and the air warm, lacking the humidity of August. After pausing to admire the terracotta pots of scarlet geraniums still blooming in her neighbours' garden, she glanced up at the sky: there was a promise of change in the air, a hint of cooler weather to come.

There was also the suggestion of change in the background noise: above the familiar rumble of traffic rose a faint, unfamiliar murmuring.

The pots standing sentinel outside her own front door contained nothing more inspiring than tired leaves and unidentifiable black stalks. And since she'd managed to kill off yet another leafy green plant in her workroom, she was on her way into town to purchase a spider plant – surely a spider plant was sturdy enough to survive her care and attention? Now she mentally added spring bulbs to her shopping list: bunchy pink and green tulips, white narcissi, maybe some tall blue alliums.

She set off up the road, crossed Walton Street and turned in to Little Clarendon Street, lingering by the windows of its boutiques as she made her way to St Giles.

While wondering whether a cowl-necked, slim-fitting top would look good with her new charcoal-grey jacket, she became aware that the background murmur was growing louder. It was coming from the direction of St Giles, and she

1

could distinguish its different elements: the shuffling of hundreds of feet, the approach of discordant shouts and chanting. At the end of Little Clarendon Street a solid figure in a fluorescent jacket had placed himself squarely in the centre of the carriageway, his back towards Kate.

So, Oxford was the scene of yet another demonstration.

She couldn't yet see the marchers, but their voices grew clearer as she walked the remaining yards to where the impassive policeman was standing.

'What's happening?' she asked.

'St Giles is closed for the march,' he replied, without taking his eyes off the road ahead.

Kate had reached the corner by now and had a view down St Giles towards Cornmarket and the town centre. To her right the plane trees, their leaves starting to turn a rusty brown, stretched up towards the perfect blue sky. And in an orderly, unending line came the marchers, placards held aloft, approaching at a steady pace, filling the road for as far as she could see.

'I want to get to Cornmarket,' she remarked. She would look for spring bulbs in the covered market and pick up something for her lunch in the deli before looking for a green houseplant.

'Cornmarket? I'd take a different route if I were you,' the policeman replied.

'There aren't all that many protesters, surely?'

'A few hundred, but they'll be stopping to listen to the speakers when they get to the Science Area.' For a moment he turned to look at her. 'There may be a few scuffles with the onlookers: this particular lot don't believe peaceful demonstration gets them anywhere. Why don't you go home and try again later?'

Kate didn't like being taken for a wimp. She could cope with the odd bit of scuffling, couldn't she? She stayed where she was.

The head of the march was approaching the spot where they were standing, so that Kate could see the man leading it and hear his shouted words:

'What do we want?'

'Stop the torture now!' came the reply from his supporters.

The man's voice rose to a scream and the banner-waving crowd behind him joined in the chant, louder and louder, so that their words reverberated off the walls of the unresponsive colleges that lined the road.

'Stop the torture. NOW!'

They must be demanding the release of the prisoners at Guantanamo Bay, Kate thought. Or maybe they were protesting against extraordinary rendition. Then she read the wording on the placards: 'Stop animal testing'.

Maybe they should rethink their priorities.

When they reached the church of St Giles, the marchers wheeled right into the Banbury Road, and Kate could read a dozen posters carrying the same message following the leaders as they turned right again into the university Science Area.

Kate retraced her steps towards Walton Street. She wasn't going to return home; she would circle back towards the High and hope that she could eventually make her way to Cornmarket. As she passed the shop with the cowl-necked top, the sounds of ragged chanting and the pounding of hundreds of feet echoed after her.

2

On hot and sunny summer days, the younger members of Blake Parker's research group congregated on the laboratory's flat roof to eat their lunch. Now that September had arrived, they were taking a last opportunity to enjoy the sun.

Behind them stood a small wooden hut with a faded sign, 'Canteen', which held a stained wooden table and half a dozen folding chairs, though it hadn't been in use for some twenty years. The hardiest members of the group would drink their coffee and eat their sandwiches inside the hut even on cold or rainy days, but today there was no need. Sam, Kerri and Conor, the youngest and most junior of those present, had pulled the chairs out into the open air to face the sun while they ate, and Greg and Lucy had come over to join them.

Sam didn't usually notice what women were wearing. He was vaguely aware that Kerri looked good in low-cut jeans and a short white T-shirt that contrasted nicely with her suntanned face and arms. But however unobservant you were, you couldn't help being struck by the eye-opening colours of Lucy's wardrobe.

'Anyone seen Candra?' asked Lucy, breaking into his thoughts.

'Didn't she follow us upstairs?' said Sam, thinking that Lucy's clothes today were not only bright but *gaudy*. That slash-necked top in gentian blue made the freckles on her pale skin stand out like frog spawn and her light green eyes gleam like gooseberries. With that sandy hair, she really should think about the colours she wore, and throw away her scarlet-and-black skirt. Now Kerri, he considered, could wear just about *anything* and look really good.

'Don't think I'm keeping tabs on you all,' said Greg, pausing as though expecting the others to smile at the joke, 'but I believe I saw her ten minutes ago, making for the University Parks with her plastic lunch box and bottle of spring water.' He took off his new glasses and started to polish them on a small cloth. He shouldn't have chosen the narrow rectangular black frames, thought Sam; they made his eyes appear closer-set than ever. It might be cool, but it did him no favours.

'Pity about the spring water,' said Lucy. 'She might have let me have some of hers.'

'Don't tell me you're too lazy to walk down a couple of floors to use the water cooler,' accused Greg.

'Don't you bet she's gone to drool over the rowing eights?' said Lucy, ignoring the dig.

'Why? You reckon that even a statistician gets turned on by guys in one-piece Lycra?' asked Conor.

'Yeah, and muscled torsos, gleaming with sweat,' said Lucy.

Greg said, 'I don't suppose she'd know what to do with a muscled torso if it came over and bit her on the ear.'

'She would if the torso belonged to Blake!' said Lucy.

'Thought you'd already warned her off,' said Conor. 'He's your property, isn't he?'

'Candra likes to sit on a bench, feeding the ducks,' said Sam, who felt uncomfortable at the way they were talking about her behind her back.

Conor's narrow face broke into a sneering smile at the idea of Candra being so childish. 'No sign of Blake today, either,' he remarked slyly, still watching Lucy. 'He duck-watching with Candra, you reckon?'

'Blake? He'll be lolling in some panelled hall, nibbling roast pheasant and talking philosophy at High Table. He's a Fellow of Bartlemas,' replied Lucy off-handedly, though Sam could see that Conor's hints were getting to her.

'College Fellows don't discuss philosophy,' said Greg. 'They talk nothing but funding. It's the most important thing in their lives. No funding, no research.'

'They're not all as crass as that,' objected Lucy.

'Good word, "crass",' said Conor. 'Covers most of what goes on here, don't you think?'

'Shut up, Conor,' said Sam good-naturedly. 'Anyway, I don't reckon they'd let this place close down even if the pharma pulled out. We're too high-profile.'

'Don't bet on it,' said Greg. 'They might have no alternative.'

'Anyone got some spare water?' asked Lucy hopefully.

'No. Why don't you drink your juice instead?'

'I like water with my meal, juice after it,' Lucy explained.

'Mental,' commented Conor, who had taken out a cigarette packet and was turning it upside down, unwilling to believe it was empty.

'And by the way, Lucy,' added Greg, 'Blake's already taken. He lives with a partner.'

'Really? How come we've never seen her?'

'Maybe he likes to keep his private life separate.'

For a few minutes there was general chat as Sam reflected that for the past forty or more years people had been climbing up on to this roof and eating their sandwiches in the shed optimistically labelled 'Canteen', and that by following them he was carrying on a venerable tradition. He hid this thought from his friends since he guessed, correctly, that they didn't share his respect for tradition.

'What's that?' asked Greg lazily, polishing an apple on the hem of his sweatshirt.

'Lentil salad,' replied Lucy.

'No, I mean the noise. Can't you hear it?'

The others stopped talking and listened. It might have been a river in full spate, approaching from a distance.

'I can hear people shouting,' said Kerri nervously.

'Sounds like another demonstration,' said Greg, who had worked at the lab for longer than the others and had grown accustomed to such interruptions.

'You mean they're shouting at *us*,' said Kerri.

'Don't let it get to you, Kerri: they're always demonstrating,' said Lucy, opening her can of cranberry juice. 'There's nothing new about it.'

'This sounds like they're serious,' said Greg. 'But I don't think they can get at us up here,' he added quickly for Kerri's benefit.

As the noise grew louder and closer, the five of them left their chairs and clustered by the low parapet overlooking the front of the building.

'I've always been scared of heights,' said Kerri, so quietly that only Sam could hear.

'Hold on to me, I won't let you fall off,' he replied cheerfully, putting an arm round her shoulder.

Conor was leaning over the edge, craning to see up the road, apparently unaffected by thoughts of vertigo.

The sound of the march was growing even louder now as the demonstrators turned the corner and approached the tall concrete and glass blocks of the Science Area. The group on the roof could even make out some of the slogans.

'What's their message this time?' asked Lucy, no longer feigning a lack of interest.

'The usual,' said Greg. 'Death to all scientists. That kind of fascist crap.' He spoke casually, but Sam could see that he didn't like the waves of aggression approaching from the town centre any more than Lucy and Kerri did.

Kerri shivered, and Sam gave her an encouraging hug.

'Greg's right: we're safe enough up here,' he reassured her.

'Maybe. But they're intimidating enough to disrupt our work, and scare off investors, not to mention terrorising the builders and cleaners, and anyone else who's employed by us,' said Greg bitterly. Below them in the street the air was still and the protesters wore T-shirts or open jackets. Up on the roof, there was a breeze that blew long strands of Greg's hair across his forehead, hampering his view of the scene below.

'You're obsessed with money,' Conor told him. 'Why should we care about the fucking investors?'

'Because they pay our fucking wages,' said Greg.

'That's overstating it, surely?' said Lucy. 'We're part of the university. We're supposed to be independent.'

Greg laughed, the sun glinting off his narrow-framed glasses. 'As if!' he said.

'You're saying that Blake's sold us out?' queried Conor. 'We're just a cog in the capitalist conspiracy?'

'STOP THE TORTURE NOW!' By some quirk of the acoustics, the words reached them as though the speaker was standing only a few inches away.

It was the leader of the march, a man with a lean build and a gaunt face, Sam saw, who had raised his head so that he seemed to be speaking directly to the small group on the roof, though Sam was sure he couldn't have spotted them. Flanked by two men built like tanks, both wearing balaclavas to hide their features, the leader, in contrast, was a slight figure, but he left no doubt that he was in charge. As they watched, he turned to say something to one of his supporters, then shouted again, 'What do we want?'

And back came the reply: 'STOP THE TORTURE NOW!'

At least it had interrupted the argument between Conor and Greg, thought Sam.

'This is boring,' said Lucy. 'We've heard all this stuff before.' She glugged down the remains of her juice to prove how unconcerned she was.

'I think maybe we should get off the roof now,' suggested Conor, looking uneasy. 'I don't like the look of that mob.'

'We're safe enough up here,' said Sam. 'And it's a crowd down there, not a mob. Who knows, maybe that bloke's got something new to say. Look.'

The leader had taken a megaphone from his assistant, and they watched as he lifted it to his lips.

'We'll be able to hear better now,' said Sam.

'Oh, great, Sam! You want to listen to the little fascist shit. Don't tell me you're a sympathiser!' said Greg.

'Murderers!' came the amplified, distorted voice from below, making Kerri jump.

'You're putting your hand up to that, are you?' demanded Greg, his face red with anger. Sam noted that Greg enjoyed being a bully when he believed he could get away with it, and liked him less for it.

'Why shouldn't Sam be a sympathiser?' Lucy joined in, liking to see the other two stand up to Greg. 'We're animal-lovers too, aren't we?'

'Yeah, you're right,' said Sam, watching the scowl on

Greg's face. 'We studied biology and environmental science because we're interested in the natural world and how it works. So it's natural that we care about animals. And anyway, I like to hear the other man's argument before dismissing it out of hand.'

'Exactly,' said Kerri, gaining courage from his support. 'I reckon they've got a point. And look at the way farm animals are treated.'

'What's any of that got to do with anything? We're not being threatened by power-mad vegans, are we?' Greg was visibly losing patience with Kerri and Sam. 'And you two may want a rational discussion, but those crazies down there aren't going to stay around and listen while you wave your certificates at them and tell them how much you love the rats in the cages in the basement.'

Kerri screwed up her face like a child about to cry. 'Don't bully her,' Sam started to say, but the activists' leader was getting into his stride and Sam's voice was drowned out by the amplified clamour from below.

The man had his back to them, and by the time his words had ricocheted off the walls of the lab and reached the watchers on the roof, they were so badly distorted, and the echo so resonant, that only his sense of outrage came through to them, and even Sam stopped trying to make out what he was saying.

'Kill them!' shouted someone from the crowd, the high, sharp imperative cutting through the jumble of words. A placard with a crudely drawn message was thrust up in front of the windows. Conor leant forward again and the others clustered round him as he read out: 'Remember Henry. Tortured, blinded, killed.'

'Who the hell was Henry?' demanded Greg, his Canadian accent stronger than usual.

'A macaque monkey,' replied Lucy. 'Captured in the wild and used in experiments. Don't you remember the row when the story hit the tabloids?'

'Never mind the frigging monkey! They should arrest these people,' shouted Greg. 'Why are they free to threaten us? Who allows them to disrupt our work like this?'

'Protesters have rights too,' said Kerri, speaking up again. Her face went pink as the others looked at her. 'They're allowed. They can say what they like, however much you disagree with them. Freedom of speech . . .' Her voice trailed away.

'It's all right for you to be so liberal-minded. You're only with us for a few more weeks, then you'll be off to college. It's not your job and your future that's at risk,' Greg responded, the scowl back on his face.

The five heads had moved close together to block out the background noise, their irritation with each other magnified by their forced proximity.

'Kerri's entitled to express her view,' began Sam, about to bring Noam Chomsky into the argument.

'Sure, everyone's entitled to a view,' said Greg. 'And which of us here is arguing against animal welfare? Lucy's a vegetarian, I eat only organically raised meat, Blake's partner Marianne's a vegan; but these people don't want to hear about us and our attitudes. They're terrorists. They're psychopaths who happen to pick on animal rights as their cause of the year. And as far as I'm concerned, terrorists should be locked up. Next time there's a pro-animal-testing rally, I'll be out there waving a banner, OK?'

'Pro-animal-testing, anti-testing, all this marching's a waste of time,' Conor interrupted him impatiently. He ran nicotine-stained fingers through his greasy hair, causing Kerri to wince as she watched.

'What's with you?' he asked her belligerently.

'Nothing,' she replied.

Conor took a couple of steps away from the group. 'You lot can waste time verbalising; I don't care whether they're terrorists or not. I'm finding something to throw back at them when they start hurling shit at us.' And he began casting around the roof for ammunition.

'Don't be so fucking dumb,' shouted Greg after him. 'They'll have you arrested if you do that. They'll sue us for damages if you hit someone.'

'They'd have to catch me first,' said Conor sulkily, but he reluctantly gave up his search. 'I'm not sticking around here, though. And if you've got any sense you'll come with me. Kerri?'

'I'm with Sam,' she replied.

Shrugging, Conor disappeared through the peeling white door to the staircase, and his footsteps clattered down the steps while the others turned back to watch what was happening below.

Occasional words reached them from the mangled sound roaring through the megaphone.

'All . . . guilty!'

'Murderers!'

'*Punishment*!'

A few minutes later Greg said, 'Hey, isn't that Conor down there?' He pointed at a slightly built figure moving round the edge of the crowd, making slow progress away from the demonstration and towards the entrance to the University Parks. 'Is he OK? Where's he off to?'

'Could be Con,' said Lucy. 'Hair's greasy enough. But from this angle it could be anybody, come to that.'

The figure paused and turned sideways so that they could see his face.

13

'Yeah, that's Conor,' said Sam.

'Looks like he's met up with a mate on the demo,' said Lucy.

'Those two don't look very matey to me,' said Sam, leaning forward so he could see more clearly. 'Looks more like they're having a row.'

'I hope that means he's telling his mate what a prat he is,' said Greg.

'He's a lot bigger than Con,' said Kerri.

The crowd below shifted and for a minute or two they lost sight of the two figures. Then Lucy pointed. 'There he goes.'

'Is he OK?' asked Kerri.

'Can't see any blood,' said Lucy flippantly. 'But he's looking pretty pissed off, I'd say.'

'Doesn't he always?' asked Greg.

Conor was mooching along, his head down, distancing himself from the lab.

'I wonder what that was about?' asked Kerri.

No one bothered to answer, for the crowd had taken up their chant again, with placards waving in time to the beat. The leader let them carry on for some minutes before lifting the megaphone once more and addressing the windows of the laboratory, speaking slowly and clearly this time. 'We're leaving now, but we won't forget your crimes. You'll be hearing from us again.'

There was a smile on his lined face as he turned away and led the protesters down Parks Road and back towards the High Street. Many of them must have drifted away already, for it was a small, straggling column that followed him along the road, and it wasn't long before the space in front of the lab was empty once more.

'The entertainment's over for today. Time to get back to

work,' said Greg, as though remembering he was the most senior staff member present.

But at that moment something stopped them dead, frozen in place, identical expressions of surprise on their faces.

Beneath their feet the roof bucked like the deck of a sailing ship before righting itself again, and they all staggered dangerously close to the parapet before regaining their balance. At the same time there was a roar like a long peal of thunder followed by a light pattering of stones.

And then silence.

'Earthquake?' queried Lucy.

At least that was what Sam thought she'd said. Her lips moved, but her voice was inaudible, even two short feet away. All he could hear was the high-pitched buzzing in his ears.

To his left, Greg was coughing and spluttering as he looked over the low wall to see what was happening below. He pointed downwards as Sam joined him.

'Christ!' Sam's comment was easy to lip-read.

'What's happened?' mouthed Kerri, white-faced, shaking Sam's arm, not wanting to look. Tears of fright shone on her cheeks, making rivulets through the grit.

Greg shook his head. Behind him, Sam saw a cloud of dust rising and a few scraps of drifting paper.

Lucy staggered uncertainly across to join Sam and they both peered over the parapet.

Not an earthquake. Must have been an explosion, Sam thought, his head buzzing.

'Is it a bomb?' shrilled Kerri, her voice reaching them like the distant piping of a small bird.

Sam reached across to reassure her, then felt her arm trembling under his touch and drew her away from the parapet. He pointed at the door and beckoned the others to follow him.

If there was another explosion and the building collapsed, this wasn't a clever place to be.

But Greg shook his head and gestured to the others to stay where they were while he went to investigate the staircase. At last he turned back, nodding his head, and then led the way down, raising his hand to urge caution as they descended.

Kerri's mouth was open. She was probably moaning, or screaming even, but none of them could hear.

Lucy gripped Kerri's free hand so that the youngster would feel more secure, and she and Sam kept close beside her as they reached the head of the stairs. The lights had failed and none of them had a torch, so they felt their way down, stumbling and shivering, as the shock of what had happened came home to them.

From afar came the discordant wail of a fire engine and the blaring of a police siren, but all they could hear was the shrill whistling inside their own heads.

3

Blake Parker had found a quiet corner of the car park, and was talking into his mobile phone. The pale dust bleaching his skin and frosting his hair made him appear older than thirty-seven, and as he frowned into the phone, the lines across his forehead and around his eyes were inked in black.

'Yes,' he was saying. 'I'm not disagreeing. This is a serious incident; no one can argue with that.' He paused to let the gush of words from the other end of the phone pour over him. 'Don't let's exaggerate,' he put in eventually. 'After all, it could have been so much worse.' But the other speaker continued as though he hadn't spoken.

Blake watched as a young woman crossed the car park and approached a red Toyota. She was wearing a white tank top and a short denim skirt that showed off her tanned arms and legs. Catching his eye, she smiled at him, briefly. Legs on the thick side, he noted, disappointed, but the contents of the tank top looked promising. As she turned to put her shopping in the boot she noticed that he was still looking at her and frowned. Blake smiled in a friendly way, but she quickly slammed the boot shut and climbed behind the wheel, revving the engine unnecessarily before pulling away and out of sight. Can't win 'em all, thought Blake, tuning back into the phone conversation. He had an almost irrestistible urge to light a cigarette, but he didn't think he could get away with a click of his lighter and the deep, giveaway intake of smoke without alerting the sharp Mr Browne to what he was doing. That was the trouble when you dealt with an American company: they had no tolerance for the reasonable use of alcohol and nicotine. Unwillingly he returned to the rasp of Browne's voice in his ear, repeating the same points over again.

'Blake, I want to be sure that every member of your staff is accounted for, and unharmed.'

'We've been through that. They're all safe.'

'Right. And now I'd like you to email me a brief report listing any damage caused to the lab, and details of any equipment that will need to be replaced. We have to get you all back to work as soon as possible. This work you're doing, it's not a race where we can afford to come second.'

'Yes, fine. Though it may take me a while to find an undamaged computer.' He cleared his throat. The bloody dust was everywhere, and the only way he wanted to get rid of it was by swallowing a large whisky. Just at this moment he wouldn't even care if they ruined it with ice and soda water.

'What kind of security measures do you have in place? You need to be safe from these maniacs.'

'The security officer will contact you direct,' said Blake wearily. 'I'd say the most important point is that no one has in fact been injured. We like to think we're pretty good on security, and the safety today of all the staff must mean we're doing something right.' The other man's pompous style was catching, he thought with disgust.

'I quite understand that you're longing to get away, Blake. I'm sure you want a hot shower and a stiff drink, but we need to get one or two things clear before you go.'

'I need to talk to my staff. And then I need—'

'Quite. You're on edge, I can tell.' There was a false note of sympathy in Browne's voice, and Blake sensed a black mark being written against his name. 'But the reality is that someone entered your laboratory and left an explosive device in the office. I hate to suggest this, Blake, but if your security's as good as you say, then there must be someone on your staff who gave them a helping hand.'

'I don't believe it. We're a small, close-knit group, completely committed to our work.' A slim female form in tight jeans sauntered across Blake's field of vision and he turned his head to watch her.

'I'm asking you to keep the thought in mind as you talk to your staff and as you go about all those tasks you're so eager to press on with. I'm not saying it was a deliberate act: the person involved may not have known what he, or possibly she, was doing. They may have been duped into it.'

'Yes, well—'

'Dr Parker.'

The voice was insistent and came from behind him.

'I'm wanted,' said Blake into the phone.

'I'm sure. But ask whoever it is to wait, will you?'

Blake looked round and recognised one of the maintenance staff. 'Can it wait?' he asked. The man nodded. 'I'll be with you in two minutes, Geoff,' he added, making sure his words could be heard on the phone.

'So, you've taken my point on board, Blake?'

'I'll ask them,' said Blake briefly. 'But it sounds unlikely: this is a group of highly intelligent people.'

'But not necessarily up in the ways of the world. Don't get me wrong here, Blake. I don't want to accuse any of your staff of being disloyal, naturally, but is it possible that you have a sympathiser in your group? Someone who believes in animal welfare – as we all do, naturally – but who has inadvertently been drawn into a group of extremists.'

'That's unlikely too.' Blake wanted to walk away from this futile conversation. His eyes felt gritty, his clothes were filthy, and he needed to know what the hell was happening in his lab, but he understood there was no getting away from Browne until he had answered all his intrusive questions.

'I was thinking of someone young and impressionable,' Browne was saying, and he paused for Blake's comment.

'I can't believe that anyone working here would put lives in danger.'

'Yes, well, let me know your thoughts when you've had a chance to wind down. And maybe you'd email me a list of your staff members with their dates of employment and anything useful you might know about them, just to be on the safe side.'

'That sounds like an invasion of privacy.'

'My company is paying a large part of their salaries, so I believe I have a right to know who they are, especially if they're putting our investment at risk.'

'If you insist.'

'How long do you think the lab will be out of action?'

'We have to wait until we're told it's safe to go back. Tomorrow morning, if we're lucky, we'll be able to use at least part of the building. The office will be out of commission for a while, but the rest of the lab has suffered only minor damage.'

'Sounds promising. But when you do go back, Blake, you will remember there's someone out there who wants to kill you, won't you?'

'I doubt that. These people don't want to be convicted of murder. If this was done by animal rights extremists, I think the explosion was intended merely to bring our work to a halt. They wanted to destroy property rather than people.'

'They were taking quite a risk!'

'The device went off at one thirty-five in the office, which closes for lunch every day between one and two o'clock. It's at the front of the building and they could have seen through the window that there was no one in there.'

'I gather there was a demonstration in the vicinity just before it happened. Have the police arrested the leaders, do you know?'

'They'll need to know more about what caused the explosion before they start arresting people. The crowd had already moved away from the science area when it happened, and it's not as though one of them lobbed a grenade in through the window. We'll have to wait until the forensic people have examined the site to know more.'

'You say the place was empty at lunchtime?'

'There were one or two people working in the lab at the time, but no one was hurt, and there's been no major damage to equipment. There was a few minutes' concern about a small group of younger staff who'd been up on the roof, eating their sandwiches, when the device went off, but they were able to make their way back down the stairs, through the rubble and out of the building. All of them are unharmed. Everyone's upset, of course they are, and the department's found us a conference room where they'll be served hot drinks while they wait for me to join them. I must get in there as soon as possible and let them know what's happening.'

'What about medical check-ups? We don't want any claims for compensation.'

'That's been taken care of.'

'And how did people behave?'

'We've had enough bomb scares for people to know what to do when it's the real thing. There was no panic: the few members of staff who'd been on the premises gathered in the car park and we checked those present against the list of people who had signed out for lunch. No one was missing. And everyone's determined to carry on with our work.'

'I'm glad to hear it. I'm sure you're doing a great job of keeping the mood buoyant.'

'Thank you for your vote of confidence. And I really should—'

'Before you go, Blake, indulge me, will you? Just briefly fill me in on the younger staff members.'

Why was the man banging on about the junior staff? 'They're hardly a group of rebels: two of them are on student bursaries, two others are postgraduates who have been with us for more than a year, the fifth is our statistician, and finally we have a lab technician who's acquiring qualifications in his spare time. Not exactly disaffected youth.' Blake spoke impatiently.

'If you say so.'

'I'll do my best to get back to you before the weekend, but I won't be allowed back in my own office until they're sure the whole place is safe,' said Blake.

'Don't think I'm putting pressure on you, Blake. I'll put in a word with my boss about the next tranche of your funding; I'm sure he won't use this incident as an excuse to delay it at all.'

Blake paused before replying. 'I'm glad to hear it.'

'But he's bound to be nervous. Just as long as you're back to work and an investigation is under way, I'm sure it will be fine. We don't want anything like this to happen again, do we? Or, God forbid, something worse. That could cost us . . . Hey,

I know I sound like the big bad corporate guy talking about money at a terrible time like this, but I thought it was worth a reminder. You wouldn't want to wake up one morning to find you can't pay the bills!'

It wasn't easy to keep his temper with the bastard. 'I'll get on to it. But now I really have to ring off.'

'You and I both know we're not in this business for the money, Blake, but there are people back at head office who aren't as idealistic as we are.'

Fucking bastard, thought Blake as he snapped his phone shut, noticing as he did so that his hand was shaking. All that apparent sympathy and then he threatens to cut off our funds! Oh yes, he made it sound like a joke, but he was deadly serious all right.

He had one more task to perform before going up to the conference room. He scanned the car park swiftly: no one from his own department in view, so he pulled out a pack of cigarettes, lit one and drew in a long, satisfying lungful of smoke. Giving up had been Marianne's idea, not his, and if ever a jolt of nicotine was justified, it was now. He didn't want the staff to see how rattled he was, though, and he waited until his hands had stopped shaking before going in to speak to them.

4

'Why are we sitting here? Are we waiting for another bomb to go off?' The high, hysterical voice cut across the low-pitched conversations in the borrowed conference room. Up to now the mood had been subdued, but now a charge of anxiety flashed through the room.

'The building was checked before we came in here,' said Greg with quiet authority. Was it, though? He sincerely hoped so.

With the windows shut against the dust, the room had the stuffy smell of too many people cooped up for too long, and there were empty tea mugs and biscuit crumbs on every flat surface. The half-dozen who had been inside (or on top of) the building when the device exploded had been checked by the paramedics, though no one had needed to see a doctor. Although their ears were still ringing, they could hear enough of what was being said.

'What the hell *are* we waiting around for?' queried Lucy, voicing the thoughts of everyone present. 'Why won't they let us go home?'

'We have to listen to the rallying speech from Our Leader first,' came a disgruntled reply.

'I wish he'd get on with it,' said Lucy. 'Where is he?' Dust coated her red-gold hair, her skin was grainy with it, and lines were etched black between her eyes, so that the others glimpsed her as she would be when she reached sixty.

'Blake has a lot on his mind,' said Greg.

'So have I,' said Lucy curtly. 'And I want to go home, pour myself a large drink, and think about the future.'

Conor had reappeared and was sitting with Kerri and Sam in a quiet corner.

'We thought we saw you disappearing down Parks Road,' said Sam. 'Where were you off to?'

'Me? No. It couldn't of been.'

Kerri frowned. 'It looked like you.'

'This town's full of geeks who look like me.'

'Didn't you meet up with a mate?' asked Kerri.

'Why're you so interested? What's it to you?' Scowling, Conor leant back violently, balancing his chair on two legs.

'Cool it, Conor. It's nothing. It's just that we're all on edge,' said Sam.

'Nah. I didn't meet a mate. I just went round the back for a smoke.' Conor glared at Kerri as though challenging her to disagree.

'Really? Did you see anything?' asked Sam, suppressing the memory of Conor vainly shaking the empty packet.

'How d'you mean?'

'You could have seen whoever delivered the bomb,' said Sam.

'You mean a man in a black mask, carrying a heavy spherical package through the back door? You're winding me up!'

'Are you sure you saw nothing? It could be important.'

'I told you. I just went out for a smoke. I could hear the crowd of nutters, but I was round by the bike shed, and there wasn't anyone about.'

'I thought you were giving up,' said Kerri.

'I'm like Blake Parker, I only smoke when I'm stressed out,' replied Conor.

'Fair enough,' said Sam, and he shifted his chair a little nearer to Kerri's. 'But I didn't think you were under much stress before the bomb exploded.'

Conor ignored him and tried to regain Kerri's attention, but she was intent on what Sam was saying.

'It'll be less than a year. More like six months,' he told her.

'China,' she said. 'It's so far away. I wish I could go too.'

'You don't need to travel that far to escape from your family,' he said.

'I don't know why you want to. I'd like it if my mum cared what I was doing.'

Sam didn't know how to answer her. Of course he was lucky to have such a large, cheerful family, but it was sometimes suffocating when he was younger, and he found himself longing to get away, with enough space to make his own decisions. Kerri, on the other hand, seemed to exist in a vacuum, with no one to fuss about what she ate, or whether she had clean underwear. Would she really still be waiting for him when he returned to Oxford, he wondered, or would she have moved on? He didn't think she was interested in Conor, though. She was taking no notice of him at that moment, certainly; just staring into her empty mug as though searching for the answer to all life's problems.

'What's bugging you?' Sam asked her.

'I don't think they like me. Do you think they'll be asking me to leave?' She turned anxious brown eyes in his direction.

'You're daft, you are. Who hates you? What you on about?' asked Conor, butting in.

'That lot.' She nodded towards the others across the room.

'Of course they don't hate you. Why on earth should they ask you to leave?' Sam provided the necessary ego-boost. And who would do that while he was away?

He was baffled by Kerri's insecurity: she was on the same Science Bursary Scheme as him, working alongside the world-famous Dr Blake Parker in a research group that was investigating degenerative diseases of the brain. He and Kerri had been given their own small corner of the project, supervised by Greg Eades, and had been made to feel like valuable members of the group during their two-month placement. He put his arm lightly round her shoulders, just to let her know he was there, looking out for her. He sensed that she smiled, faintly, in response. After a few seconds he removed his arm so as not to embarrass her in public.

'They think I support the animal rights movement,' she said.

'But you don't, do you?'

'It's true. Of course I do,' said Kerri diffidently. 'At least, I believe that animals have rights, and that we shouldn't abuse them.'

'So what about the work we do here?'

'I support that too.' She stopped, knowing she was getting into a confusing argument. 'And I don't go along with the extremists. But Greg was really angry with the demonstrators, wasn't he? And I think that Lucy and Candra agree with him. And Blake, too.' Sam could tell that she was counting the people ranged against her. 'But I think the demonstrators have got a point. I don't go along with violence or anything like that, but I think people should care about cruelty to animals and whether it's possible to carry out research in some other way.'

This was one of the longest speeches Sam and Conor had heard from Kerri, and they both nodded in encouragement.

'Anyone would agree that the bomb today was way out of line,' Kerri continued, getting into her stride since she'd found no opposition so far to her views. 'And I know what we're doing's important for people with Parkinson's and—'

'Only old gits get Parkinson's,' scoffed Conor, breaking in, quickly tiring of Kerri's earnest arguments. 'Old gits whose lives are over. Why should animals be sacrificed to keep boring old farts alive?' Conor, who was two or three years older than the other two, and who worked as a lab technician while he studied part-time, spoke flippantly, as though he enjoyed winding Sam up. Maybe he was jealous of the way Kerri looked at him and allowed his arm to rest on her shoulder.

'They're not all old,' said Sam reasonably. 'There's a friend of Emma's . . .' But he could tell that he'd lost their attention and he stopped. 'At least Kerri's consistent in her care for animals.'

'I care for animals too, don't I?' said Conor belligerently. 'It's part of my job.'

'But do you support what the protesters are doing?'

'It's just a bit of laugh,' shrugged Conor.

'Not today it wasn't,' said Kerri.

'And you'd be the first one out of a job if animal testing was banned,' said Sam smartly.

'There's other labs. I'd soon find another job.'

'Kerri's a vegetarian, but what about you, Conor?' asked Sam, pursuing his point. 'Or do you believe animal testing is wrong but killing animals for food is OK?'

'Oh, I dunno, I just think Blake and that lot are a load of pretentious wankers, and why're you talking like some git of a teacher anyway?' said Conor, taking out a new pack of cigarettes. 'Do you think anyone would make a big fuss if I lit up?'

'Blake would.'

'Oh yeah!' Conor laughed. 'He's given up, hasn't he? When he thinks no one's looking.'

'And you're sitting under the No Smoking sign,' said Kerri.

There was one more thing Sam wanted to find out. 'Did you know any of those people who were demonstrating this morning?' he asked.

'I might of recognised one or two, maybe,' replied Conor, giving him a searching look. 'Why do you want to know so much about my friends?'

'Just interested.'

'You think I had something to do with planting the bomb?'

'Should I?'

'Why are you picking on Conor?' asked Kerri, joining in. 'Friends of mine go on demos too. That doesn't make me a mad bomb-maker, though, does it? Why should you suspect Conor?'

'I wasn't—' But they were interrupted by the entrance of Blake Parker before a serious argument could develop, and they turned their chairs so that they formed part of the larger group, each of them glad to drop the subject.

Blake had washed his face, but his hair and clothing were still coated with the dust he had picked up when he inspected the damage to the building. His manner was consciously upbeat, but Sam noticed that he was unable to control the tremor in his hands, and he realised that Blake was more shaken by what had happened than he wanted them to know.

'Well, it's good to see you all here, and even better to see you're all unscathed,' he began. 'You'll be relieved to hear that no one was injured in the blast, and that most of us were out of the building when it happened.' He looked around at the silent faces. 'We don't yet know the extent of the damage, but it does look as though most of it occurred in the office rather than in the labs, so once the building has been declared structurally safe we'll be able to get back to work. We're not going to let these extremists stop us, are we?'

Sam could hear the false note of cheer in his voice, and could imagine the awkward phone calls Blake had been fielding.

'And what about the future?' asked Greg.

'Our future lies in our research, as always,' said Blake smoothly.

'I meant, what's being done to stop the violence? How are we to be protected from such an attack in the future?'

'Good question. And we are going to review security immediately, as a priority. You're quite right, Greg. Such an outrage must never happen again.'

The faces opposite him had the blank look of people who were unconvinced by his words: they sounded too pat, too rehearsed.

'And what effect is this outrage going to have on the bodies who provide our funding?' asked Candra. 'Won't they lose confidence in our ability to produce useful results? They must be asking themselves the question, at the very least.'

'And that's why I've already spoken to our sponsors in the pharma industry,' said Blake. 'I've reassured them that this was a minor incident' – ironic cheer from Sam and his friends – 'and that it will interfere with our work for no more than a couple of days.'

'That's a promise, is it?' asked Lucy.

'Until I know more, it's a reasonable guess,' said Blake. 'Now, before we take ourselves off home, since I can't get at the computer records for the present, could you all write your phone numbers and email addresses on these sheets of paper, and I'll contact you with an update of the situation as soon as I know anything.'

There was a murmuring as people stirred themselves and did as he asked.

'Could you stay behind for a minute, Greg. And you, Candra, please. There are a couple of points to sort out.'

As the others left, he reassured them again that the damage to the lab was minimal, that tighter security would be put in place and that none of them was at risk from the activists. 'It's all done for publicity, to keep their faces on our screens and in the press. If they hurt one of us, or our families, the public would turn against them. That's the last thing they want,' he told them.

Has he convinced himself yet? wondered Sam.

Conor was the only one who was delighted at the idea of an unscheduled holiday, but then Blake called him back too.

'You'd better check on the animals' welfare, Conor,' he said. 'And make sure they're looked after over the next few days, even if the lab is closed.'

When Sam and Kerri left they discovered that they wouldn't be able to get their bikes out of the shed until the police had finished their work, so they set off on foot.

'What did you think of Blake's morale-booster?' asked Sam.

'I don't think he knows much more than us, and he's not letting on even if he does,' said Kerri.

'No. And I reckon he's shit-scared about losing funding too. That's why we all have to behave as though nothing's happened.'

'Do you think that's it?' asked Kerri.

'How do you mean?'

'Will they do it again?'

No need to ask who 'they' were. 'I shouldn't think so,' said Sam, recognising the false upbeat note in his own voice.

Kerri was quiet for a moment. 'I keep imagining that the

ground is lurching under my feet,' she said eventually.

'Me too, but it'll pass off soon,' promised Sam. 'How are your ears?'

'Still stuffed full of manic bees.'

'Come back to my place,' said Sam. 'My mother will get us a meal and find a bed for you. There's plenty of room.'

'Thanks,' said Kerri.

'I've spoken to the pharma,' began Blake when he was alone with Greg and Candra. 'And as usual their man Browne got straight on my tits. They want a preliminary report asap – as though I haven't more urgent things to get on with! – so we have to make this brief.'

'Did they mention our funding?' asked Greg.

'They want to see our latest results before they release the next tranche of the money.'

'You've reassured them that our work won't be held up by this little glitch?'

'Don't worry, there's no blood in the water, but he's still wary. I was talking to a non-scientist who just cares about profits – his profits. "Of course, we're not in it for the money," he said, the lying shit. Just typical of MegaBucks,' Blake added disgustedly.

'Better not let them hear you call them that.'

'Big Uglies, then.'

Candra laughed nervously, but Greg said, 'They're not so bad: they've given us sums of money that would be considered generous by any lab. I know they hope to get something out of it, but remember that we need them more than they need us at the moment.'

'OK. I'll remember. I just wasn't in the mood for grovelling after what's happened.'

'What do you want me to do?' asked Candra.

'Always the practical one,' said Blake.

She was the only one of Blake's staff that afternoon who managed to look as clean and tidy as when she had left her flat that morning: her polished hair in its elegant bob, her make-up carefully applied, her jacket and trousers newly brushed. Then Blake noticed smudges of grey dust on her shoes, and was reassured that she wasn't as impervious to recent events as she wished to appear. Neat ankles; pity she doesn't show us her legs more often, he thought, before returning to business.

'The report I send in this afternoon can only be a preliminary one, but I'd like the two of you to get working straight away on something concrete: the case for giving us more money. This incident with the activists has come at just the wrong time, and we don't want the pharma to grab the chance of holding back on the wonga.'

Candra pinched her lips together at this frivolous term for money.

'I mean funding, of course,' said Blake, noticing her reaction. 'Candra, I know you'll want more time, but I need you to produce some encouraging figures from the latest results.'

Candra frowned. 'The figures don't lie, Blake. You know that.'

'I'm not suggesting they should, but we all know that there's room for interpretation, and I'm asking you to be flexible.'

Candra's expression gave no hint of flexibility, but although it often irritated him, Blake respected her for it. In an ideal world he would never have suggested that she give an optimistic slant to the results if they didn't warrant it.

'And Greg, as soon as you have the figures from Candra, I

want you to write the submission for the next tranche of funding.'

Greg nodded. He was the group's most persuasive writer, and the most diplomatic, so Blake always landed him with this job.

'I know the situation's tricky at the moment, but I'd like it if you treated this task as a priority. Can you both work from home for the next few days?'

'It would be easier if we could have access to a terminal in one of the undamaged offices,' suggested Candra.

'I'll fix something and email you from home,' said Blake, glancing again at his watch. 'I must go now and get on with my own report.' And he left the room.

If it had been anyone other than Candra, Greg would have proposed a visit to the pub for a large brandy before going home, but there was an aloofness about the statistician that discouraged him from suggesting it.

When Greg too had left, Candra wondered whether she should have offered him a lift home in her car, but most of the lab staff rode bikes to work and she felt that they disapproved of what they saw as her unnecessary use of fossil fuels. She would have suggested to Greg that they call in to the pub for a much-needed drink, but he had disappeared before she could overcome her shyness enough to suggest it, so she made her way home on her own.

Before settling down at the computer in a borrowed office, Blake fished out his mobile and dialled his home number. Marianne, his partner, might have heard about the explosion at the lab by now and be worrying about his safety.

'Hello?' came a woman's sharp voice after half a dozen

rings. 'Blake? Is that you? I've been waiting! Where the fuck are you?'

'Marianne? Is everything all right?'

'If that's you, Blake, then no, it fucking isn't. It's fucking awful, if you want to know. And no one's been answering the phone at that fucking lab of yours. Where the fuck are you?'

Blake sighed. So she hadn't heard the news by the sound of it, and in this mood was unlikely to feel any sympathy for him. He softened his voice. 'There's been a bit of bother at the lab and I've borrowed an empty office in the department so that I can complete an urgent piece of work, but I'll be home around six, OK? I'll deal with whatever's wrong then.'

'What's so fucking urgent?'

'Making sure we get our hands on the funding.'

'Oh. *Money*.' Marianne invested the word with scorn. 'Does that mean you'll be closeted for hours with Candra?'

'On my own,' he said. It was easy for her to sneer, with Blake providing the roof over her head.

'There'll be nothing to eat till you've given me a hand here.' There was a quiver in her voice now, but at that moment. Blake had little sympathy left for anyone outside the lab.

He disconnected, wishing that Marianne would deal with her own problems without waiting for him to turn up and solve them for her. He needed a cigarette to calm him down, and reached for the pack he'd bought earlier, but then he remembered that it would only set off the smoke alarm and cause further disquiet in the department. With a sigh, he turned back to his computer.

5

Later that day, a brisk wind was scurrying round Jericho, snatching leaves from the trees before they were ready to fall, chasing them along pavements and into gutters, hounding the early days of autumn into a premature November. This same wind was drumming its insistent fingers on the windows of Kate Ivory's house, and moaning and whistling down her chimneys. The light was already fading from the sky, reminding her that summer would soon be nothing but a memory.

Kate was attempting to ignore the enervating weather. She had a book proposal to write and she was sitting at her computer, her back resolutely towards the window, concentrating on the blank screen. *Just write a few words,* she told herself. *Anything. Any old rubbish. Once you've made a mark on the pristine white then you'll be able to carry on. The ideas will arrive.* But the screen remained blank.

It was past six o'clock in the evening and she had managed somehow to waste a whole day, helped by the fact that after her enforced detour to Cornmarket, and before arriving at the library, she'd bumped into her friend Camilla and they'd sloped off to the nearest coffee shop.

'So tell me, how are you and Jon Kenrick getting on? You must have been together for, oh, six months or so by now,' Camilla had asked when she was halfway through her latte.

'We're fine. We've been "together" for a couple of years, and living together for the last eight months.'

'Time flies! Why, that must be a Kate Ivory record!' Camilla caught sight of Kate's expression and quickly softened her observation with a smile.

'You sound as though you expect us to be splitting up by now,' said Kate.

'Sorry, Kate. I'm delighted that things are working out for you this time, but you must admit, your previous record wasn't so great. By the six-month mark you've always noticed some habit that irritates you to distraction, or else you uncover the fact that his view of life is incompatible with your own. And then you pack up your belongings, push the cat into her carrying basket and move out – though in this case I suppose it will be poor Jon who has to leave, since he's living at your place.' Dear Camilla, direct and tactless as ever: Kate put it down to the years she'd spent battling with teenage girls. But there were a number of perceptive comments in there, she had to admit.

'No cat,' she said briefly. 'Susanna . . . died.' An image of the spot under the apple tree where her beloved cat was lying came into her mind, but she didn't want to go into the gruesome details of her death with Camilla. 'And anyway, this time it's different,' she said firmly. 'Jon may be living at my place, as you put it, but that means he's given up his London flat and we're going to look for a house together, somewhere outside Oxford, probably in one of the villages. I might learn how to grow vegetables.'

'You might even get married,' suggested Camilla.

'Not just yet.'

'Moving away from Oxford will be a bit of a wrench for you, won't it?'

'How do you mean?'

'Your lovely house! You've only just settled in, and now you're planning to sell it.'

'But we have to start afresh, don't we, if we're really going to make a life together?' She hadn't meant to sound so indecisive.

'You're probably right. After all, I'm the last one to know anything about taking up with a suitable man and making a new life together.'

That was true: in the past Camilla had taken up with a young man who was not only unsuitable but had walked out on her just as all her friends had grown used to his youthful, flamboyant presence in her house.

They walked back along Beaumont Street together before going their separate ways: Camilla down the Fridesley Road to the school where she was headmistress, Kate to her desk in Cleveland Road.

When she reached home she felt she needed to relax for an hour or two, and then she made a cup of tea and took another short walk, thinking about what Camilla had said. It was true that she didn't want to move out of her house. But she admitted that she wasn't making a good job of sharing it with Jon. In theory there was plenty of room for both of them, but each time he tried to take over a space, however small, she felt it as an invasion of her territory. Give it another month or two, though, or maybe three, and she might be reconciled to the idea of leaving Cleveland Road.

By the time she'd checked her emails and spent twenty minutes chatting on the phone to her mother, it hardly seemed worth sitting down at her desk and starting on some serious work. But she was a professional, and so, late as it was, here she was, glaring at her computer and hoping for inspiration.

A little later she heard Jon come in and she was aware of the silence that meant he was afraid that if he called out, 'Hello! I'm home!' he would break her concentration. She felt guilty that he was being so considerate while she was so unproductive. She made one final effort, forcing her fingers to move across the keys. *This is me, trying to write a proposal. Why can't I think of anything? Once upon a time* . . . No, that was no good. *It was a dark and stormy night.* Even worse.

Jon's subdued footsteps were approaching up the stairs and she quickly deleted what she'd written in case he entered her study, looked over her shoulder and saw how pathetic it was. It could be tough work living up to his opinion of her.

There came a gentle tap at the door, it opened a foot or so, and Jon's apologetic head appeared in the gap. He had discarded his jacket and tie and apparently run his hands through his hair a few times to get rid of its daytime neatness.

'How's it going?' he asked.

'Fine,' she said, trying to sound upbeat.

'I hope I'm not interrupting, but it's well past six. How about taking a break?'

'Is it really that late? I'd better stop what I'm doing and get us something to eat.' She clicked the 'Turn off computer' button, feeling illogically that if only she'd stared at the screen for another thirty seconds she might have come up with a usable paragraph.

'I'll get the supper on if you like,' said Jon. 'If the work's flowing it's a pity to break off.'

He was being far kinder than she deserved. 'Oh no, it's my turn to cook,' she replied quickly, as she squared the oddments of paper on her desk and tucked her pen and notebook away in a drawer.

While she did so, Jon was looking round at the room. 'There's not much furniture in here, is there?'

'There's enough for me,' said Kate. 'Why? What's missing?'

'Wouldn't you like another bookcase? There's room for one against that wall.'

'I don't really need—'

'It's just that I've got one going spare,' he said. 'It's in storage at the moment, but I could put out a few more of my books if I brought it over.'

'Wouldn't it fit into the dining room, next to your desk?'

'It's getting a bit crowded in there.'

'We could shift things around. It's not as though we eat in there more than once or twice a month.'

Frowning, Jon paused for a moment before replying. 'I'm getting the feeling you're not really happy with me living here, Kate.'

'Of course I am!' This was too near Camilla's view for comfort. 'It's just that I prefer having my study to myself. You wouldn't like it if I took some of my stuff over to your office and laid claim to a shelf or two of yours, would you?'

'Fair enough. But you're not keen on moving out of here into somewhere bigger either.'

'I'm getting used to the idea, but I need more time. Let me make a start on the meal and we can talk about it.'

'You keep avoiding the subject, but I think we should work out a timetable for the move.'

'Yes.' Kate suppressed her feeling of dismay at his words. Couldn't they drift along for a while yet?

Before going downstairs, she took a look at her study, seeing it through Jon's eyes. It was above the living room and the same size, and it had polished wooden floors, off-white blinds at the windows, a large desk and chair, a two-drawer filing cabinet, a small stationery cupboard and a bookcase for her reference books. What else did she need? If she had another bookcase she'd only fill it with enticing novels, and then she'd sit and read them instead of writing her own. As it was, she had plenty of space for walking around and thinking. She could even lie on the floor and stare at the ceiling, waiting for inspiration, if she felt like it. But she could see that Jon might see it as, well, rather bare.

The only thing missing, in her opinion, was a lock for the door.

'I need my surroundings to be neutral, then I can let my imagination run free,' she said. 'I don't even like too many books in here – just the reference books I use when I'm writing.'

'Fair enough. Let's go downstairs, I'll pour you a glass of wine and we'll talk about something else while we eat.'

Ten minutes later their supper was in the oven and they were sitting on the pink sofa drinking wine.

Jon sneezed. 'Hay fever,' he said.

'I thought the season was over; you haven't had an attack for days.'

'It could be the flowers over there,' he said.

Kate had placed a large arrangement of cream-coloured flowers and bronze leaves by the window. Now she picked them up and moved to the door. 'I'll put them in my study,' she said. 'They shouldn't bother you in there.'

When she returned to the sitting room, Jon was blowing his nose and blinking.

'I'll have to use my eye drops,' he said, finding the small bottle in his jacket pocket and leaning his head back to drop liquid into his eyes. 'How's that?' he asked a few minutes later. 'Are they looking any better?'

'Yes. Much better. Still a bit puffy, though.'

'Maybe I should take an antihistamine.' Jon sneezed again and then fumbled in his pocket for his pills. Kate fetched a box of man-sized tissues and a glass of water, and placed them on the table next to him. Then she took a gulp of her wine.

Jon turned on the news as Kate was about to disappear back into the kitchen to wash some green leaves. His eyes on the television screen, he called, 'Wait a minute, Kate. Look, that's central Oxford. What's been happening?'

Kate sat down again. 'It's just another animal rights demonstration,' she said. 'They were marching up St Giles this morning when I went out, so I had to go round by George Street to get to Cornmarket.'

The newsreader took up where Kate left off. 'At lunchtime today, animal rights supporters were demonstrating in Oxford's Science Area. The demonstration was orderly and law-abiding, but only a few minutes after the demonstrators – and our camera crew – had left South Parks Road and dispersed, there was an explosion in one of the laboratories.'

The scene changed, the camera jerkily homing in on a glass-and-concrete building nearly obscured by a cloud of grey dust.

'It has been confirmed that no one was injured in the explosion, though part of the building has been damaged.'

The camera advanced towards the dust cloud, then stopped again. On the soundtrack the wail of a police car approached rapidly, merging with the lower notes of a fire engine.

'No one has yet claimed responsibility for the blast, and there is nothing to connect it directly with the demonstration, one of a series taking place this year in the Science Area,' the newsreader continued, 'but we will keep you informed about any developments. On this evening's edition of

Newsnight there will be interviews with a spokesman for the animal rights group who organised today's march, as well as a senior scientist from the university. We are hoping that someone from the Home Office will feel able to join the discussion.'

Kate and Jon sat stunned in front of the television.

'Didn't you hear the explosion?' asked Jon.

'No.'

'It can't have been a very serious one, then.'

'It was almost at the end of our road. Any explosion a few hundred yards away is serious!'

'Nearer half a mile, I'd have thought.'

Kate realised that he was attempting to allay her anxiety.

'Everyone knew there was trouble over animal experiments,' said Kate. 'There's something on the news nearly every week, but I didn't realise it had gone this far.'

'I notice they're not making a definite connection between the demonstrators and the explosion.'

'There was a strong hint.'

'We'd better watch *Newsnight*. They may know more about it by then.'

'I must have been in the town centre when it happened, and it's noisy there,' said Kate, unable to leave the subject. 'I wouldn't have heard much if I was inside the library, I suppose. Or maybe I was sitting in the coffee shop, chatting to Camilla. Did I tell you I bumped into her at Carfax?'

'No. Wasn't it at her house that you and I first met?'

'You're right.'

'We must have her over one of these evenings.'

'Good idea.' But Kate wasn't to be diverted so easily. 'We hadn't seen one another for ages: it would have taken quite a large bomb to interrupt our flow of conversation, let alone make itself heard above the clatter of crockery and the loud voices.'

'Shall I pour you another glass of wine?' asked Jon.

'You want to change the subject?'

'There's not much to say about it until they release more news, is there? So, how about the wine?'

'I'd better wait till I've dished up,' replied Kate, returning to the kitchen to finish preparing their supper.

After they had eaten and while Jon was making coffee, the phone rang.

'Kate? It's Emma here.'

'Hello, Emma. I haven't heard from you for ages. How are things?'

'We're all well. Mostly, that is.' Emma Dolby had at least half a dozen children, and a husband, and it was unlikely that they were ever simultaneously free of problems of some kind. She had a habitually distracted air, as though she had forgotten to do something but couldn't quite remember what it was. Her own work, as a children's author, tutor in English literature and teacher of creative writing, seemed to have disappeared, buried under the mountain of her family's needs.

'I was worried about Sam and Kerri when I heard about the explosion, and of course when they turned up here this afternoon their clothes were covered in dust. Kerri was quite shattered, poor girl, though Sam was putting a brave face on it—'

'Young Sam, do you mean? He was actually there at the time?' Kate had always thought it would have been simpler if they hadn't named Sam after his father, but doubtless it was an old Dolby family tradition, and family was important to the Dolbys.

'Yes, Young Sam and his girlfriend, Kerri: they're working at the lab where the bomb went off, and they were standing on the roof when it happened.'

'My God! How awful!'

'Sam rang me on his mobile to say they were all right, but he could hardly understand a word I said in return. He says his ears are better now, but I don't think they've stopped ringing yet.'

'Who did it, Emma? Have they arrested anyone? Does Sam know? Was it the animal rights protesters?'

'Give me a chance, Kate! The protesters have every right to express their opinion about animal testing, and they were quite peaceful and law-abiding, from what I gathered. We suspect one of the extremist fringe groups may have had something to do with it, but we don't know that the police have arrested anyone yet.'

'Why not?'

'Kate, I have no idea what the police are doing. But I imagine they're taking it seriously. And Sam tells me the Science Area was crawling with men in white overalls by the time he left.'

'It must have been the marchers I saw in St Giles. He struck me as a fanatic even then.'

'How do you mean?'

'Thin and intense. Long hair. Staring eyes.'

Emma managed to laugh. 'Perhaps you should offer your services to the police as a profiler.'

'But aren't you furious with those people?'

'If you're referring to people who object to experimenting on animals, actually I agree with them, in principle,' said Emma slowly.

'But you have to condemn violence, especially when it's aimed at the innocent. A bomb! It's so random!'

'I don't know why I'm arguing, Kate, since it was Sam and Kerri in the line of fire. But I've always believed in free speech and the right to protest. I can't ditch my principles just because this time it's personal.'

'They could have killed Sam! Or injured him. Isn't that irresponsible, to put it at its lowest?'

'But we don't know they're the ones who caused the explosion. If I'd set a bomb to go off I wouldn't hang around to watch,' said Emma. 'I'd want to be a mile or two away.'

'If the protesters weren't responsible, who was? Doesn't anyone know? Have they got any ideas about it?'

'I expect they're questioning all the local tearaways,' said Emma. It didn't sound nearly good enough to Kate.

'Poor Sam! What a horrible experience! What's he doing at the lab, by the way? I thought this was his gap year.'

'It is. I have to go in a minute, Kate, but I was wondering if you were free for coffee one morning. I could tell you more about it then.'

'Yes, I can manage that. Your place or mine?'

'How about going out somewhere? In town, maybe.' Emma sounded wistful, as though a short trip into the centre of Oxford was a distant dream.

'Of course.' And Kate mentioned a place where the coffee came in two varieties – black and white – but was fresh and strong and would be within Emma's stringent budget.

At Emma's end of the line the sound of childish voices demanding their mother's attention could be heard. 'Tomorrow? Eleven o'clock?' she asked hurriedly.

'See you then,' said Kate. 'And please give my love to young Sam, and tell him to take care.'

'That was Emma,' she said to Jon when he came in with the

coffee pot. 'Her eldest, Sam, was on the roof of the lab when it was blown up.'

'Is he all right?'

'Apparently, though I think he's playing down the effects of the blast for his mother's sake.'

'He can't be too bad if they sent him home, Kate. You don't need to get too worked up about it.'

'I'm worked up about people who think they can kill and maim innocent bystanders – and then get away with it. Poor Emma's torn between her liberal principles and her concern for her family. Aren't these the sort of criminals you dealt with in your old job? Can't you ring someone up and find out what's happening?'

'No. I've moved on. It's no longer my concern.'

Kate could tell by his closed expression that she would get nowhere by continuing this line. 'I'm seeing Emma for coffee tomorrow morning and I get the impression she's more stressed out than usual, even before Sam's near miss, but I'll find out what it's all about when I see her.'

'It'll be the usual,' said Jon. 'Too many children. Husband who takes her for granted. Not enough money.'

'I don't think they're really hard up,' said Kate, picking up on the one point it was possible to argue about.

'Anyone with that many children to educate must be skint. And I don't suppose Sam makes much money.'

'Sam Junior's just left school, and Abigail must be leaving in another year or so. That should help.'

'University fees,' said Jon succinctly. 'But maybe all she needs to set her straight is a morning off, window-shopping with her only carefree friend.'

Carefree? He should try sitting in front of a computer screen trying to come up with three good ideas every morning.

'And by the way,' said Jon a little too casually, so that Kate's antennae twitched. 'How do you feel about embarking on a journey like Emma's?'

'Writing children's fiction? Morphing into J.K. Rowling? Settling down with a husband who takes me for granted? Or do you mean acquiring a huge family?'

'It needn't be like that. I thought we could start with one child, and see how we went.'

'Shouldn't we find a bigger place to live first?' said Kate, giving herself time to consider the proposition. Naturally, it had occurred to her before now that if she wanted children she'd better get a move on. Her thirties were coming to an end and her chances of conceiving would start to go down dramatically over the next few years. Even so, she and Jon hadn't given themselves a chance to get used to living together yet: it was too early to think of starting a family. 'It's getting a bit crowded here with the two of us. We'd need more room if we had a baby.'

'You can always squeeze in a cot,' said Jon, as though he'd been doing it all his adult life. 'I don't think we should leave the decision much longer, Kate.'

'Pass over the stuff from the estate agents,' she said. 'Though they never seem to send us anything we like the look of.'

'Nothing we *both* like the look of,' amended Jon, and sneezed.

6

'Ten thirty, time for *Newsnight*,' said Kate. 'I'll switch on the television.'

'I hope they get to the lab explosion soon. I don't want to stay up too late,' replied Jon, yawning.

Luckily for him it was the first item.

After a brief introduction the arguments began. A well-dressed, articulate woman spoke for the university, explaining how important the work of the laboratory was in defeating major degenerative diseases; an expensively suited but less articulate man from the Home Office explained what demonstrators were, and were not, permitted to do, and then it was the turn of the spokesman from an animal rights group – Razer, according to the caption on the screen.

'A one-word name? He made it up!' said Jon.

'Very likely. I think it's the same man who was leading the march in St Giles,' remarked Kate. 'Or at any rate, out of the same mould.'

'Just another fanatic,' said Jon, echoing Kate's own words to Emma. Kate noticed that he had lost his earlier detachment now that he saw Razer in action. 'He wasn't even bothering to listen to what the other two were saying,' he added as Razer started to speak.

The activist addressed the camera rather than engaging with either of the other speakers or their host.

'Of course, none of us in the animal rights movement condones violence,' he began in a reasonable voice. 'But if those who inflict violence on innocent animals won't listen to our protests, you cannot blame some of our supporters if they decide to take direct action. Vivisection is a filthy practice and its perpetrators deserve to be treated as criminals. If the law won't punish them, don't be surprised if someone else does.'

The Home Office spokesman started to interrupt, but he was silenced by the show's host, and Razer continued.

'Today's incident in Oxford – which had nothing at all to do with the organisation I represent – is a wake-up call to the guilty – and that includes the torturers, their families, their friends and anyone who is employed in any capacity to work in these so-called laboratories.'

'You're issuing a threat, then, to hundreds – perhaps thousands – of people?' asked the host.

'This is not a threat, but a warning of what will happen if they continue their unnecessary work.'

'It sounds like a threat. And it applies to innocent bystanders too, does it?' The host's eyebrows were raised in incredulity.

'In the matter of animal experiments there are no innocent bystanders. Certainly no one connected to the university is innocent in this. All are guilty, if only by association. If you work for the murderers, then you are guilty – office staff, cleaners, maintenance men – all of you, guilty of murder. And you can expect to be punished for your crimes.' The voice was still reasonable, but the man's mouth had twisted into a grimace and he was staring fixedly into the camera.

'So you approve of today's explosion?'

'Like I said, I can't approve of violence, but I do

understand those who feel so frustrated that their anger explodes in this way.'

'Unfortunate turn of phrase,' remarked Jon.

'And what have you got to say to the sufferers of diseases such as Parkinson's, whose only hope of a cure lies in the research carried out in these laboratories?' The interviewer was jabbing a finger at Razer as he spoke.

'We all know that the use of animals in research is unnecessary. Alternatives do exist. And in any case, rats and humans are not the same; they react in different ways to the same drug, so nothing is learnt by sacrificing rabbits or rats: animal testing is pointless.'

'Why don't the other two reply to this rubbish?' asked Jon.

'I think Razer's being allowed to demonstrate how extreme he is,' said Kate. 'No one's going to believe what he says.'

'Don't underrate public stupidity! He shouldn't be given air time like this. He's a fanatic. A terrorist!'

Inconclusive as ever, the discussion on the screen was drawing to a close, and a few moments later a new subject was introduced. Jon picked up the remote and switched off the television.

'I call that another reason to move out of Oxford,' he said.

'It's a reason for us to find out who did it, and make sure they can't do it again,' said Kate.

'Us?' queried Jon. 'You can't just join in whenever there's something you feel strongly about.'

Kate didn't reply, but she thought, *But that's who I am.*

That night, as she lay awake in bed, Kate wondered why she felt so unhappy about Jon's suggestion that they should have a child. If he wanted her to have his children it must mean that he loved her, that he wanted their relationship to be permanent.

And surely, if she loved him as much in return, she would feel the same way. As he'd said, they didn't have to have a family as large as Emma's. One child would be enough. Or two at the most. She wouldn't even have to give up her work, or only for a few months.

She needed time to think about her decision, she told herself. It would have to wait until the next day, for she was drifting into sleep.

On his side of the bed, Jon was wondering whether he had been hasty in selling his London flat and moving to Oxford to live with Kate. It had been the offer of the job that had clinched it, of course, but there were other jobs out there waiting for someone with his qualifications and experience.

Kate had lived in Oxford since she was a child and she loved the place; after eight months, he wasn't so keen. Maybe he shouldn't have absorbed so many rosy views of the city from the television before coming to live here. He had been hankering after a photogenic Arcadia that no reality could ever live up to, a city touched by magic, but all he saw was damp grey stonework, gum-strewn pavements, and streets full of frazzled shoppers, exhausted from queuing for a parking space.

Not that he was blaming Kate for any of this. He was the one who had been so keen to relocate to her house in Jericho while they looked around for somewhere that they could buy together. And now he admitted to himself that when it came to cities, he would always be a Londoner at heart. When he saw himself in Oxfordshire it was as a countryman, striding across a furrowed field, the sun on his face, the wind in his hair. He hadn't mentioned it to Kate, but he was dreaming of acquiring a waxed jacket, maybe a tweed hat and a labrador or two.

He could understand that Kate was loath to move from her house in Jericho: five minutes' walk from the town centre, ten minutes from the rail station, and close to some good food shops. But the real problem was going to be Kate's inability to commit herself to a future that included a husband and children. Her view was influenced by her own childhood, and the early death of her father. And much as Jon liked Kate's mother, Roz, he could see that she might not be the best role model. Then there was her friendship over the years with Emma Dolby. The Dolbys' set-up would put anyone off marriage and parenthood.

Weren't there friends of his own who would provide a more attractive image of domesticity? He would have to approach the idea obliquely, convince her that it was what she really wanted. And just as he, too, was drifting off to sleep, the ideal method slid into his head. Tomorrow he would make a phone call.

7

In spite of his assurances to Marianne, Blake Parker was still dealing with the effects of the bomb into the evening. It was getting on for nine before he left his makeshift office and cycled back to the house they shared. He had phoned her again before leaving to let her know how things were going, hoping for an offer of a lift home in her car, but she was in one of her combative moods. She seemed to treat his brush with death as an attempt to gain sympathy and get out of doing his share of the household chores. She didn't appreciate that he was exhausted after a day of answering questions from both press and police, as well as organising the clean-up and repairs necessary for the lab staff to get back to work.

'It hasn't been all joy and sunshine here either,' she had said acidly. 'But you'll see what I've had to put up with when you finally get here.'

'I'll be back within the hour to deal with it,' he'd said. Whatever 'it' might be. When he'd disconnected, he went in search of cigarettes. No point in trying to give up when he was being landed with so much grief. He might as well treat himself to a pint and a smoke before heading towards home. The weather was still balmy enough to sit at a table on the pavement and watch the passing parade. Skirts were being worn well above the knee this year, he noticed appreciatively, and the latest intake of women students was as attractive as ever. He was in no hurry to face another of Marianne's tantrums, so it was nearly an hour later that he arrived back at the terraced house in north Oxford.

The door opened just as he reached it, as though Marianne had been looking out for him, and she stood there, spots of colour on her cheekbones, hair slightly tousled, expression belligerent.

'You look like shit,' she said. 'And you stink of beer and fags. Where the hell have you been?'

'Do you mind if I come in first, before we start the row?' he asked mildly. Wordlessly she stood aside to let him through into the hall. 'OK, so tell me, what's it all about?' he said.

'As if you didn't know!'

There was an odd smell in the hall: something unpleasant, heavily overlaid with chemical citrus spray. 'I can't guess, Marianne, and I'm too tired to play games. You're going to have to tell me what this is about.'

'First it was the phone calls,' she said accusingly. 'Every time I get started on a piece of work the fucking phone goes. Is it for me? No! It's some fucking madman asking for you. Asking for the animal-killer. I told him to piss off, you weren't here, and I had nothing to do with your fucking work, and anyway I didn't care how many rats you strangled.'

'What did he say?' asked Blake, intrigued.

'He laughed. Not a nice laugh, in case you were wondering. A fucking unpleasant laugh. "When he gets home, tell him we know where to find him when we want him," he said. I said, right, I've got the message, so now just piss off. Then he told me I wasn't to think I was so bloody innocent. Through my connection with you, apparently, I'm as guilty as all the other murderers.'

'Yes, I can see it was upsetting for you.'

'Upsetting! Don't be so fucking patronising, Blake. And anyway, that wasn't the end of it, was it?'

'Apparently not.' It was odd the way he was feeling disassociated from Marianne just when he should be at his most sympathetic. But she was making all this fuss about a phone call while he was worrying about a bomb at the lab. And if he couldn't persuade the pharma to keep up their funding, the whole group would be finished. No good telling Marianne any of that, though, even if he could get a word in edgeways.

'Then came the Jiffy bag, addressed to both of us, by the way, "Marianne and Blake Parker", like we were fucking married or something. As if!'

Blake didn't feel it was the right time to mention that he was just as pleased as Marianne that they hadn't formalised their relationship. 'Yes?'

'Dog shit!' she screamed at him. 'I pulled it open here in the hall and it went all over the fucking carpet. Can't you smell it?'

'Well . . .'

'As soon as I realised what it was, I dropped it, of course I did. And now whatever I do I can't get rid of the fucking smell. It's following me all over the house.' At this point her anger dissipated suddenly and he saw that there were tears leaking down her cheeks. 'Who hates us this much, Blake?'

He took a couple of steps forward and put his arms round her. 'Never mind,' he said, breathing in the camomile scent of her hair and the disinfectant smell on her hands. 'I'm here now. I won't let it happen again. We'll be all right.'

After a minute or two she moved back and took a good look at him. 'You poor bastard,' she said. 'Why don't you run a hot bath while I get on with making the supper.'

As he turned to leave the room, she added: 'And you can hand over the pack of cigarettes you bought today.'

Wordlessly he passed it across. There was no hiding his smoking from Marianne's X-ray eyes; he'd have to leave his cigarettes in his desk drawer in future.

Later, lying back in the hot water, he allowed his mind to drift back to the events at the lab and to wonder about who might be responsible. Much as he hated Browne's accusations, he had to face up to the possibility that one of his own staff had either placed the bomb in the office, or let in an outsider who'd done it. He reviewed the list of suspects and came to the conclusion that it was likely to be one of the younger ones: someone who had no stake in their future, or who didn't understand just how competitive a field they were working in. Someone who cared about the bloody rats, he supposed.

He liked them all, that was the trouble, and he didn't want to think that one of them had committed such a stupid, such a *criminal* act. Or had it been that they didn't know what they were doing when they opened the door and let in the man in the balaclava and the heavy backpack?

OK, so the bomber probably didn't fit the stereotype. It was just as likely to have been a pretty girl wearing a short skirt and an inviting smile. With the way Marianne had been these last weeks, he might have invited her inside himself.

Were the police thinking along the same lines? They weren't likely to take him into their confidence, so he really didn't know. As far as they were concerned, all the lab staff would be potential collaborators with the bomber. They were probably digging into their files at this very moment, looking to see who'd been a tearaway in their student days. Well, who hadn't thrown a bottle or two in their alcohol-fuelled youth? Probably not Candra, he admitted. He couldn't see her dropping her high moral standards and getting her white-gloved hands grubby.

The thought of Candra brought his mind back to his other problem: ensuring that their funding continued. Without it, their existence was threatened, and it was Candra who was his greatest obstacle to success. He needed to talk her around, but he didn't look forward to facing that uncompromising stare of hers.

8

Half an hour before Kate was due to meet Emma in town, the phone rang.

'So sorry, Kate. Plans have changed at my end and I'm afraid I can't make it into Oxford.' Emma sounded upset as well as in a hurry.

'Do you want to fix another time now?' Kate knew that Emma needed these infrequent breaks, and unless she pinned her down to a precise time and location, the demands of her family meant she was unlikely to see her friend for another three months.

'I wondered whether you'd like to come over to my place this morning instead.' Then she called out, 'I'll be with you in just a moment,' and Kate realised she was addressing someone at the other end of the line.

'Is everything all right with Sam and Kerri?'

'Oh, yes, of course.' It sounded as though Emma had already put their frightening experience out of her mind.

'I'll be with you in twenty minutes.'

'Good. I could use the adult company, to be honest.'

After Kate had rung Emma's doorbell, there was the usual interlude in which sounds of activity from within – a door closing, footsteps on the stairs and across the hall, the demanding voice of a small child – reached her before the door opened and Kate was greeted by the sight of her friend's back.

'Don't worry, Geraldine,' Emma was calling up the stairs. 'Why don't you colour in some more of the pretty pink sheep? I'll be back in just a moment.'

Geraldine? Emma's daughters had romantic names like Poppy, and Flora. When she had named her babies, Emma had imagined they would grow into winsome little girls dressed in Laura Ashley florals, romping in meadows starred with wildflowers. (The reality had turned out to be somewhat different: one of them refused to wear anything but dungarees and looked like a miniature prizefighter.) But Kate was nearly sure that none of the girls had been given the name Geraldine.

'She's a bit upset by everything,' said Emma, turning round at last and speaking directly to Kate as she led the way to the staircase. 'And who can blame the little mite?'

'Is this a good time? Would you like me to come back later?' As Emma shook her head, Kate handed over the chocolate biscuits she had brought with her just in case Emma hadn't managed to hide a packet for adult use from her family.

'Thank you, Kate. How kind of you. Now, before we settle ourselves in the kitchen, just come upstairs with me so that I can introduce you, otherwise Geraldine will think you're the doctor.'

Doctor? No one had taken Kate for a doctor before: the look she aimed at was creative and original, with a touch of designer style; she was never seen in the crumpled grey suit, faded blue shirt and harassed expression worn by her own GP last time she had visited her.

Emma took her into one of the many bedrooms in the rambling Dolby family house in Headington. Her husband had inherited it from his parents and luckily it was large enough to accommodate Emma's numerous children. If they de-cluttered it and slapped a coat of fresh paint all over the walls it would be worth a fortune, thought Kate. But she couldn't see Emma and Sam moving somewhere else: if Emma had her way, she would continue to fill the house with babies until her exhausted ovaries finally gave up the struggle.

'Here we are, Geraldine,' Emma said brightly. 'This is my friend Kate.'

Geraldine sat at the table on a chair piled up with cushions so that she could reach the paper and crayons that Emma had set out for her. She was a fair-haired, washed-out-looking child with a thin face and dark smudges under her eyes. She looked unblinkingly at Kate, her mouth pulled down as though she was ready to burst into tears at any moment.

'Are you a doctor?' she asked, lower lip trembling.

'No. Definitely not.'

'Kate's a writer,' said Emma. 'She writes lovely books full of exciting stories.' Kate had never heard Emma refer to her books as 'lovely' before, let alone 'exciting'. Was it a compliment? Probably not.

'Can you read me one of your stories?' asked Geraldine, obviously testing out such an unlikely proposition.

'They're stories for grown-ups,' explained Emma, still in an unnaturally cheerful voice.

Geraldine continued to stare balefully at Kate, who felt compelled to explain herself further.

'I haven't got a bag or a briefcase, let alone a stethoscope or a thermometer,' she said. 'And since I'm not wearing a white coat, I can't possibly be a doctor.'

'Oh, no! Kate's a totally frivolous person,' explained Emma, a little unkindly in Kate's view, and shooting a look in Kate's direction that ordered her to be frivolous immediately.

'The doctors have taken my mummy away,' said the child. 'And I want her back.'

'They've only borrowed her for a little while,' said Emma gaily. 'She'll soon be back home again. Now, while you draw me some more lovely pictures, Kate and I are going to be downstairs in the kitchen, talking nonsense and drinking coffee.'

'I was hoping we could talk about the bomb,' said Kate.

'Bomb! No nasty bombs round here, are there, Geraldine?' And Emma attempted a light-hearted laugh.

'Are you going to eat biscuits with your coffee?' asked Geraldine, who knew where her priorities lay.

'Chocolate ones,' said Emma coaxingly. 'I'll bring you up a glass of juice and a biscuit, shall I?'

'Yes. But I'll need two biscuits, please,' said Geraldine, turning back to her drawing.

Outside the room, Kate said, 'That child outwitted you, Emma.'

'I know. And I let her.' Which wasn't at all Emma's usual method of child-management.

'Where are, er, Flora and, er, Jack?' asked Kate. She always had difficulty remembering the names of Emma's younger children.

'Flora's at her playgroup this morning, and Jack's at school.'

'Goodness! And I thought Flora was still in her pram.'

'She's three and a half,' said Emma. 'And Jack's seven now.'

Kate thought it wise to move on, as Emma was getting the wistful expression that indicated she was about to rehearse the arguments she used to persuade her husband that they should have just one more baby, so she quickly led the way back to the kitchen.

Emma found juice and poured it into a plastic beaker

decorated with a befrilled rabbit as Kate opened the biscuits, put the kettle on and scooped coffee into the press.

'I think these should keep her happy for a while,' said Emma, indicating the tray with its plate of four chocolate biscuits arranged in a fan shape.

While Emma was upstairs, and the sound of the two voices in conversation drifted down, Kate looked around the kitchen. There were changes from when she was last here, though at first she couldn't quite put her finger on what they were.

A large carton full of the sort of healthy vegetables that most people's children refused to eat, but which Emma's had doubtless been trained since babyhood to spoon up with delight, stood on the table. On the windowsill rested a fat little squash, matt green with yellow freckles, its segments deeply indented. Beside it lay a child's sock, the belt belonging to a green dress and a packet of cat food. A battered violin case leant against a dresser from whose half-open drawers dangled oddments of string and a school tie. Two mismatched trainers sprawled in a corner and a heap of ironing was piled up on the floor near the utility room.

Next to the cooker, an ageing cat with moulting beige fur and ragged ears slept peacefully in its basket. Well-thumbed children's books covered every surface.

All the familiar, comfortable Dolby clutter. A long way from animal rights extremists and bomb threats.

When Emma returned with the empty tray, Kate said, 'You've got your hands full at the moment, looking after young Geraldine as well as your own children.'

'You mean the house looks a tip?'

No more than usual, thought Kate. 'No, not at all, but I wondered how you were managing to fit your own work into such a crowded day.'

'Work? I'm not like you, totally free from domestic respon-sibilities. Running this family is enough work for anyone!' Emma ran a hand through her hair, which only pointed up the fact that she needed a decent haircut. 'Especially now.'

'Of course it's a full-time job for anyone,' said Kate. 'It's just that you usually manage to do so many other things as well.'

'Yes, I did, didn't I,' said Emma, sitting down and pouring the coffee. She pushed the chocolate biscuits over towards Kate, then took a couple for herself. 'I'm sorry Kate, I shouldn't take it out on you.'

'Don't worry: I can see you're under pressure.'

'I can't think how I ever found the time to do any writing. I thought when the children got older things would be easier, but it hasn't worked out that way. What with keeping an eye on my mother now she's getting frailer, and seeing to the house and children, I can't see how I'll ever be able to start writing my next book.' She stared at her chocolate biscuit as though it held the answer to all her problems, then broke it in half and stuffed it into her mouth, since, after all, only an unending supply of chocolate-covered food could make up for her disappointment.

'You'll get back to it once the crisis with your friend is over.'

'Do you really think so? Sometimes I wonder whether I'll ever have another publishable idea.'

'You know you have real talent, Emma. That won't leave you: it's just hibernating for the present.'

'Yes. Maybe you're right,' said Emma, a little more cheerfully.

'Don't the older ones give you a hand? Sam and, er . . .'

'Sam and Abigail? Sam's a good lad, but you know what

boys are like! Or maybe you don't, but it's hard for them to think of anything but their own concerns at this age. And of course, with the explosion at the lab, he has quite enough on his plate without my adding to the demands on him.'

'You must have been terrified, knowing he was so close to the explosion.'

'It was a small bomb, apparently, but I couldn't help thinking about what might have been. Sam seems more worried about Kerri, to tell the truth.'

'His girlfriend?'

'Yes. They met at the lab. She's not his usual type – she's a nervous little thing, and always seems scared stiff when she comes here for a meal. We're hardly intimidating, though, are we, Kate?'

'Maybe she's not used to such a crowd.'

'Oh, we're hardly a crowd! Sam's very protective towards her, but I just hope he isn't being *used*.'

'He's a good lad. I expect he knows what he's doing.' He sounds as though he's growing up to be just like his mother, Kate thought.

'Well, they're both very young. They'll not feel the same about each other when he gets back from China next year.'

'You think? But tell me, Emma, have the police decided yet who was responsible for the bomb?'

'We've heard nothing definite, but Sam's father's sure it was the animal rights people.'

'Well of course it was!' exclaimed Kate. 'That was obvious. Did you see that man who calls himself Razer on *Newsnight*? He refused to condemn the violence, and said that anyone who worked in a lab was fair game for his thugs.'

'I think you're exaggerating, Kate.'

'Hardly. Of *course* Razer and his friends were behind it. I can't think why the police haven't arrested anyone yet. Suppose they decide to have another go!'

'Sam and his colleagues are taking it more calmly than you, Kate.'

'I bet they're worried, even if they're not telling you about it.'

'There have been so many false alerts, they're taking bomb threats in their stride these days. I suppose it's something we're all having to learn to live with.'

'Well I certainly don't want to get used to it. I want someone in a blue uniform to go out and arrest the bombers.'

'It does disrupt their work at the lab, certainly, and Kerri's like you, she gets very upset about it. After the explosion she was really in shock, poor girl.'

'I'm not surprised!'

'But she should pull herself together. I'm fond of her, but she is always in need of reassurance. I know it's unkind of me, but I do wish Sam had picked a less needy person. Such a white face and huge dark eyes when they got here. I ran a hot bath for her, then wrapped her in a duvet and made them both a comforting meal. I put her in the spare bed in Amaryl's room for the night. Sam was relieved, I know. He was much more concerned for her than he was for himself. But I wish Kerri would show a little more *backbone*. Sam shouldn't have to prop her up all the time.'

'He's always been good-natured. You wouldn't want him to change.'

'No. I wouldn't. It began with rescuing abandoned kittens and injured fledglings, then he moved on to raising money for starving children and AIDS victims in sub-Saharan Africa. I suppose I should take it in my stride when he falls for a girl like Kerri.'

'But you don't think it's serious?'

'For the moment, perhaps, but I don't think it will survive Sam's gap year away.'

'And what about the others? How's Abigail?'

'Abigail! All she thinks about – and talks and dreams and eats and sleeps – is her wretched boyfriend.'

'How old is she?' asked Kate, who still pictured Emma's daughter as a tomboy with a flat chest, riding a skateboard through town while wearing her brother's cast-offs.

'Abigail's sixteen. "And three-quarters", as she would say. And the boyfriend is a man, a postgraduate – really much too old for her. Still, he's very steady and dependable. I don't think we have anything to worry about there.'

The likelihood that a sixteen-year-old would fall for someone steady and dependable seemed remote to Kate, but as she didn't wish to add to Emma's cares, she kept the thought to herself.

'Maybe you need to concentrate on your own needs for a while instead of taking on everyone else's problems,' she said.

'I can't just leave people to flounder around on their own. And I still have children who need me full time. I can't be so detached.'

Recognising that they were about to embark on their well-worn discussion about the advantages to Emma's family of her taking time off for own relaxation, they both paused.

'I'm afraid Fungus is getting to the end of his days,' said Emma in a desperate non sequitur.

Kate saw that the Dolbys' dog – patched with yellow fur, bleary-eyed, deaf – had wandered into the kitchen through the open door and now sat with his grey muzzle on Emma's knee, staring at the second chocolate biscuit as it disappeared into her mouth. Long strings of drool dripped on to Emma's trousers. Absentmindedly she took another biscuit from the packet and gave it to the dog, who crunched it up contentedly. The drool was now chocolate-coloured and dripping on to her shoes.

'The poor thing isn't so well these days. There's a problem with his hips, and a discharge from his ears; and he's permanently moulting; and his digestion doesn't seem to work as well as it used to.' Fungus dutifully farted to illustrate the point. Kate buried her nose in her coffee cup until the air cleared.

'So what's up with Geraldine?' she asked, feeling she'd learnt more than enough about Fungus by now.

'Apart from being an anxious little thing, Geraldine's doing very well, really. It's her mother who isn't. Have I mentioned my friend Jenny Lindley to you? She's married to Bob, who works in the same department as Sam at Brookes.'

'I think I remember their names, but I don't believe we've ever met,' said Kate cautiously. They weren't the couple who had been present at the disastrous dinner party in a fashionable restaurant, when Emma drank too much and became obstreperous, were they? No, she remembered on that occasion the woman had been called Megan.

Kate was always wary of Emma and Sam's friends. For a while she and Sam's brother George had been an item and had lived together for some months while Kate was recovering from the effects of a knife attack. After she and George broke up, she had the feeling that the Dolbys disapproved of her for walking out on him for no good reason.

'Jenny tries to make light of it, but there's obviously something very wrong and she doesn't seem to be getting any better,' Emma was saying.

'What seems to be the matter?'

'To begin with, she was forgetting things, and getting muddled.'

'That will happen to us all eventually! How old is she?'

'Not much over forty.'

'Oh.' Twenty years too young to start getting forgetful, surely? It sounded as though Emma was right to be worried.

'It's out of character. Jenny has a very good mind – at least she used to have.' In Kate's experience, most of Emma's friends had very good minds, also superior educations and socially responsible jobs.

'Has she seen a doctor?'

'Her GP could find nothing wrong. But I don't think she was telling him everything. He asked her to come back in six months' time, so I think he was just trying to get rid of her. But now she's getting worse. I spoke to her the other evening and I thought she must be drunk. I could hardly understand what she was saying.'

'You don't think perhaps she *had* been drinking?' asked Kate tentatively.

'I've never seen her drink more than the odd glass of wine. Certainly not enough to cause such slurred speech. When I mentioned it, she said she hadn't had a drink for a couple of days, so I sent her back to her GP. He's referred her to a neurologist, so perhaps they'll get to the bottom of it now. To be honest, Kate, I thought she might have had a small stroke.'

'They're pretty good up at the JR hospital. I'm sure they'll sort it out soon,' said Kate.

Emma shook her head. 'And then this morning I had another call. She was so incoherent that I could hardly understand her, and I could hear Geraldine screaming in the background. The other child was at school, so the two of them were on their own. I couldn't tell what had happened so I got in the car and drove round there as fast as I could.'

'She's lucky to have you for a friend.'

'It took me several minutes to persuade Geraldine to open the door to me, and then I found Jenny in a heap at the bottom of the stairs. She'd lost her footing at the top, apparently, and fallen the length of the flight.'

'Was she badly hurt?'

'She was bruised, and there was a graze on her forehead where she'd hit it on the hall table. She didn't seem to have broken anything, so I helped her to her feet and sat her down in the kitchen, dealt with the graze and made her a cup of tea. But then I noticed something else.'

'Yes?'

'There was another bruise, yellowing, on her cheekbone, and a plaster covering a gash on her elbow.'

'You're not suggesting that someone has been hitting her? Could it be her husband?'

'I asked her how she got the other injuries, and at first she looked vague, but then she said, "Oh yes. I must have slipped and fallen down the stairs yesterday. Or maybe it was last week. I forget now." So that's when I rang for the ambulance. At least they might take a proper look at her in the hospital. And Kate, she didn't even seem particularly concerned about what had happened to her – I'd say she was detached from her own life, if that doesn't sound far-fetched.'

'I think I understand what you're saying.'

'I let Bob know what had happened, and after I'd seen Jenny into A & E, and Bob had turned up, I brought Geraldine back here with me. I'll be picking Lucas up from school this afternoon and I'll give him his tea, too. Bob's bound to be worried about Jenny, and the children need some stability in their lives.'

Kate took another biscuit and thought about what Emma had been saying as she ate it.

'Why don't you ever put on weight, when you eat so many biscuits?' asked Emma.

'Me? Oh, I have a brilliant metabolism. I can eat whatever I want. It's just good luck, I suppose.'

'It doesn't seem fair,' and Emma looked down at her own expanded waistline with despair.

'Auntie Emma!' called a high, insistent voice from upstairs.

'Coming, darling!' and Emma disappeared again.

Kate placed their coffee mugs in the dishwasher, brushed the biscuit crumbs from the table, and wondered whether it was time to leave Emma to concentrate on Geraldine. She picked up her bag.

'No, don't leave yet,' said Emma, returning with Geraldine's empty plate and mug. 'I'll just take her up some more juice, and then we can talk some more.'

'Are you sure?'

'I haven't got round to asking you to the party, have I?' And Emma whisked upstairs again before Kate could answer.

Party? Surely Emma's hands were full enough without a party to organise?

'It's for Sam,' Emma explained when she had seated herself back at the kitchen table. 'Young Sam. He's coming up for eighteen.'

'And how time flies,' said Kate.

'So we're celebrating his eighteenth birthday and also the fact that he's off to China for part of his gap year.'

'Isn't he a bit young for that?' said Kate, remembering the gangling adolescent she had seen last year.

'He was only seventeen when he took his "A"s,' said Emma with warranted pride. 'But he'll be eighteen when he leaves for China. Old enough to get drunk or to marry, and to vote. I think he'll survive a few months abroad on his own.'

'I'm sure, said Kate hastily.

'Sam and his friends will be celebrating in their own way during the evening, of course, but we're putting on a lunch party for friends and relations of all ages, in the garden if it's warm enough; otherwise we'll all have to squeeze into the house.'

'Sounds like fun,' said Kate. You could 'squeeze' a hundred or more friends and relations into the Dolbys' house, she calculated.

'I'm planning a buffet lunch, then strawberries and champagne, all quite simple.'

'But still a lot of work.'

'It is, rather, but I'm sure I'll manage. I haven't got round to sending out all the invitations yet, so please put it in your diary.' And she mentioned a date that sounded remarkably close. 'Of course, all the family know about it, but I really must get round to inviting the friends he wants to see too.'

'Couldn't you ask Sam to do that himself?'

'Sam? Oh, he's such a scatterbrain. I always have to do things like that myself.'

For a moment Kate wasn't sure whether Emma was referring to her son or her husband, but it struck her that they might both be less scatterbrained if Emma occasionally showed more faith in their abilities. But then, who was she to pretend to know anything about husbands and sons?

'Let me know if there's anything I can do to help,' she said, picking up her bag again.

'I expect I'll manage,' said Emma. 'I generally do.'

As Kate stood by the front door, preparing to leave, she paused for a moment and turned back to Emma, whose attention was already back on Geraldine.

'I know you've got too much on your plate already, Emma,

but hasn't anything new surfaced about the explosion? Hasn't Sam – your husband, I mean – heard anything?'

'Kate, leave it! It's nothing to do with you and there's nothing you can do to help.'

'I was there when the protesters marched down St Giles. The bomb went off less than a quarter of a mile from my house: of course it has something to do with me!'

Emma sighed. 'I don't know why you have to get involved in these things, I really don't.'

'But?'

'Sam – yes, my husband – did mention that a colleague of his named a number of organisations active here in Oxford that believe in direct action.'

'Why Oxford, do you think?'

'The university – well, both the universities – is the target, naturally, because of the research they're doing.'

'Did he give you any names?'

'Stupid made-up things.'

'Yes?'

'Sorry, Kate, I really can't remember. Now I must get back to Geraldine. And please leave it all alone. There's nothing you can do that can't be better done by the police.'

'I won't do anything stupid.'

'No? I recognise the expression on your face, the manic light in your eye.'

'I'm off home to work on a new book. It's the light of creativity you're seeing.'

Emma closed the door behind Kate. She looked unconvinced.

9

'Hi, Susie.'

'Is that Jon? Jon Kenrick?'

'You recognised my voice after all this time: I'm flattered.'

'Oddly enough, I was thinking about you, wondering what you were doing and how you were getting on. And then the phone rang and I heard your voice. It must be telepathy.'

'Or coincidence,' said Jon prosaically. 'Think of the number of times the phone rings and it isn't the person you were thinking about.'

'Oh, Jon, you haven't changed!'

'It's been a while: I expect we've both changed these past few years.'

'Is it that long?'

'I'm afraid so. Though I did glimpse you briefly in Green Park earlier this year.'

'Why didn't you come up and speak to me?'

'You were heavily involved with your family: Gary was tangled up in someone's dog lead, the dog was barking and Freddie was clinging like a limpet to your knees, howling, so I thought it wasn't a good time for a chat.'

'What a pity! I always enjoyed our little chats.'

'Actually, there's something specific I wanted to talk to you about.'

'And what's that?'

'Freddie.'

'Freddie? You weren't thinking that perhaps . . .'

'No, of course not!'

'Good. Because he couldn't possibly be.'

There was a short silence at Jon's end of the line.

'I had worked that out for myself,' he said eventually.

'I'm glad about that. So what's happening in your life?' she asked.

'I have a new job, in the private sector this time. And I've moved from London to Oxford.'

'That's a surprise: I've never seen you as a provincial type.'

'Oxford's a very lively city,' he insisted. 'And anyway, it's only an hour from London.'

She laughed. 'That's what I mean – *provincial*! What prompted the move?'

'I told you about Kate, didn't I?'

'Frequently. And enthusiastically.'

'Well, now I've moved into her place.'

'That's quite a commitment, isn't it?'

'Definitely. And we're looking to buy our own house,' he said, ignoring Kate's reservations.

'Wonders will never,' Susie said, and Jon noticed a wistfulness in her voice, so he hurried on.

'To get back to the reason I was ringing, I was wondering – we were wondering, I mean – whether you'd like to come down for the weekend.'

'All three of us?'

'Of course.'

'Because there's no way we'd leave Freddie with the nanny for the weekend. We spend quality time with him when we're not at work. Well, if I'm honest, I'm quite besotted with the child. We both are. I couldn't bear to be parted from him.'

'Yes, well—'

'You can't believe how clever he's getting. We've enrolled him in a Talented Toddlers group, and as soon as we can persuade him to sit still for ten minutes at a time we're starting him on a musical instrument. We think he'd love to get his hands on a cello.'

'Isn't that rather big for a toddler?'

'They have small-scale instruments for children.'

'Really?' Jon was wondering how to get off the subject. 'Well, to get back to the reason I was ringing . . .'

'About Freddie's music lessons? I didn't know you were interested in music.'

'No, not the music specifically. More the whole family situation.'

'Jon, you phone me up out of the blue, you ask about Freddie, and you invite us all down for the weekend, so the obvious question to ask is why.' Susie's tone had cooled noticeably. 'I'm getting the impression you're not really interested in Freddie; more in a token toddler, so to speak.'

'Freddie sounds wonderful. I'm really looking forward to meeting him. And of course it will be lovely to see you, Susie, and catch up with what you and Gary have been doing for the past year or two, but as well as that I'd like Kate to meet you all – as a family.'

'I was right: you're trying to sell her the joys of marriage and parenthood!'

'I wouldn't put it quite that way.'

'I guess she's holding on to her freedom for a while yet – sensible woman.'

'Look at you: you've got your career, and Gary and Freddie. I'd say that your life was a great success.'

'So you want her to see us as role models?' A sharpness

had entered Susie's tone that indicated to Jon that this conversation wasn't going exactly the way he had planned.

'What's wrong with that? I'd have thought you'd be flattered.'

'I suppose you have asked yourself whether you've chosen the right woman to be a domestic goddess? Maybe she's happier the way she is. Maybe she doesn't want to change. There are women like that, you know, who are perfectly contented with a life that doesn't include a family.'

'Once we've found a house of our own to buy, I'm sure we'll settle down together and she'll see things my way.'

'Don't bank on it, Jon; you could be setting yourself up for a big disappointment. And were you thinking along these lines when we were together?'

'I'm forty-six, Susie. I must be a late developer: but now it's time I got serious, isn't it?'

'Maybe I was serious about the future in those days. Had you ever considered that?'

'I'm really sorry if you wanted more from the relationship, but there's no going back now.'

'I understand that,' she said briskly. 'I live the perfect life and you'd like the Browne family to show your Kate just how wonderful if would be if she fell in with your plans.'

'I'd like to see you again, Susie,' said Jon, realising that he hadn't played the scene quite to Susie's liking. 'We can be friends now, can't we? We always got on really well, and it would be good if we could spend some time together. If it convinced Kate to see family life in a different light, then that would be a bonus.'

'I'm not so sure it would work, but if it's that important to you, we'll give it a try. Let's hope we can put on a convincing show for you, Jon.'

'Thanks, Susie. I really look forward to it.'

'Just like old times,' and again he thought he heard the suggestive note in her voice, but then she added casually, 'And maybe you – and Kate, of course – would like to come over to France and see what you think of the place we've found down near Aix-en-Provence. We're hoping that lots of our friends will come down to join us there next year when we've finished the renovations. It's such a lovely spot and there's plenty of room. I'm sure you'd both enjoy the life there.'

'Yes, I'm sure we would,' he replied, managing to keep any hint of envy out of his voice. 'Shall we get out our diaries and fix the date of the weekend in Oxford?'

Afterwards, Jon wondered whether he was imagining it. When he and Susie had broken up it had been a joint decision, but once or twice during the conversation he had felt that Susie was hankering after their old relationship. No, it couldn't be: she had Gary and Freddie to occupy her. Why should she need Jon too? Susie, he remembered, was a woman who couldn't help coming on to any man who ventured within flirting distance. It meant nothing. It was just the way she was.

10

'How's your day been?' Jon was opening the fridge, pouring them both a generous glass of white wine, humming tunefully under his breath.

'Up and down,' replied Kate, remembering her visit to Emma and her unproductive afternoon in front of a blank computer screen.

'Here, have some wine. I'm sure you deserve it. Would you like me to get the supper?'

'But it's my turn.'

'I don't mind. I'll do it.'

'Thanks,' she said, noticing he was more cheerful than usual. 'Anything special happened today?'

'I may have solved a niggling problem at last.'

Maybe it was a good moment to put in her own request. 'How do you feel about a few days away?' she asked.

'Where were you thinking of going?' He didn't sound enthusiastic.

'Somewhere really luxurious. A country house hotel where we can stroll in the grounds before dinner, and sit in front of a log fire to drink our coffee afterwards, maybe.'

'It sounds extravagant. Why don't we look for somewhere less ambitious?'

'Because that would miss the point.'

'The point?'

'To go somewhere special. Get out of the rut. Do something just for fun. It's only for two days, and it doesn't have to be in the country if you don't want. We could go to London: dinner at a really good restaurant, the best seats at the theatre, stay overnight instead of getting the train home. I think it's called a treat.'

Jon looked at her with a slight frown as though she was speaking a foreign language. 'I still don't see the point,' he said.

'I'd like to go somewhere where I don't have to worry about bombs going off at the end of the street and injuring my friends.'

'It was hardly the end of the street, and no one was injured. You're exaggerating, Kate.'

'OK. Forget it,' said Kate. She had a feeling that the foreign word that Jon failed to understand was 'fun'.

As he chopped an onion with precision, Jon said casually, 'I thought I'd take a look at the spare room after we've eaten.'

'Spare room?'

'The one at the back where we've been piling up our overflow.'

'What's brought this on?'

'Oh . . . nothing in particular. But you're right, we could do something different one weekend. We don't have to leave Oxford, though, do we?' Jon blinked and sneezed. 'Onion,' he said in explanation.

'Hm.'

It was around ten o'clock when Jon reappeared in the living room looking dishevelled and with a layer of dust sticking to the sweat on his face and neck. Kate had studiously ignored the regular tramping up and down stairs, and now she asked casually, 'How's it going?'

'Nearly finished.'

'You probably need this after all your effort.' She handed him another large, cold glass of wine.

'Thanks.'

He was halfway to the sofa before noticing that there was dust on his clothes too, so he remained standing as he drank the wine.

'What have you done with all the stuff?' asked Kate.

'It's in the back of the car. I'll get rid of it tomorrow.'

'But those are your much-loved possessions! I'm not bothered about the back room at the moment. You could have left them in there.'

'I've been thinking how few of them I really want to keep. There's no reason why I shouldn't stow them in the storage unit with my furniture. I'll get rid of the stuff I no longer want: there's no point in hanging on to it.'

'You're very brave, breaking with the past like that,' Kate said as she got to her feet. 'I'm just going up to admire what you've done.'

Jon followed her upstairs and stood at her shoulder as she opened the door.

'I see,' was all she said.

'I'll get the Hoover,' said Jon. 'And a duster. It'll look better after I've cleaned it.'

'It'll look like an empty room,' said Kate. There was a query in her voice which Jon ignored. 'But it's larger than I remember it, now that you've cleared it out.'

She went back downstairs and sipped her wine thoughtfully. As she listened to the hum of the Hoover overhead she wondered what, or even who, Jon intended to bring into her house (yes, *my* house, she thought resentfully) and install upstairs. And why couldn't he bring himself to talk to her about it?

A little while later she heard Jon in the shower, singing as he always did, and when he came back into the sitting room he was dust-free and smelling sweetly of her Roger & Gallet soap.

'I thought of going over to the storage unit this evening,' he said. 'But maybe it's getting a bit late. I'll drive over there straight after work tomorrow.'

'Fine,' said Kate, resolutely not asking him anything more about his plans. 'Were you proposing an early night?' she asked, taking in his attractively tousled damp hair.

'That sounds like a good idea,' he said, looking enthusiastic.

'Why don't you go up then? I'll just watch *Newsnight* and join you later.'

She saw the eager light fade from his eyes, but she hadn't quite forgiven him for keeping his plans for her house from her, nor for squashing her idea of a weekend away, so she didn't relent. She wanted to catch the local news too, to find out if any more was known about who was responsible for the explosion. After that she'd be in the mood to enjoy watching Jeremy Paxman savage an evasive politician.

And before she went to bed, she might just spend ten minutes Googling 'animal rights groups.' She might turn up something useful, or come across a name she recognised. Jon might not be interested in finding out who these people were, but she definitely wanted to know more.

'Hi there, Sooze. Had a restful day?'

Gary Browne slung his jacket over the arm of a chair and placed his briefcase on a console table next to a tall vase out of which trailed sprays of small cream flowers.

His wife frowned. 'Not exactly restful, no,' she said. 'If you remember, I stayed at home to blitz through some work without interruptions.' Susie stared pointedly at his jacket, which, together with his briefcase, was ruining the carefully contrived elegance of the room. Her own work was kept in her study and not allowed to stray outside its confines.

'Good for you. I expect you feel like a decent drink now, don't you? I know I do.'

'Yes, in a minute. But aren't you going to go up to say good night to Freddie first? You don't want to breathe whisky fumes all over the child. And you haven't even asked how he is.'

'Oh, sure, if you say so. I thought he'd be asleep by now.' Gary pushed his narrow-framed glasses further up his nose, then flattened his coarse reddish hair above his ears, looking admiringly at his wife. In spite of her busy day, she was dressed in immaculate silver-grey, a couple of shades lighter than her eyes so that they appeared dark and inviting against her fair skin. How lucky he was that such a beautiful and talented woman had fallen for *him*, out of all the men she might have chosen.

'You can't expect Freddie to be asleep yet. It's not even eight o'clock and he's been waiting up for you.'

Gary picked up his jacket but left his briefcase where it was and went upstairs to see his son, hoping that Susie would have stopped sniping at him when he returned.

'Hi there, Freddie,' he said.

Freddie was sitting up in his small bed. Above his head dangled a brushed-steel mobile of shining spacecraft, planets and stars.

'Want story!' He pushed his lips out and screwed up his eyes in the way that Gary recognised could lead at any moment to a full-volume bellow of rage.

'I just couldn't make it any earlier,' said Gary

apologetically. 'Daddy had to stay at the office to make us all lots of lovely money, but I'm here now and reporting for book duty.'

Freddie stared at him for a moment while he worked out what his father was telling him, his forehead wrinkled just like Susie's when she was puzzling something out. In fact, his whole face was a miniature version of his mother's, with wide-set eyes in a face that would one day lengthen to an oval, a small, straight nose, and a smile that he was learning to use to get whatever he wanted from his parents. His hair was a couple of shades darker than Susie's and cut rather longer than Gary liked.

Freddie made up his mind; he stopped preparing to throw a tantrum and produced a highly coloured book from under his pillow.

'This one,' he stated firmly and handed it across to his father. 'Read!'

That was the wonderful thing about his son, thought Gary fondly as he opened the book: so articulate, so bright and intelligent, and so clear about his wants and needs. He was bound to go far in life.

Half an hour later, his stomach rumbling with hunger, his mind numb from the third repetition of the story about a talkative tractor, his voice hoarse from making the appropriate sound effects, Gary finally laid the book down. Freddie's eyes had drooped shut at last and his head had flopped back on to the flat pillow as he lost his battle with sleep. Gary covered him gently, placed a fatherly kiss on his forehead and tiptoed to the door. Susie had just come quietly up the stairs to join him and they both turned to look at their son. Susie walked across to the bed and bent down to stroke Freddie's hair and give him another kiss.

'His hair's so soft,' she said lightly. 'And they're still so vulnerable at this age, I feel I have to protect him every hour of the day.'

'Don't worry. He's a tough little fellow really,' said Gary, but he looked just as fondly at Freddie lying so snugly in his bed.

When he had turned the light out, he flicked the switch that animated Freddie's mobile, so that the stars and planets began to twinkle restfully in the dark, revolving at a speed calculated to soothe a restless child back to sleep if he should happen to wake in the night.

Downstairs, he looked for the whisky that Susie had poured for him earlier.

'Afraid the ice has melted,' his wife said. 'You shouldn't have spent so much time reading him a story. I'd already read him two, complete with sound effects.'

'He's so keen to learn something new, and we don't want to discourage him from reading, do we?'

'He is a little star,' said Susie fondly. 'But you must be exhausted. I'll get the dinner on the table right away.'

'Thanks.' Gary was reaching the stage when he felt too tired to eat, but he knew he must make an effort to do justice to Susie's efforts in the kitchen.

Once they'd started on their marinated grilled tuna steaks which she had served with a bowl of mixed green salad, Susie said brightly, 'How do you fancy a weekend away in the country?'

'Away from home? What about Freddie?'

'Oh, he'd come with us. We could introduce him to sheep and cows and meadows full of buttercups,' said Susie. 'He'll love it. What do you think?'

'Yes, we do both need a break, don't we? Where were you

thinking of going? Should we try that manor house hotel in the Cotswolds that everyone's been raving about?'

Gary forked in a large mouthful of assorted leaves, spluttering as the balsamic vinegar hit the back of his throat, while Susie said, 'I thought we'd go to Oxford. It's not too far to drive, it's full of history and culture – and Freddie's not too young to start appreciating art – and yet at the same time it's really quite rural.'

'Hardly,' said Gary, regaining his voice. 'It's a city, not a little market town, and with a bad pollution problem, they say.'

'The pollution's only bad in the middle of the summer. There'll be no problem in September or October.'

'And what about the animal rights criminals? They set off one bomb recently, so I imagine they could do it again.'

'Bomb!'

'Yes. Didn't you hear about it?'

'No. How many people were killed?'

'None,' said Gary, sounding as though he was disappointed not to be telling a more exciting story. 'It was only a small bomb,' he conceded. 'It did some minor damage to a research lab. Might have killed a few of those rats they're so keen on, but that's all.'

'Oh, well there's nothing to worry about, then. It's no more dangerous than London, is it?'

There was a pause while they both chewed on tuna. Susie leant across and refilled Gary's wine glass. As she did so, her accurately cut, shining platinum bob swung across her perfect jawline and obscured one of her slate-blue eyes so that he found it difficult to read her expression. 'And it happens that we've received an invitation – for Freddie, as well as for us,' she continued.

'Who from?'

'Kate and Jon.'

Gary looked blank. 'Who are they? Have I met them? Did they come to our wedding?'

'Oh, I expect so. He's just moved into a new job in Oxfordshire, with a private security outfit, I believe, and she's a writer. A successful writer,' she added, knowing that Gary wouldn't want to meet any other sort. 'They've asked us down for the weekend and I said I'd check with you, of course, but that I was sure we could find a date free in the next month or so.'

'Does she write children's books? Is that why they want to meet Freddie?'

'No, I don't think so. Lightweight novels, I believe.'

'It sounds as though he's dull and she's arty.' And Gary didn't use 'arty' as a compliment, Susie knew.

'Don't be so negative. They're a charming couple and highly amusing,' she said brightly.

'Do we have to go? We'll be slumming it, won't we?'

'Jon's used to a comfortable single existence, so I hardly think it will be a squalid little place. I believe she's a wonderful cook, too.' Should she ring Jon tomorrow and ask him to persuade Kate to sign up for an urgent cookery course? she wondered.

'Talking of good cooks, this is a brilliant meal, darling. I don't know how you get everything done, and done so well, at that.'

'Well thank you, darling. It's good to be appreciated.'

'But getting back to your friends, how come you haven't mentioned them before? Why don't I remember them?'

'Admit it, darling, you're not very good at names and faces.'

'I remember them if they're important.'

'Important to your work, yes. But this will be a social occasion. A break from routine; a chance to get away so that we can relax.'

'Well, Sooze, I can see you've got your heart set on it.'

'I've made the chocolate dessert you're so fond of. I'll just go and get it. Would you like cream with it, or vanilla ice cream?'

'You don't think I'm putting on weight?'

'You? No, of course not. You're even sexier than the day I married you.'

'Cream then, please.'

'And we might get some fresh air and exercise while we're away from London,' said Susie, returning from the kitchen with two glass bowls.

'Oh, why not?' said Gary. 'If we get tired of your friends' company I suppose we can always go for long walks with Freddie in search of Oxford's sheep and cows.' Susie looked at him doubtfully: was he making a joke? 'Have they got children, by the way?' he asked.

'Not yet.'

'Oh well, never mind: they're bound to love Freddie. Give them a ring and fix up a date.'

A couple of evenings later, Jon found Kate standing in the open doorway of the empty spare room, looking thoughtful.

'I was wondering if you had any plans yet for this room,' she said.

'How do you feel about having a couple of friends to stay for the weekend?'

'People from London, do you mean?'

'Yes.' There was a slight note of enquiry in his reply.

'Good thinking. You don't want to lose touch with old friends now you've moved out to the sticks. When were you thinking of asking them?'

'We're pretty well free at the weekend for the next month or so, aren't we?'

'Apart from Sam Dolby's eighteenth bash, and anything you have planned, yes.'

'How about the week after Sam's party, then?'

'Sounds OK to me.'

'I'll do some phoning.'

'Haven't you forgotten something?'

'What's that?'

'This room. I'd have thought our contemporaries were getting too old for sleeping bags. Unless these friends of yours are going to sleep on the floor, we'd better organise some furniture.'

'Don't worry about it. Leave it all to me.'

'And I'll get out the cookery books. One way and another I've got into a bit of a rut recently. It's time I tried something a little more adventurous.'

'I look forward to it – not that your cooking's been at all boring, of course!'

'Now you're being tactful. How many people were you thinking of inviting, by the way?'

'Just two.'

'Let me know when you've fixed the date.' Kate asked for no more details. Somehow she had the impression that Jon's plans for the proposed weekend were further advanced than he was letting on.

'Oh, and Kate, do you think you could take a look at my shoulder?'

'If you like. Why?'

'I think I may be growing a small lump. I can't quite see it, even in the mirror. There, by the shoulder blade.'

Kate tried not to let him hear her sigh. 'I'm sure it's nothing to worry about,' she said. 'But of course I'll look at it for you.'

11

Blake was right in thinking that his staff would be able to get back to work once the forensic team had left, the security people had pronounced the place to be safe, and the necessary clearing-up and repairs had been done. He'd made himself unpopular with a lot of people, but it had taken only a couple of days.

The staff were a bit subdued, even the younger ones, but that was only to be expected. And they were all making an effort to compensate for the time that had been lost. Blake didn't need to remind them that in their line of work, there were no prizes for coming second.

After their first day back, Sam and Kerri had retrieved their bikes (which were unharmed, though dusty) and cycled together down the High Street to the Plain, where Sam took the left fork towards Headington, while Kerri pedalled down the Cowley Road towards the house she shared with a group of friends.

Sam had offered to escort her all the way home, but Kerri was feeling much more cheerful after Emma's care and attention and insisted she was fine on her own. Emma had been wonderful with Kerri, of course, but Sam wondered whether Kerri had noticed the occasional flash of disapproval in his mother's eyes when she looked at her. Emma would come round, he thought, once she got to know Kerri for the wonderful person she was.

In Headington, Sam pushed open the back door of his parents' house, took a step forward and stumbled over a tricycle that was standing just inside.

'Shit!' he exclaimed, but without resentment. There had been children's toys strategically placed to trip up the adults in the Dolby household ever since he had left his own roller skates on the stairs a dozen years ago.

He could hear sounds of activity upstairs – his mother's voice soothing, a child whingeing – as he called out, 'Hi, Emma! I'm back!'

There was no response. But that, too, was getting to be the norm these days.

Once her children reached sixteen, Emma lost interest. He and Abi were aware of it, but were secretly glad that they could live their own lives without too much interference, or 'concern', as Emma would put it. Babies, that was Emma's thing. She had at last stopped producing babies of her own, he and Abi were relieved to see, but now she appeared to have taken on the offspring of her friend Jenny.

Much as he loved his parents, Sam knew that it was time to strike out on his own, which was why he had chosen to go to China for his gap year.

Abigail was the nearest in age to Sam, seventeen in three or four months' time, and Sam thought it would be a good idea if Emma actually took more notice of her. He wasn't at all sure that his sister had made the right choice with her new boyfriend, but Emma hadn't listened to him when he had tried to discuss it with her. And it didn't look as though Abi would get tired of Eric any time soon. It wasn't a serious relationship; there was too much of an age gap for that, but there was something – sex, probably – that was keeping them together.

Then there was Kerri. While Sam was away, she'd need a

motherly eye on her, and he hoped that Emma would take her under her wing when he left the country – feed her some decent food, put a load of laundry through the washing machine. She had been very kind when they had turned up at her door after the explosion, but her attention had soon been diverted back to the young ones again.

He pushed his hands through his hair in a gesture he unconsciously copied from his father. When he was younger he had worn his hair cropped really short, afraid that his school mates would laugh when they discovered that his name was really Samson – Sam attended the sort of school where the pupils were familiar with stories both biblical and mythological, and had immediately picked up on the origin of his name. But now he was approaching eighteen, he felt confident enough to grow it long (though just at a time when his contemporaries were shaving their own heads nearly bald). His decision had certainly been influenced by the way his hair grew thick, wavy and a dark red colour that the young women of his acquaintance, especially Kerri, found attractive.

Sam went upstairs to his room, circumnavigating a wooden scooter, assorted limbless furry animals and a football on his way.

'Oh, there you are!' Emma emerged from Tris's room holding a tennis racquet, though she had never been known to play the game.

From inside the room came his sister Amaryl's voice: 'But why can't I have Sam's room when he goes to China?'

'Hi, Emma. Is anything up?' Sam thought his mother looked more careworn than usual.

'Nothing special, not once I've made enough space in Tris's room to put down the camp bed for Lucas. I don't want to send him back to Jenny's just yet.'

Sam thought it better not to disentangle the complexities of his mother's remark. 'OK if I do a load of washing?' he asked.

'Of course. If you're doing pale colours, could you put in the things on the floor by the machine. I have sorted them. And I nearly forgot, there were several phone calls for you today.'

'Really? Who was it? Why didn't whoever it was try my mobile?'

'He didn't leave his name, but I must say he didn't sound a very nice person, Sam. When I asked him what it was about and whether I could help, he laughed quite nastily and said you'd know what it was about, a criminal like you, and I'd find out soon enough when retribution caught up with you.'

'Sounds like a nutter to me.'

'Do you know what he was talking about?'

'No. Really, Mum, I've done nothing criminal recently. If he calls again I'll speak to him and put him right.' In his eagerness to soothe Emma's worries, he forgot that he hadn't called her 'Mum' for more than a year.

Emma returned to Tris's room, still holding the tennis racquet, and Sam disappeared into his own room to gather a load of dirty clothes together. He felt a twinge of resentment that Emma was more interested in her friend's children than in her own first-born. She hadn't even asked him about the conditions at the lab: one might almost believe that she found the subject of Sam's work boring.

And then there were the mysterious phone calls. Did they have anything to do with the animal rights people, or the explosion at the lab? But why would they target someone as insignificant as Sam, and how would they even know who he was, and where he lived?

Even as he pondered the question, the phone rang. Knowing his mother was busy, Sam went to answer it.

'Sam Dolby,' he said, unusually formal.

'That would be the younger Sam Dolby? The animal-experimenter? The murderer?'

'What?'

'This is just to let you know that we know where to find you, Sam Dolby, and we know what we're going to do to you if you don't stop the torture. This is your final warning.' And the connection clicked off.

Candra drove home in her silver Peugeot 207. Blake frowned whenever he saw her driving it, but she didn't like being trapped in a hot, crowded, smelly bus with strangers who would be shouting into their mobile phones and poking her in the ribs with their bulging shopping bags. She had paid for the privacy of a car and that was how she would travel.

It was a relief to be on her own again, away from the stressful atmosphere of the lab, she thought, as she turned into the quiet backwater where the low blocks of flats, 'suitable for one or two professional people', as the estate agent had described them, sat serenely in their grassy surroundings.

She parked in her designated space, and walked into the entrance hall. It was so peaceful here: no loud televisions booming out into the stairwell, no inconsiderate playing of music, and everything kept clean by the woman who came in to Hoover and dust twice a week. Candra lived at the top of the block, on the first floor, and since she was feeling more tired than usual, she took the lift instead of running up the stairs.

The walls were painted a fresh cream colour, the woodwork was sparkling white, and there were prints of picturesque mountains and lakes on the landing. At least, that was what Candra was expecting to see when the lift doors opened opposite her flat.

MURDERER.

The word was spray-painted in red letters two feet tall across her door, spilling over on to the wall.

The lift door slid shut behind her. Candra opened her mouth to scream, but managed to stop herself. How many of her neighbours had seen the accusation? Thank goodness they were all out at work during the day and perhaps had no reason to walk upstairs. She looked around. On the wall next to the lift there was more graffiti, smaller letters, in blue this time.

ANIMAL TORTURERS WILL DIE.

Shaking, she opened the door to her flat, dreading what she might find inside. But it was all right. Everything was as she had left it, she found, as she made a tour of the rooms.

She needed a cup of tea. She needed a drink. She needed to phone the police. And Blake. But before she did anything else, she had to scrub those filthy words off her door and wall. There were a couple of bills and half a dozen pieces of junk mail on her doormat, and she could only hope that the postman had arrived too early to see what had been written about her.

She shivered to think of the man who had planted the bomb, or any of the mob marching into the Science Area, coming so close to her private space, and she sniffed the air as though gauging how recently a stranger had been there. Now you're being fanciful, she told herself. But he must have come during the daylight hours, while the outside doors were unlocked. Surely none of the other tenants would have opened the door to someone wearing a balaclava and holding a can of red spray paint?

She filled a bucket at the sink, pulled on rubber gloves, found scouring powder and scrubbing brush and set to work.

* * *

Arriving back at the house in east Oxford she shared with four others, Kerri parked her bike inside the back gate then dumped her backpack in the hall before sticking her head round the kitchen door.

'Hi, everyone! I'm home!' The room smelled reassuringly of takeaway pizza and instant coffee, but she was hoping that there was someone else in. Since the explosion she hadn't liked being on her own and she was already feeling nervous. Then she heard footsteps behind her and a familiar voice.

'Kettle's just boiled if you want a coffee,' said Mel.

'Might as well,' said Kerri, finding the last clean mug on the rack and digging a spoon into the catering pack of instant. Then another of her housemates appeared, and the kitchen felt reassuringly full of people.

'Have you seen your post?' asked Lynne. 'It looks like someone's sent you a prezzie.'

'I'll look at it in a minute,' replied Kerri, wondering if there was any of the pizza left.

'Pizza's all gone,' said Mel, as though reading her mind. 'But there's some kidney bean and veggie casserole in the fridge. You could heat that up if you like.'

'Thanks. I'll do a grocery shop tomorrow,' Kerri promised.

'Everything OK at work?' asked Lynne.

'Yeah. We're getting back to normal,' said Kerri.

'The man who did it must be mental,' commented Lynne.

'I suppose.' Kerri didn't want to talk about it. The sooner she could think about something different, the better. 'Shall I make us a batch of soup tomorrow?'

'If you like.' Lynne drifted away.

After her meal, Kerri left the dishes in the sink to be dealt with later, helped herself to an apple from the communal bowl on the table, and went out into the hall.

103

The mail was in an untidy heap on the table and she picked out two pieces addressed to her. One was junk mail, which she stuffed in the recycling bin by the front door, but there was another package that looked more interesting, which she took upstairs to her room.

Though she hadn't changed the colour of the walls when she moved in – they were still a brilliant electric blue – she had cleaned the paintwork and the windows, and pinned up her own posters. A shelf held her books, and the few papers on her desk were held in place by a blue glass paperweight. Her small collection of clothes was hanging on the chrome rail which she had wheeled into the corner. The cream shade on the table lamp was draped with a purple fringed scarf so that the room looked shadowy and mysterious in the evening (though Sam had inserted a low-energy bulb in case it caught fire). Yeah, this was her place and she was glad to be back. No mad bomber could reach her here.

She took a bite out of the apple and chewed it while she turned over the book-sized padded envelope: there was no return address. Her birthday was five months ago, in April; she hadn't heard from her mother for over a year, and she couldn't think who else might have sent her something. Sam wouldn't have posted a present, he'd have handed it to her, eager to see her reaction when she opened it. She prodded the package. It was slightly lumpy, and addressed to her in capital letters. Her name was spelt wrong, she noticed, but lots of people put a y at the end of Kerri instead of an i.

She took another bite of apple and started to pull open the flap, but even as she did so she felt a sudden presentiment of danger and hurled the packet away from her.

There was a flash, a blast of heat, and a loud report. Kerri started to scream.

12

'So tell me something about these friends of yours,' said Kate, staring at the patch of warm sunlight on the carpet where a cat would be dozing, if she still had a cat. It was that time after lunch on a warm Saturday when neither she nor Jon felt like doing very much.

'Friends?' Jon looked up from the magazine he was reading.

'The ones you've invited to stay for the weekend,' she answered patiently. 'You told me that a couple of friends had accepted your invitation to come down to Oxford for the weekend after Sam's birthday party.'

'You're not annoyed about it, are you?'

'No, of course not.' She tried hard not to speak through gritted teeth. 'We agreed it would be a good idea, but I just wanted to find out a bit more about them.'

'Didn't I say? They're called Susie and Gary Browne.'

'And?'

Jon frowned. 'Why the sudden interest? You're not going to write them in to one of your books, are you?'

'I doubt it. I'd just like some basic information about them: where do they live, how do they earn their living, how did you meet – stuff like that, just so that I can make reasonable small talk, if nothing else. And so that I can plan the shopping. Are they vegetarians, for example?

'I'm pretty sure they're not vegetarians; at least I know that Susie isn't, but I'll have to ask about Gary.' He turned back to his magazine, and Kate recognised that she came a poor second to anything with sails.

'What do they do?' she tried again. 'To earn a living, I mean,' she added.

'Hunh? Oh, she does something clever with numbers: she studied maths before getting a Masters in business studies in the States. She's the sort who's successful at whatever she puts her mind to – a real high-flyer. And Gary's in marketing, or sales maybe. They both work for LDPharma, but in different departments; big company, you know. It's where they met, I believe.'

What Kate wanted to ask was whether Susie was very good-looking as well as being successful, and how long she and Jon had known one another, since she was inferring from what he'd said that he knew Susie much better than he did Gary. But although she believed she would get an honest reply, she wasn't so sure that she wanted to have her small but niggling suspicion of their past involvement confirmed. 'You haven't mentioned them before, have you?' she asked.

'They've been away for a year or so, working in the company's Brussels office, so I haven't seen them for a while.'

'Yes, I can see you'd want to catch up with their news,' said Kate.

'What should cheer you up is that they've invited us down to their place in Provence next year,' added Jon, reluctantly putting his magazine aside.

'Their place in Provence?'

'In the south of France. *That* Provence. It might even be fun,' he added, as though he had at last learnt what the word meant.

'Sounds pretty good,' she conceded. 'But what about—' she began, when she was interrupted by the phone ringing.

'That's bound to be for you,' said Jon. 'Probably your mother.'

Kate remembered that she had last used the phone in the kitchen, so she went to find it and left Jon to his scrutiny of yachts and expanses of salt water.

'Hello?'

'Kate? Roz here.' The phone call *was* from her mother.

'Hi. What's up?' she asked.

'You're sounding very scratchy and impatient,' said her mother. 'Is there something wrong with your sex life?'

'That's none of your business!' She paused for a second and added, 'And no, there isn't.'

'That's good. I'm glad that you and Jon are getting on so well.'

Why could she never be sure whether her mother was being sarcastic? 'Yes, we are,' she said firmly.

'But you're finding that life as half of a couple isn't perfect,' said her mother, with the hint of a query in her voice.

'I have to admit that he can sometimes be, well, a bit of a hypochondriac,' said Kate, whose gaze had rested on the row of pill bottles and eye drops sitting on the kitchen worktop.

'All men are. Haven't you discovered that?' Then Roz's tone changed and she asked, 'Have you seen the local paper?'

'I skimmed through it. I saw the piece about the Jericho boatyard—'

Roz interrupted her. 'No, I'm not talking about that. It wasn't a very long paragraph and it was hidden on an inside page, so you probably missed it, but the police have been investigating the discovery of a car containing three bodies in an old gravel pit, somewhere west of here, near Witney.'

'Three, you say?'

'Yes.'

'Did it say whether they were male or female?'

'I don't think they know yet. I suppose they'll have to wait until the post mortems have been done.'

'But you're worried that they might turn out to be your friends the Freemans.'

'And their son, Jefferson. Yes, I am.'

'They've been gone for several months, but there's no reason to suppose that they're—'

'Dead,' said Roz. 'That's what you believe, isn't it?'

'I know you don't like to think badly of them, but they did disappear just when we found out what crooks they were. They probably knew they were about to be questioned by the police and—'

'Absconded? It's true that they disappeared suddenly and completely.'

'But that's what they were good at. That's why they were successful for so long. Each time people became suspicious of them, they moved on to a new location and changed their names.'

'I suppose so.' Roz didn't sound convinced. 'I did think they might have packed up and taken themselves off to somewhere like South America where they could start again. They weren't all bad, you know. They did a lot of good with their healing.'

Kate had her own opinion about this. Her mother seemed to have forgotten that the Freemans had tried to steal her money and then murder her in a house fire. But then Roz always did have a highly selective memory.

'I suppose I'll have to wait until the identities of the three people in the car are confirmed before I know for certain whether it's them,' said Roz.

'I know it's corny advice, but you should try to put the whole thing out of your mind.'

'I'll try.' Her mother sounded doubtful.

'I thought those flooded gravel pits were really deep,' said Kate, whose imagination was working as it always did when she was given the elements of a story. 'How did they discover the car?'

'Can't you leave the subject alone?'

'Sorry. You're trying to forget about it and I'm being insensitive, aren't I?'

'You are rather.' Roz sighed. 'But you won't be happy until I give you all the details, will you? After the scorching-hot weather in July and August, the water level in the gravel pits dropped by several feet. They are fenced off and surrounded by warning notices, but naturally kids take no notice. A group of boys saw the roof of the car just beneath the surface of the water, and one of them ran home and told his mother what they'd discovered. She reported it to the police.'

'If you find out any more about it, let me know, won't you?' said Kate, who could hear that Roz was more upset than she was letting on about the gruesome affair. In spite of their behaviour, Roz had liked the Freemans and considered them to be good friends.

Kate changed the subject and they chatted for a few minutes longer before hanging up.

When she returned to the sitting room, thinking about the conversation, she found Jon hadn't moved from the sofa, though he had put down his magazine and was now watching television. On the screen, cars were whining round a race track and she didn't feel like competing with them for his attention. There seemed no point in involving him in her mother's concerns, though he too had met and distrusted the Freemans.

'I'm going to do some filing,' she said eventually, just for something to say.

'Hunh?'

'Yes, filing, wearing nothing but strappy green four-inch heels, scarlet lippy and a big smile.'

'Hunh?

Was that a flicker of interest from Jon? No, apparently not.

'Never mind,' she said, and left the room. Susie Browne, however beautiful, was welcome to try her luck when Jon was reading about boats or drooling over fast cars, she thought as she went upstairs.

In her study, she switched on her computer and checked her emails – not that she expected to receive many on a Saturday afternoon, but it was a good way of doing something that looked like work, even if it wasn't. To her surprise there was a message waiting for her:

Hi Kate,

I gather Emma's asked you to my birthday bash. I hope you can make it, there's some people I'd like you to meet and also important stuff happening here I'd like to talk over with you before I leave for China.

Cheers, Sam

PS: Maybe it would be a good idea to talk even sooner.

What was that about? she wondered. She hoped that Sam wasn't following his mother and taking the world's problems on his shoulders. Eighteen, after all, was an age to be preoccupied with oneself, exclusively. But she mustn't forget that Sam was a Dolby, and therefore a Good Person.

She picked up her phone. She had the Dolbys' number on speed dial and she pressed the green button to connect.

Emma answered.

'You want to speak to Sam? I'm not sure he's in. He seems to spend all his time with Kerri these days. Well, after what happened to the poor girl, I can understand that she needs all the support she can get, and yes, I am glad he's being so caring.' Emma didn't sound at all pleased, Kate noted. 'Let me go upstairs and try his room.'

Emma still used a phone attached firmly to its base by a cord. Probably just as well in that household, thought Kate. If they owned a cordless, she could imagine Emma frantically searching the house for the receiver every time the phone rang. A few moments later, in the background, she heard footsteps and Emma calling her son, and eventually more footsteps and Sam's voice: 'Hi, Kate. Thanks for getting in touch so quickly.'

'Your message sounded urgent.'

'Yeah. Right. Look, can we meet somewhere for a talk?'

'Now?'

'Yes. If you can make it.'

'OK.' Jon wouldn't even notice she'd left the house. 'The pub round the corner's open all day. Would you like to meet there?'

'Cool. I'll cycle down. Twenty minutes?'

'Fine.' She gave him the name of the pub and rang off.

Ten minutes later she put her head round the sitting-room door and said, 'Just going out,' then left before Jon had even turned his gaze away from the screen.

13

At the pub, Kate ordered a pot of coffee for two and took it
into the courtyard garden at the back. She had just settled at a
table when Sam turned up.

'Thanks for coming,' he said, polite as ever, and accepted a
cup of coffee without mentioning that he might have preferred
a cold Stella at four thirty on a warm afternoon.

'So what's this all about, Sam?'

Sam stared at his coffee cup for a few moments as though
working out where to begin.

'It starts at the lab,' he said eventually. 'I'm working there
on a bursary for two months. We're doing research into
neurological diseases, really interesting stuff, and one day it
will make a big difference to a lot of lives, but of course we
use lab animals, rats mostly, for our experiments. You can do a
certain amount in a test tube, but you have to try things out on
animals,' he added ruefully.

'No need to apologise about it to me, Sam.'

'But there are people who feel strongly about it. Have you
seen the local news on the telly recently?'

'The protests in the Science Area against animal experiments? They've been going on for years, haven't they?
The protesters have been trying to stop the building of a
new research facility, but I thought the university had
taken out an injunction to prevent them harassing their staff,

as well as builders and office workers.'

'They still have the right to protest – and I agree with that, of course. They're not allowed to have so many people targeting the building at the same time, but even so it can be intimidating. And then there's the barmy fringe, the ones who are really violent – I think they're psychopaths who attach themselves to any passing protest, and no injunction's going to stop them.'

'You haven't been attacked since the explosion, have you?'

'No. Well, just a few unpleasant phone calls. Everyone in the lab's been getting them, and graffiti sprayed on to walls and garage doors, excrement through the letter box, that sort of thing.'

'What!'

'It's Kerri who copped it, though.'

'How do you mean?'

'A letter bomb.'

'My God! Was she badly hurt?'

'She realised what it might be just as she started to open it, and threw it across the room. It scorched her duvet and left black marks on the wall, but she wasn't really hurt. Except that she was in shock after the explosion at the lab, and now she's so nervous that she hardly dares leave the house. And one of her flatmates has to open her post for her.'

'You really care about her, don't you? You two are close.'

'She's on the same bursary scheme as me – she's really bright, though she has no confidence in herself. And yes, she's my girlfriend.'

It was as Emma had said: Kerri was intelligent, also damaged and vulnerable. Kate said, 'I can see why you're worried about her. You're taking it very calmly, but the situation's horrible. Aren't the police doing anything to stop these people?'

Sam shrugged. 'Like I said, it's Kerri I worry about, especially since I'm not going to be around for a while. She'll be on her own again.'

'I imagine she reported the letter bomb to the police?'

'They say it was a pretty amateurish attempt, but that it would have injured her face and hands when it went off if she hadn't thrown it away. It could have scarred her for life.'

'And all of you at the lab are on your guard now?'

'After the bomb there, do you mean? That was just a minor incident too. The place is operational again after only a couple of days. Security's tight at the moment: we all have to remember to carry our ID with us, or the porter won't let us in, and even internal doors have keypads to stop intruders. Luckily the bombers don't seem to be very competent, whoever they are.'

'You're being very laid back about all this destruction!'

'There's not much point in panicking, is there? And anyway, I don't want Kerri to go to pieces. One of us has to stay calm, and it will have to be me.'

'I wonder why they picked on your lab specifically. Why didn't they target one of the others? Your group's not famous, is it?'

'It will be one day,' said Sam loyally. 'And I've no idea why they chose us. It was just bad luck.'

'Maybe. But you mentioned phone calls and graffiti. How did they find out where you live? I don't suppose your department gives out your personal details to anyone who phones up and asks.'

'I shouldn't think they're that difficult to find. Dad's in the phone book, after all.'

'I bet Kerry isn't, if she's in a shared house.'

'True,' said Sam, frowning. 'It is worrying that they've bothered to track so many of us down.'

'How does Emma feel about the phone calls?'

'I suggested we should go ex-directory, but she wouldn't like it if people couldn't phone her up, and I don't want to scare her and get her as jittery as Kerri about what's happening.'

'I don't think Emma's easily scared.'

'No, but she'd go ballistic if someone threatened to harm one of the kids. It wouldn't take the activists long to find out that the way to get to me would be to threaten my family.'

For a moment Kate imagined an interesting package sliding through the Dolbys' letterbox and one of Sam's cheerful young siblings rushing to see what it was.

'It mustn't happen,' she said.

'No. But apart from closing down the lab, I don't see what we can do.'

'Is there some way I can help?' asked Kate, though it occurred to her that Jon was the one who knew about security and would be a lot more useful in a dangerous situation.

'That's why I wanted to see you. It's Kerri. I don't want to leave her alone – and she is alone, Kate; she's fallen out with her family big time so she doesn't keep in touch with them. I don't think they even know where she's living. She needs me around at the moment, but this trip to China is a chance I don't want to miss. I'll be away for about nine months, working in a school in a rural area and then . . . Sorry, you don't need to hear about that now, do you? This is about Kerri. I'd been hoping that Emma would do her usual mother act, but you know what she's like at the moment. Her time's fully occupied with her friend Jenny and Jenny's two kids. Even Jack and Flora aren't getting much of her attention at the moment, let alone Tris and Amaryl, or Dad, of course. I couldn't expect her to find the time to listen to Kerri when she's talking about her nightmares, or to coax her out of the house into the dangerous world outside.'

'So you hoped I'd take her on?'

'I can see it would be asking a lot – you don't even know her. But yes, I'd be really grateful if you would.'

'I'll give it a try,' said Kate doubtfully. 'But she might not like me.'

'You'll meet her at my birthday bash. And I know the two of you will get on. Anyone would like Kerri, and I don't see why she shouldn't like you.'

Kate wasn't so sure, but seeing Sam's anxious face, she said, 'I'll give it my best shot, Sam. You go to China, and take the long way home, too. I'll turn myself into Kerri's best friend and be just as motherly as I know how.'

Sam laughed. 'Don't overdo it!'

'You don't think I can do motherly?'

'Um, well . . . perhaps. Actually, Kate, there'll be some other people from the lab at the party, so you'll be able to meet them too. Blake, who's our boss, for example. And Greg, who's my supervisor. Maybe you'll notice something the rest of us have missed and then you'll be able to answer your own questions about the lab.'

'Are you saying you suspect one of them may support the activists?'

'It's a possibility.'

'And that they could have passed on useful information?'

'I don't want to be looking over my shoulder when I'm at work, wondering if there's someone I shouldn't trust.'

'So you'd like me to look them over for you. You have great faith in my ability to read character.'

'You're good at observation,' he said.

'OK. I'll turn up with a checklist and chat up anybody you think will be useful.' She spoke flippantly, but they both knew this was in deadly earnest.

'It's not long now to the party,' said Sam.

'And it's not long until you leave for China, either, so I'd better make some progress in getting to know Kerri while I have the chance.'

It seemed to Kate that what Kerri needed was a bodyguard rather than a lightly built novelist to look after her, but she doubted that Sam's bursary would run to such an expense, so she would have to do.

They'd finished the pot of coffee and Kate said, 'Would you like a beer before you cycle back to Headington? It must be thirsty work pedalling up that hill.'

'Thanks.' Sam brightened.

'A Stella?'

'Great.'

'I'd better remind Jon about the party, when I get back. I'm not sure he listens to what I say if it's not about boats.'

'Boats?'

'Ones with sails. I always knew it was an interest of his, but now I'm discovering that it's his passion. That and cars. And motorbikes.'

'We're all set for next Saturday at the Dolbys, aren't we?' she said to Jon when she returned home. He had turned off the television and set down his magazines, and she found him in the kitchen, looking out the ingredients for their supper.

'Next Saturday?' he queried.

'Yes, the invitation's on the mantelpiece in the other room and I've mentioned it several times. Emma's arranging a buffet lunch in the garden and I believe the celebrations will extend well into the afternoon.'

'Yes, of course you told me about it – and then it just slipped my mind.'

'You mean you can't make it?'

'I meant to tell you before this that I've been invited down to Havant on Saturday. I'd forgotten about the party. I'm really sorry, but I said I'd crew for Tim, so I can't let him down. I'll have to leave early in the morning and I won't be back until late.' Jon ran out of breath and looked at Kate appealingly.

'I see.' It wasn't that she minded going to a party on her own; it was the way Jon didn't bother to check the joint diary before arranging to go away.

'I'll have to miss the party, but it won't stop you from going, will it? And young Sam's more your friend than mine. I'm sure he finds me middle-aged and boring anyway.' He waited a couple of seconds for Kate to disagree.

'It's the middle-aged and boring party we've been invited to,' she said. 'Sam's off partying with his own friends in the evening, so Emma said.'

'Emma,' said Jon, nodding. 'Has that woman stopped taking on the troubles of the entire world yet?'

'Not as far as I know,' said Kate. 'It's one of the things I particularly like about her.'

'You'll have a good time there without me,' said Jon encouragingly. 'There'll be loads of people that you know and I don't, after all,' and he turned back to the chopping block.

It was true that the Dolbys and their circle were Kate's friends rather than Jon's, but surely it was time they became 'their' friends rather than 'hers'?

119

She would have liked to have Jon at her side – it made the aftermath of a party so much more enjoyable when you had someone to discuss it with. On the other hand, it left her free to get to know Kerri, as well as Sam's colleagues at the lab, and that would be easier without Jon dogging her every move.

'I'll set the table. Where would you like to eat?' she asked.

'At the kitchen table, I guess,' he replied, turning away from his saucepans for a moment. 'You know what you should do with this place, Kate?'

'Tell me.'

'You should knock the whole of the ground floor into a single living space: cooking, eating, relaxing. It's what everyone's doing now.'

'I'll give it some thought,' she said. Did this mean that Jon was reconciled to the idea of remaining in Jericho rather than moving to the country, at least for the present? If so, it might be worth considering reorganising her living space according to his plan.

It was on the Friday afternoon, the day before Sam's party, that Kate heard from her mother.

'I don't suppose you've seen the local paper today?' asked Roz.

'I don't see it very often, I'm afraid.'

'Avril and I take it every day so that we can keep up with local affairs.' Avril and Roz ran a small property company, so this made sense.

'And is there anything new to report about the car in the gravel pit?'

'I'm afraid there is.' Roz sounded unwilling to continue.

'Bad news?'

'The bodies are confirmed to be those of Marcus and

Ayesha Freeman, together with their son Jefferson. They'd been shot: two bullets each, in the head.'

'How horrible! You must be devastated. Do they know who did it, and why?'

'If they do know, they're not saying yet. And I'm not blind to Marcus and Ayesha's faults, you know. They swindled vulnerable old women out of their property, and even shortened their lives. It was a mean and despicable crime. And they were trying to do the same to me. But I can't forget their concern for me when I was ill: I still believe that feeling at least was genuine, whatever their later intentions. And you must admit they were a very entertaining couple.'

'I met Jefferson once and I didn't take to him.'

'Really? I can see that Marcus and Ayesha must have come across some unpleasant people during their adventures. Perhaps they misjudged the victim of one of their swindles and paid the price.'

'I doubt whether there's much evidence to be found after . . .'

'After several months under water? I suppose not.'

'Is that the end of the story, do you think?'

'I'd like to think that their murderer will be found.'

'Don't you think it would be a good idea—'

'You're about to tell me to drink a cup of sweet tea and then take a little rest for an hour or two, aren't you, Kate?'

'Would I dare?'

'Yes, if I forget to remind you that I am still perfectly fit for my age, or any other if it comes to that.'

'Of course, Mother.'

'And don't call me Mother.'

'Bye, Roz.'

14

For Emma and Sam's sake, Kate was glad that Saturday yielded a golden autumn day. As the sun burned away the mist and the temperature edged upward, it grew warm enough for a partygoer to wear something more attractive than yesterday's thick pullover, woolly hat and jeans.

At half past six that morning Kate had slipped down to the kitchen to make Jon's coffee and put the bread into the toaster.

'Shall I cook you eggs and bacon?' she asked when he appeared, unshaven and yawning. 'And we still have some mushrooms, I see. And a couple of sausages. How about a proper artery-clogging fry-up?'

'You're being very generous with your time. I didn't think you'd want to get up at this hour.' He ran his hands through his tousled hair and yawned again.

'It's no earlier than usual,' she said cheerfully.

'It feels like it on a Saturday. Well, if you're offering, then yes, that would be great. Can you manage fried bread, or should we make toast?'

'Better make it toast. It won't all fit in the frying pan.'

'Leave the toast to me. You concentrate on the serious stuff.'

It felt good to be working together in the kitchen: it was some time since they'd been in harmony like this. Maybe they should clobber their arteries more often.

'I'll stoke up with as much solid grub as you can produce,' Jon was saying. 'Thanks, Kate. I'm not sure when I'll get to eat again today.'

When they were tucking into their breakfast he said, 'Sorry about the party this afternoon. I know I should have remembered about it before agreeing to crew for Tim, but you know how I forget everything when there's a chance of sailing. Somehow it just slipped my mind.'

'I can't expect you to be as keen as me. The Dolbys are old friends of mine and I'm fond of young Sam, but you hardly know them, after all.'

'I do feel I'm letting you down, though. I'm sorry, Kate, really.'

'Don't worry about it.'

'I expect you'll enjoy the party just as much without me.'

'Maybe not quite as much.' But Kate found she was looking forward to a day in the company of her old friends, and with the possibility, too, of making some new ones.

'I'll make it up to you when I get back tonight.'

Kate laughed. 'Have a great time on your friend's boat,' she said. 'And I won't expect you back before midnight.'

When he'd cleaned his teeth he returned to the kitchen, looking anxious.

'Could you take a look at my eyes, do you think?' he asked.

'What's up?'

'I can see a white ring starting to appear around the iris.'

'No, I can't see anything. It must have been a reflection.'

'You could be right,' he said doubtfully. 'But I'll pop down to the surgery and get my cholesterol level checked, just in case. I may have overdone the saturated fats this morning.'

'I don't think one breakfast is going to do anything life-threatening: you can revert to muesli and fresh fruit tomorrow.'

Jon shook his head and went back upstairs to dress. He'd soon forget about it when he was out with his friends, she thought.

And once she'd waved him goodbye, finished up the toast, scrubbed out the frying pan and washed up the dishes, Kate wandered round the empty house with a smile on her face. It was only seven thirty on a Saturday and she was going to enjoy a morning all to herself, in what was once more her own place.

As Kate walked up the Dolbys' drive at twelve forty-five, she could hear a faint buzz of voices and the distant beat of music. Someone had weeded the gravel and put away the toys that usually littered the front garden; even the mulch of wellington boots and trainers had vanished from the porch.

The house, with its eaves and patterned brickwork, had been built in the prosperous late Victorian years and stood in an unusually large garden. The trees planted in the nineteenth century now towered over the house and screened it from its neighbours. To Kate it had always had a forbidding, dis-approving air, as though pointing out that the Dolbys were solid members of society while she was nothing but a frivolous novelist. No, she replied to the silent rebuke, I have no intention of getting myself a proper job at this stage in my life. Or ever, if it comes to that.

The front door stood ajar, so there was no need to lift the heavy dolphin knocker to summon someone to let her in, and she passed down the passage into the large family room at the back of the house (also thoroughly tidied for the occasion) and through the open glass doors into the garden.

'Hi, Kate.' It was Sam Dolby Senior, Emma's husband, large and hairy as ever, sporting a brand-new shirt in electric blue, topped with a darker blue pullover. His red hair was sandier than young Sam's, and although worn quite long at the back, it was receding fast from his forehead.

'We're drinking fizz,' he said jovially, handing across a glass of what turned out to be real champagne rather than his usual supermarket plonk – it was, after all, the coming-of-age of his eldest son that they were celebrating. 'Emma and the food are under the beech tree at the bottom of the garden. You should find Sam down there too,' he told her.

The Dolbys' garden, large as it was, was filling up with guests. Emma had mentioned that Sam would go partying with his own friends that evening, and sure enough, the majority here appeared to be his parents' friends, and members of their families, rather than other eighteen-year-olds.

'Hi, Kate!' It was one of Emma's children, the small prize-fighter, growing taller and more recognisably female, but still wearing dungarees, albeit pink ones on this festive occasion. 'You'd better get yourself some food quick. It's all getting eaten!'

'Thanks, Amaryl.' Somehow she managed to remember the right name. 'I'll get down there straight away.'

'And Sam's there with his putrid girlfriend. Yuck! I'm never going to get like him and Kerri.'

The garden sloped away from the house towards a screen of tall trees that separated the Dolbys from their neighbours at the back. From where she was standing, Kate had an overview of the party: the further down the garden, the younger the guests, and the brighter and scantier their clothing. And threading through them, a sprinkling of small children, enjoying a parallel party at knee-height.

She recognised Geraldine, solemn in a flowery dress, holding the hand of a boy a couple of years older who resembled her closely enough to be her brother. They were standing silently, enclosed in their bubble of unhappiness, looking around them as though they had just dropped down into Headington from an alien planet.

Kate planned a route through the crowd, towards Emma and the food. Emma and Sam's friends were fellow academics, or people who worked for aid agencies, or reporters for the more earnest parts of the media. All brainy, mostly high-minded with it, occasionally dowdy. The general impression was of solidly built women dressed in shades of beige, wearing sensible shoes. (Kate's own heels, though not unreasonably high, were gradually sinking into the grass.) And their husbands (or partners, for many of them were not willing to submit to the servitude of marriage) were dressed in crumpled jackets and trousers that were either an inch or two too short (showing white ankle above sandal), or baggily long (hiding scuffed and unpolished brogues). There were a few determinedly bright and colourful figures, but still no one Kate would describe as stylish. Or carefree.

As the champagne emptied itself from the Dolbys' flutes into their friends' worthy gullets, the buzz of conversation grew louder and cheeks grew pinker. There was, to Kate's eye, even a little flirtation going on, in a suitably serious manner, of course.

It was time to take Amaryl's advice and aim straight for the food: there was a competitive streak in the Dolbys that meant that, given the chance, they would all fill their plates, wolf down the contents and be back for seconds before anyone else could get to the table.

She made her way towards the beech tree, taking occasional sips at her champagne, listening in to conversations as she passed.

'He's always been such a dear boy.' This from someone

elderly and carefully spoken. Kate glanced round and saw a tall, thin woman, dressed in a tweed suit with a beige raincoat over it, in spite of the clear blue skies above them and the warmth of the sun. There was no hint of red left in her white hair, but her eyes were the bright Dolby blue and Kate felt sure this was a family member. If she was talking about Sam, how would he react to being called a boy?

'But I'm not sure about this girlfriend of his.' The puckered mouth turned down at the corners as she spoke.

'She does look rather dreadful, doesn't she?' Her friend's voice was higher-pitched and lighter, and she too was wearing a buttoned-up blouse and a warm coat against the nonexistent chill in the air. 'But then they all do nowadays, don't they? No pride in their appearance. Showing off their bare bellies and goodness knows what else.'

'At least she's a quiet little thing, with no visible metalware about her,' her friend replied.

'Do you know what she's called and who her people are?'

'Isn't she named after some Irish county?'

'How bizarre!'

'I have no idea where she's from, but perhaps her name indicates that it's somewhere in Ireland. One only hopes they're not Romans.' Kate inferred she was referring to the religion rather than the inhabitants of the Italian capital.

'Do you think Sam could possibly be serious about her?'

'Surely not. And in any case, he's far too young to choose himself a wife. He's off to China and then to university. He'll have forgotten all about her this time next year, with any luck.'

'It's true that the Dolbys always have their heads screwed on when it comes to choosing a spouse.'

Kate wondered for a moment what the Dolby aunts had said when she and George Dolby had been living together. She imagined that the comments had been no more charitable than they were about Kerri. A novelist was hardly a good prospect when it came to solid worth.

She listened to no more of the conversation: she preferred to make up her own mind about Sam's girlfriend, so she overtook the women and edged past two men in pale chinos and sandals, also in earnest conversation but not, this time, about young Sam, as far as she could tell.

'He'd better get the submission right or we'll all be in the shit,' one of them was saying.

'He'll have to resign if he's got it wrong,' replied the other. 'How could he face us if he failed?' This was the younger of the two speaking, and he wasn't bad looking, Kate noticed approvingly.

'It's his own future on the line as well as ours, so I suppose he'll do his best.'

'Let's just hope it's good enough.'

'If it's not, you'll have to prepare to shoot the puppy.'

'Not a phrase to use round here, even as a joke!'

'Really? Of course, it's all going to depend on the results in the end, isn't it? Any indications yet, Blake?'

'It's a bit early to say.'

'Not giving anything away, as usual. Well, don't take too long, or everyone will assume you're holding back because you're having no success.'

The younger man laughed unconvincingly. 'I'm sure Candra will come up with the goods.'

'It's all a question of interpretation when it comes down to it, after all.'

'Up to a point. But the last thing I'm worried about is failure.'

'If you say so.'

The two men sipped their champagne as though they'd been forced to drink cider vinegar. Ah! The stresses of the academic life! Kate just wished that she had all those weeks of paid leave every year, not to mention the sickness benefits and the pension scheme. She looked around, planning her final route towards the food.

Scattered across the grass were small clumps of Dolbys. She could recognise them by the mode of their dress (bought to last), their height (they were, in general, taller than average), and the redness of their hair. To her right she saw an elderly beige woman with a small redhead clinging stickily to her knees, and recognised Emma's mother, Joyce Fielding. She was looking older and more careworn than she had a few years back when she went missing and Emma had employed Kate to find her. Patting the head of the toddler and taking her by the hand, Joyce moved slowly towards one of the child's older siblings. Kate hung back for a moment, stifling memories of the confrontation with a murderer in the cathedral, which the sight of Joyce brought crowding back.

It struck her that if she hadn't walked away from George, Sam's younger brother, these people would be her family too. There might even be one or two more red-headed moppets playing with Emma's brood and spilling their Coke down their party dresses. How would she feel about having lively little carrot-tops instead of the raven-haired, solemn children that Jon was likely to father? The red hair around her ranged from marigold (three-year-old Flora), through dark mahogany (young Sam) to brown with only a hint of red (his uncle George).

George Dolby! Why hadn't it occurred to her that he'd be here? And even as she took in the fact that he was looking just a year or so older and a little thinner, and that the thick brown hair was receding elegantly at his temples, he turned and saw her too.

'Kate! Emma told me that you'd be here. I'm so glad you've come.' And abandoning the Dolby aunt he was speaking to, he was standing at her side, giving her a hug, kissing her on the cheek.

'Are you here on your own?' he asked. 'I thought Jon would be with you.'

'He left first thing this morning for a day's sailing in the Solent. I was glad of the excuse not to join him, to be honest. But I don't see Fiona, either. Is she here with you?'

'Fiona and I agreed to go our separate ways a couple of months ago,' he said cheerfully.

'You don't sound too heartbroken,' said Kate, perking up.

'Are you going to join Emma in telling me how shallow I am and how bad at long-term relationships?'

'Certainly not. You're no worse at them than me.' They both laughed. And if Kate was pleased at his news, she didn't mention it.

'I've been hearing from Emma how you and Jon are as happy as larks in your house in Jericho,' said George.

Kate didn't say that Jon was far from lark-like these days, whereas she appeared to enjoy herself best on the days when he was absent. 'We're fine. Really fine. We're doing really well. Yes, it's all working out fine.' And if George considered that she was repeating herself a little too much, he didn't mention that, either.

'Emma's put on a marvellous spread,' he said, leading her towards the table under the beech tree. 'Let me make sure you help yourself to a large plateful of everything on offer before I return to entertaining my aunts.'

'I'm afraid you're going to have to answer a lot of probing

questions about me if the piercing stares are anything to go by.'

'Don't worry. I'm used to it by now. And it's good to see such a turn-out for young Sam, isn't it?'

'Yes. Though I haven't seen him yet. Where's he hiding?'

George pointed to a group in the opposite corner. 'He's with his colleagues from the lab. But he really should circulate and chat to some of his great-aunts. I'd swoop in and drag him away, but he's in full protective mode with his little girlfriend at the moment.'

'Well, yes, he would be. Kerri must be shattered at receiving a letter bomb. I imagine she's still in shock.'

'Luckily she wasn't hurt at all, just transformed into a gibbering wreck,' said George. 'I'd have thought she could pull herself together and get over it by now, but Sam's encouraging her to take it very seriously. He's his mother's son in that.'

'I'd have been terrified, wouldn't you?'

'Maybe.' George didn't sound convinced.

'Who do you think was responsible?'

'Some extremist group, I imagine. They must be amateurs – they haven't managed to inflict much real damage yet, have they?'

'Perhaps they've just been practising.'

'Well, that's a cheerful thought! I should keep it to yourself this afternoon, if I were you.'

Kate had been watching the group of scientists. 'His friends are looking rather glum, aren't they? Not exactly in the party spirit.'

'They're all feeling under siege, my brother tells me, and are huddling together for mutual support. They've pulled up the drawbridge and the boiling oil is balanced on the windowsills.'

'That bad, huh?'

'You bet. Not only are they under attack from the animal activists, but the providers of their funds are threatening to stop writing any more cheques unless they start coming up with something specific that guarantees large future profits.'

'Where do you hear all this?' asked Kate.

'The academic grapevine, Katie. There's nothing to beat it. We all gossip like mad over our pinot grigios in the pub after a hard day in the seminar room.'

'I didn't think you lot at Brookes spoke to the fuddy-duddies down the hill.'

'Don't you believe it. Personally, I think young Sam's crowd might feel better, at least for one afternoon, if they split up, downed some more of my brother's perfectly decent champagne and then socialised with my excellent aunts.'

'I'll go and do my cheerful best with them in a minute and put your suggestion to the vote.'

'You need something to eat first. I'll see what I can forage.'

George was as good as his word, and made sure that Kate's plate was heaped with a portion of everything on the table before he went off to make conversation with another cluster of aunts and cousins.

'I'll catch up with you later. You won't leave until we've had a chance to chat, will you?' he said before he left her.

As he moved away, Kate caught Emma looking at her enquiringly. Emma was too busy at that moment to pass on a warning to Kate about George, but Kate could see that her friend was busy calculating what might or might not be happening between the two of them, and doubtless coming to a ridiculously overblown conclusion. Emma had nothing to worry about. George and Kate were perfectly happy as they were: nothing more than good friends.

15

Kate tucked into Emma's excellent potato salad, forked up a red-fringed lettuce leaf, then took a bite of home-made quiche to give herself energy to face the group of gloomy scientists standing in the shade of a tall conifer. They looked as though they weren't even up to handling a glint or two of sunshine.

'Hi, Sam!' she called as she walked across the grass. 'And congratulations.' As he turned to greet her she realised that someone was walking close behind her, then standing at her shoulder: it was the younger of the two men who had been talking together a few minutes before. She turned her head so that she could see him properly. Not bad. And he could get away with the jeans and skinny T-shirt worn under his jacket: there was no sign of a beer belly there. Then she reminded herself that she was in a happy partnership with Jon and not on the lookout for new talent.

'This is my friend Kate,' announced Sam to his friends.

'Hi, Kate. I'm Lucy.' A woman a little younger than Kate smiled back at her. She had sandy blond hair and a pale complexion, but was dressed in a cotton top and skirt of harsh scarlet scattered with black flowers that drained her skin of colour and overwhelmed her light green eyes. 'I expect you've gathered that we all work in the same lab as Sam.'

Kate nodded.

'We'll try not to talk shop, but I can't promise on behalf of the young geeks on my right.'

'Geek yourself, Lucy!' said Sam mildly.

'And I am Candra.' There was disapproval in her voice and no friendly smile this time, just a calculating stare that included the man who was standing at Kate's side. Candra was wearing a pale green and aqua silk tunic and trousers that reminded Kate of a shalwar kameez. Perhaps it was this elegance, and the care with which she had applied her make-up and arranged her hair, that made Candra look older than she was.

'Candy's the one who does our sums for us,' said the man at Kate's shoulder.

'He means that I'm a statistician,' said Candra stiffly. Kate saw that she hated to be called Candy, and that she preferred her proper job title – and who could blame her?

'And my name's Blake,' said the man who had followed Kate. Just as she was wondering whether this was his first name or last, he added, 'Blake Parker.'

'Our brilliant boss,' said Lucy, with a glance at Blake that made Kate think that she, as well as Candra, could be interested in him, and not only in a work context.

'They're jealous,' said Blake close to her ear, and she felt his warm breath on her neck and knew he was smiling at the thought.

'Have you not brought your partner with you today, Blake?' asked Candra, with a sideways glance at Kate. 'Marianne, isn't it?'

'Marianne prefers to stay at home and get on with translating some dreary French novel,' said Blake stiffly. 'And anyway, you should know by now that we're not permanently joined at the hip.'

136

Someone sniggered; probably one of the younger ones whose name Kate hadn't yet taken on board.

Another young man introduced himself then: Greg, the Canadian with the ponytail, suntan and big smile, but before he could say anything, another red-haired Dolby cousin barged into the group.

'Sam! I'm worried about the children,' she said. 'I haven't seen them for ages. Where can they have got to?'

'They'll be OK. They're probably just being beaten to a pulp by my young brothers,' said Sam. Then, seeing the young woman's startled expression, he added: 'Only joking.'

'Oh, Sam!' she exclaimed, and darted away again.

'You're a wicked man, worrying the nice lady like that,' murmured one of his companions.

'That's Conor,' Blake told Kate. 'Our lab technician.' Conor was young and skinny, with a pinched, narrow face and speckled eyes like a wild cat's. He moved his feet restlessly while he was speaking, as though ill-at-ease in this solidly bourgeois setting. 'He likes to pretend he's too cool to take anything seriously, but he's very good at his job, very responsible. And then next to him is Eric, who's Belgian, though I suppose he can't help that.'

Kate heard Conor mutter, 'Racist wanker,' and wondered whether Blake had heard. He didn't seem the type to overlook such an insult.

'Eric's our resident baby-snatcher,' murmured Blake in her ear. She raised her eyebrows and took another good look at Eric and his companion.

'You remember Abi, don't you?' said Sam, smiling as though he realised full well that she didn't. Abi had been a child last time Kate saw her, but now looked in her twenties, though she was not yet seventeen, she remembered, and, as Blake had indicated, surely too young for Eric. The Belgian had draped a possessive arm across her shoulders, in case Kate didn't get the message that this was his girlfriend.

'Hi, Kate,' said Abi, leaning in towards Eric. Maybe she wanted to signal her relationship to the assembled great-aunts, but Kate felt that they were interested only in young Sam and his intentions towards Kerri.

'Oh, yes. Of course I remember you, Abi,' she said quickly.

'And Kate, I'd like you to meet Kerri,' said Sam, and his tone told her how important this was to him.

Kerri was slightly built, wearing low-slung jeans and a cropped black top; she had large dark eyes in a pale face and appeared to be very shy, looking up at Kate from under her lashes, her head tipped slightly to one side. Nervously she lifted her hand to her forehead, inadvertently drawing attention to the pink skin and stubbled eyebrow. The poor girl must be reminded of the exploding letter bomb every time she looked in the mirror, thought Kate with concern.

She smiled at her, eliciting a faint smile from Kerri in response, and waited for an opportunity to talk to her one-to-one. She ate another mouthful of Emma's excellent quiche while she thought about it.

'I guess you're not a scientist, Kate. What is it that you do?' asked Greg, his small rectangular glasses turned in her direction.

'I'm a writer. Freelance,' she said, hoping he wouldn't ask her whether she was famous.

'That must be exciting,' said Greg, looking interested to learn more.

Behind him, and a little to the right, Kate glimpsed two other elderly female Dolbys talking earnestly to George, their heads close to his, their eyes on Kerri, their mouths turned down in disapproval. George was nodding in agreement.

'I'm sorry?' She turned back to Greg.

'I just thought a freelance writer must have an exciting life,' he said.

'Sometimes it's positively dangerous,' she replied, recalling moments in the past that had very little to do with the sedate life of a writer and much more to do with her innate curiosity about people.

Blake said, 'Your glass needs a top-up. Let me do it for you.' There were younger Dolby cousins making themselves useful by circulating with champagne bottles, and Blake went off to find one of them.

'What do you write?' asked Greg.

'Fiction,' Kate replied.

'Fiction? In our department we leave that to Candra,' said Lucy slyly. 'And Greg, of course.'

'Don't believe a word of what she's telling you, Kate' said Greg.

'I'm only saying what a great writer you are,' said Lucy. 'If the department closes down and we all lose our jobs, you'll be able to earn a fortune as a science fiction author.'

'This is most unfair,' said Candra crossly. 'You mustn't say these things in front of outsiders; they might not understand that it's all a joke to you.'

Kate had no idea what they were talking about, but she saw that Kerri and Conor were both smiling at Greg and Candra's discomfiture, so she supposed it was some kind of in-joke.

'Yeah, take no notice, Kate,' said Lucy. 'It's nothing but a wind-up.'

Kate took her chance during the pause in the conversation to move across to Kerri and Sam's side of the group.

'Hi, Kerri,' she said, swallowing the last mouthful of quiche. 'How are you enjoying the party?' It was a pretty dull opening, but she wanted to get Kerri to herself.

'Yeah. It's cool,' said Kerri. Behind her the Dolby aunt shook her head again. It was possible that she and her companion were discussing the weather, but Kate doubted it. George had moved on, she was pleased to see. She didn't like to think that he was ganging up with the aunts against the unfortunate Kerri.

'A great setting for a party, don't you think?'

'Yeah.' Kerri's voice was so low that Kate could hardly catch what she said. The poor girl was overwhelmed by her surroundings as well as by so many strangers, many of them intent upon judging her as wife material. Kate moved closer. 'I didn't know Sam's dad's place was massive like this.' And she probably hadn't realised how daunting his relations were, either. 'There's nothing like it where I come from.'

'Where's that?'

'My mum and her bloke live on an estate in Didcot.'

To Kate, Didcot meant only a cold, windy station where she waited for a train that would carry her the rest of the way to Oxford after an evening out in London: another conversational dead end.

'It's a bit livelier here in Oxford?'

'Yeah. I live at the end of the Cowley Road and it's lively enough down there.'

'How do you like working at the lab?' Kate glanced around at Kerri's fellow-workers.

'The work's really interesting. I'm lucky to get into a lab like that.' It sounded as though Kerri was reading from an approved script.

'But?'

Kerri smiled at Kate's insistence.

'Sorry,' said Kate. 'I'm curious about people. I probably shouldn't ask so many questions.'

Kerri even managed a short laugh at this. 'You don't sound sorry,' she said.

'Have Sam's relations been putting you through their standard questionnaire?'

'More or less. And staring at me when they think I'm not looking.'

It was Kate's turn to laugh. 'Gruesome,' she said.

'And as to working at the lab, I'll be out of here in a few weeks,' Kerri volunteered.

'Really?' asked Kate, surprised.

'They call it a bursary, but it's just a form of work experience, and my time will soon be up.'

'You'll miss having Sam around at the lab, I imagine.'

'It's not just that. There's stuff happening I don't like much.'

'Trouble?'

'You must have heard about the bomb.'

'I heard about both of them,' said Kate. 'I'd have been terrified if I'd been in your shoes, so I thought I'd avoid the subject.'

'Maybe it's good to get it out into the sunlight. It's when you hide things away and deny they exist that they have such power over you.'

'I'd agree with that.'

Kate was congratulating herself on encouraging Kerri to open up when Conor appeared between them, obviously wondering what they could be talking about.

'Is she telling you her great bomb story?' he asked Kate.

'No,' said Kate shortly.

'Our Kerri's an innocent victim of the evil animal rights mob, aren't you, Kerri?'

Kate was about to weigh in on Kerri's side when Kerri herself said, 'We don't know who was responsible for either of them. You shouldn't jump to conclusions.'

'Kerri's a secret sympathiser, you see,' Conor told Kate, who was wondering why he was being so snide.

'I don't know about that, but I don't think we should be using animals to experiment on, not as much as we do. Animals have rights, don't they?' Kerri had found her voice.

'You see, Kate, I told you so,' crowed Conor. 'She's a closet activist.' He flicked a strand of greasy hair back from his forehead. 'You want to watch out for her! Check out your post before opening!'

'I don't believe in violence,' said Kerri vehemently. 'No violence to animals, and none to people, either. That's right, isn't it?' She appealed to Kate for support.

'Sounds fair enough to me,' said Kate.

'And she doesn't want people to eat dead animals,' Conor said to Kate. 'You'd better be a vegetarian if you want to be her friend.'

Feeling got at, Kate started to reply, 'What's wrong with that?' but she was interrupted by a voice at her elbow.

'Here you are, Kate.' Blake was back with a full glass of champagne. 'Sam's father is working himself up to make a short but embarrassing speech and then we'll all need to drink Sam's health.' He looked around at the others. 'Everyone got some fizz?'

'Mine is apple juice,' said Candra.

'I'm sure it'll work just as well for a toast,' said Blake.

Lucy emptied her glass rapidly and went to find herself another drink, casting a despondent glance in Blake's direction as she went. Blake frowned slightly as he watched her go, then his attention was diverted by the ringing of his mobile.

Kate noticed that he was scowling at the screen as he said, 'Hello?' She could hear the sound of a woman's voice, raised and complaining at the other end, before Blake interrupted to say impatiently, 'But you know exactly where I am. The invitation's pinned to the board in the kitchen. It's addressed to both of us, so you could be here too if you wanted.' More from the raised voice. 'Maybe it does say "and partner", but that's what you are, aren't you? Why should you expect Sam to know what your name is?' Louder, crosser words in response this time, and Blake replied, 'Later. Probably much later.' And he snapped the phone shut.

'Sorry about that,' he said to Kate. 'I'll switch the thing off so it doesn't interrupt us again.'

A few feet away from them, Lucy, halfway through her latest glass of champagne, was standing close to Eric and whispering in his ear. Abi had pointedly moved away from them and was talking animatedly to Greg while Kerri and Conor were glaring at one another in silence. Oh dear, thought Kate. Relationships in general are in a bad way. And no one in this group seems to have got off with the right person, except for Sam and Kerri, of course.

Blake was speaking in confidential tones in her left ear: 'The trouble with this sort of lunchtime party, Kate, is that you leave in the middle of the afternoon, full of champagne and good cheer, wearing your best T-shirt, feeling at a loose end. Don't you agree?' Kate, who did agree, but who was looking forward to an evening of DVDs and a tub of luxury chocolate ice cream, was saved from replying by the sound of a spoon rattling in a wine glass at the other end of the garden. It was

143

time, as Blake had warned them, for Sam's father to give his short, but doubtless embarrassing, speech.

He began by welcoming them all to his eldest's son's coming-of-age party, then moved on to list young Sam's virtues and achievements. Fond as she was of Sam, Kate found her concentration faltering after the first minute of this, and as usual she switched her attention to the people around her. Just don't take out a notebook and pencil and start writing, she reminded herself.

Candra looked bored, but was trying not to show it. Eric and Greg were sucking in their stomachs and attempting to impress Lucy and Abi. Conor was sneering slightly to show how cool he was, but his eyes still darted back and forth and his restless feet stirred the grass. Abi looked embarrassed by what her father was saying and was watching Eric and Lucy, pouting slightly. And from the warm feeling in the vicinity of her left ear, Kate guessed that she in her turn was being closely observed by Blake.

Sam Senior's voice rose in volume as he came to the end of his speech: 'So, I want you all to raise your glasses and drink the health of my son!'

There was a rustling as the guests returned their thoughts to the present and faced Sam as he stood by Kerri's side under the cypress.

'To Sam!' came the ragged chorus of voices, young and mocking, old and quavering, but mostly heartfelt and genuine. Sam himself looked self-conscious at all the attention, while Kerri looked bewildered.

'I reckon we all get a slice of cake now,' said Blake, lightening the mood. 'Then we can pick up our balloon and goodie bag and go home.'

'Do we really get a goodie bag?' asked Candra.

'Joke, Candra. Though I expect the children will be given balloons,' said Blake patiently. He leant closer towards Kate. 'Or we could go to the pub, perhaps?'

'I don't think so.' But she was unable to keep a hint of regret out of her voice.

'No, you're right. On a lovely afternoon like this, and wearing that frock, you should be drifting down the river in a punt.'

Before they could develop this interesting conversation, they were interrupted by Emma, bearing slices of cake, and for the next few minutes they were too busy dropping crumbs and licking their fingers to continue.

Blake had just started to speak to Kate again when Emma reappeared.

'I don't want to drag you away, Kate, but I was hoping that you could spend a few minutes to talk to my friend Jenny.'

Jenny? Wasn't she the woman who was ill, the mother of Geraldine and Lucas? 'Yes, of course. Where will I find her?' It gave her a valid excuse to escape from the scientists, and she could catch up with Kerri again later.

'She's sitting in the shade, up near the house, and people seem to be ignoring her. Come with me and I'll introduce you.'

'What does she do, by the way? What should I talk about?'

'She's a teacher and a writer, rather like me.' Emma disregarded the fact that she had done very little of either for the past few years.

'And what does she write?'

'Poetry. Very sensitive, very feminine, delicately succinct poems.'

'Published?'

'By one of the small specialist presses.'

Ah well, thought Kate, since she and Jenny would have

nothing in common on the literary front, maybe they could stick to the subject of Jenny's children.

It was the two children they saw first, still isolated in their bubble of misery, standing some feet away from their mother.

'Hello, Geraldine,' said Kate brightly.

Geraldine stared at her sandals and didn't reply.

'You remember Kate, darling, don't you?' encouraged Emma.

'Mummy's not feeling well,' said Lucas, since Geraldine refused to speak.

'Really? Well, Kate and I will have a chat to her. I expect she'll soon be feeling better.'

Lucas looked reproachfully at Emma, knowing that he was being conned.

At first sight, Jenny Lindley was a woman in her late fifties, exhausted by life. Then she looked up as Kate and Emma approached her chair, and she smiled. Kate saw the intelligent blue eyes of a younger woman and realised that it was her recent illness that was stealing the youth from her face. She saw, too, the bruises, some fading to yellow, others still purple. There was a gash, healing now, just above her right eyebrow, where she had caught it on the corner of the table as she fell.

'Why don't you . . .?' Jenny spoke the first words very slowly and distinctly, but then the effort was too much for her and the rest of her question was too blurred and indistinct for Kate to make out.

'Yes, of course we'll sit down, and then I'll introduce her,' said Emma, who was obviously more adept than Kate at understanding her friend. They pulled up a couple of chairs and sat down so that they were on the same level as Jenny. 'This is Kate Ivory. Do you remember, I told you about her?

She's a fellow-writer, of course, and I know the two of you have lots in common.'

Emma was always the optimist, thought Kate, visualising small, delicate poems, printed in grey on handmade paper, while one of her own books flaunted its brightly coloured cover.

'Hello, Kate,' said Jenny, with an effort.

Emma stood up. 'Now come along, Geraldine and Lucas. Let's go and find you a piece of the lovely birthday cake, and some new friends for you to play with.'

They didn't look enthusiastic about Emma's proposal, but they were polite children and followed her dutifully. The last that Kate saw of them was Geraldine's pale, wistful face looking back to make sure that her mother was still there.

'Tell me about . . .' Jenny paused as though to prepare her next words. 'About your books,' she finished. Her eyes were still interested and alive, but the rest of her face was expressionless, as though someone had fastened a mask over it.

'They're not exactly highbrow,' began Kate.

Jenny made an odd noise that worried Kate for a moment until she realised that it was laughter. 'I've no time to be highbrow,' she said. With practice Kate found she was understanding her more easily, and they launched into a one-sided, but interesting, discussion of popular fiction.

Ten minutes later they were joined by a man who introduced himself as Jenny's husband, Bob, and who then took the seat vacated by Emma.

'How are you doing, darling? Sorry I've only just made it.'

Jenny said something that sounded reassuring.

'Yes, I know you can manage perfectly well on your own, but I thought you might be feeling tired.'

Jenny replied impatiently, but Bob seemed determined to be over-solicitous.

'Yes, well, you don't want to overdo things, do you? The party seems to be breaking up, in any case. Why don't I round up the children? I expect they're ready to go home by now.'

Across the garden, Kate could see a child in a party frock bouncing high on a trampoline, encouraged by a red-haired Dolby. Geraldine at least had forgotten her cares for the moment, and it seemed a pity to remind her of them, but Bob had set off across the grass before Kate could suggest that he leave his daughter to play like a normal child for just a few minutes more.

'Hi, Kate. I've caught up with you at last.'

It was George, minus his tie, his shirt open at the neck, his hair sticking up in clumps, suggesting that he had been playing energetic games with the youngest of the children. He probably had, at that, and enjoyed himself somewhat more than when he was talking to his stately aunts.

'Have I got your Jericho phone number?' he asked.

'Probably not.' He'd been a former lover rather than a friend at the time she had moved from Fridesley to Jericho, so he hadn't been on her list when she had sent out her new address. 'Why don't I give it to you now?' There was no harm in giving an old friend your new phone number, surely?

'I thought we might have lunch one day, and catch up with one another's news. It seems ages since we really talked,' he said.

'It must be three years. Or maybe four?'

'Far too long, in any case.'

Kate wrote down her number, tore the page from her notebook and passed it to him.

A high, demanding voice called, 'Uncle George! We need

you!' and he shrugged, putting the paper into his jacket pocket.

'No peace, as they say.'

For the wicked, did he mean? She watched as two children ran up and attached themselves to his hands, dragging him back to the area where the Dolby young had congregated.

Would he really get in touch again? Not that it was important whether he did or not. After all, their relationship was in the past and now it was evolving into the mildest of friendships.

Kate walked back to where Kerri and her colleagues were still standing under the cypress. If she gave anyone her details it had to be Kerri.

'Hi, Kerri. Before I leave, do you think we could swap phone numbers so that we can keep in touch?'

'I could give you my mobile number,' Kerri said doubtfully.

'Great. I'll write down mine, and my email address. We must get together while Sam's away.' She fished out her notebook again and tore out another page.

Kerri was looking suspiciously at Sam. 'Hey, you haven't . . .'

'Would I do a thing like that without consulting you?' he countered, all innocence.

Kerri wrote her email address and mobile number down in Kate's notebook. Kate handed her the page with her own written in her clearest handwriting. If Kerri didn't get in touch, then Sam certainly couldn't blame her.

'There you are. I thought you might have left.' It was Blake, accompanied by a cloud of cigarette smoke. The others sniffed the air ostentatiously.

'OK! Stop the silent nagging. I'll give up when I choose to. It wasn't my idea in the first place, now was it?'

The group wasn't as tightly packed as it had been earlier and Kate guessed that people were preparing to leave.

'I should be going now,' she said to Blake. 'The expression on Emma's face indicates that she's calculating how many people she can commandeer to join her plate-clearing and washing-up squad.'

'You're right,' said Blake, looking around at the thinning clumps of people. 'But the day is still young, and warm, and the punts are waiting at Folly Bridge. How about it?'

Kate thought for a moment about the hours ahead of her. There would still be DVDs to watch and the tub of ice cream in the freezer, whatever time she reached home, so why not enjoy herself in agreeable company for an hour or two?

'You're on,' she said.

16

Much later that evening, while sitting comfortably in front of *Balzac and the Little Chinese Seamstress* with a glass of cold white wine (having left the chocolate ice cream in the freezer for a time of greater need), Kate was interrupted by the ringing of the telephone.

She dived for the receiver, thinking it might be Jon, feeling irrationally guilty.

'That was quick,' said her mother. 'Were you sitting by the phone, waiting for it to ring?'

'Not at all. It just happened to be to hand, that's all.'

'So, did you and Jon have a good time at your friend Sam's birthday party?'

'Very enjoyable, thank you. Except that Jon wasn't there. He's abandoned me for something with a keel and sails.'

'Well yes, I suppose he would.'

'What does that mean?'

'Only that he's the outdoors type.'

Kate decided to ignore the insult to her own powers of attraction. 'I did meet a very interesting friend of Emma's, another writer, who has a husband and two young children, but who's suffering from some horrible disease that they haven't managed to diagnose yet.'

'That does sound like fun, certainly.'

'She was easier to chat to than Young Sam's colleagues

from the lab, I can tell you. They were all in an odd, edgy mood and I should think he's glad to be escaping to China next week.'

'And most of the other guests were ancient Dolby relations, I suppose?'

'Either that or small children eating crisps and bouncing on trampolines. I had no idea before today what a really big extended family looks like.'

'Did you feel you'd missed out?'

'No, I can't say I did. I felt they disapproved of anything remotely original in the young ones.'

'So, all in all, you had a dull time of it?'

'You could call it that, yes.'

'So when Avril, out walking her dog along the towpath this afternoon, thought she saw you sitting in a punt, trailing your fingers in the waters of the Isis, accompanied by an attractive, youngish man, she must have been mistaken?'

'Completely. I wouldn't do a thing like that while Jon was away, would I?'

'Obviously not.'

'Is that why you rang?'

'Not really. I was interested to hear whether you had a decent cover story ready for when Jon returned tonight, but he'll probably be tired from all the bracing sea air, and full of the beer that he drank with his sailing friends, so I suppose he won't quiz you too closely about your day.'

'Thanks for that, Mother.'

'No, what I really phoned to tell you was that I'm planning another trip.'

'A long one?' It was odd how much she cared whether her mother was within reach, just a couple of miles away. It wasn't as though they had ever been really close.

'I won't be gone for too long. Avril and I are still in partnership but we're going to take a break before moving on to our next project. We've had to admit we're not quite as young as we were, but six weeks should give us a chance to recharge our batteries.'

'Have you decided where you're going?'

'Portugal.'

'That sounds rather tame for you.'

'I have an old friend I'd like to look up.'

Alarm bells were ringing in the distant cells of her memory. Portugal? Who did her mother know in Portugal?

'When are you leaving?' she asked.

'In a week or so.'

'Are you sure you're up to it?' asked Kate.

'Try to forget that I was ill last year, please. I've forgotten it, my anaemia is under control, and I'm back to being fighting fit. So drop it, Kate.'

'Oh, very well.'

And after a few more exchanges in which Kate attempted to extract more information from her mother, and Roz remained obstinately vague, they ended the conversation.

Kate returned to her wine. And eventually it came back to her: her mother had been married in Portugal. Or rather, she had been married to a Portuguese with a multi-barrelled name when she had lived in California. Kate had forgotten the details. The marriage had taken place long after the death of her father, and Roz hadn't bothered to tell her about it until she stumbled upon a photo of her mother and stepfather on their wedding day. (Stepfather! Surely not! A relationship like that didn't hold if you were well over twenty-one and had never met, did it?)

She wasn't even sure that Roz and António – yes, that was

his name – had ever been divorced. Was yet another con man going to appear in her mother's life? Might they even set up house together in Oxford?

It served her right for fussing over her mother when the Freemans' bodies were discovered. Roz was getting her own back by winding her daughter up; that was all, surely.

She finished her wine and went to the kitchen. When she peered into the freezer, she found she had stocked up with several tubs of calorie-packed food therapy. She could see that Roz's trip was going to be a problem requiring a chocolate ice cream solution.

Her mother was right about Jon. He let himself into the house and stumbled upstairs some time between one and two in the morning. The next morning he awoke late and showed no more than a polite interest in the Dolbys' party when Kate brought him up a pot of coffee, a couple of croissants and a pot of apricot jam.

When he emerged in the kitchen a little later, showered, dressed, but still unshaven and bleary-eyed, Kate wondered for a moment whether he had passed a less innocent Saturday afternoon than she had. But no, when it came to Jon's infatuations, what woman could compete with a boat?

'My turn to stack the dishwasher,' he said amiably, then, 'Do you fancy some more coffee?'

'Why not? It's Sunday morning, after all.'

Sunday mornings for Jon usually involved a two-foot-high pile of newspapers to accompany his coffee, but this morning he left the stack of newsprint on the doormat and poured the coffee for both of them.

As he passed across her mug with an ingratiating smile, she wondered whether he was about to produce a big bunch of roses from a garage forecourt. That would make her really, really worried, she reflected.

'Have you had any thoughts about next weekend?' he asked casually.

'I was still working on enjoying this one. Have you got any plans for this afternoon?'

'I thought we might go house-hunting.'

'But I thought we were happy here for the present.'

'We've let it slide for several months now. Don't you think we should at least take a look at what's on the market? I'll get out the map and we'll make a list of likely villages. In fact, why don't we go out for a pub lunch? I'll map out a route.'

She should be feeling excited, but she couldn't raise much enthusiasm. Still, a pub lunch wasn't such a bad idea.

'OK,' she said.

'But right now I wanted to talk about next weekend, when Susie and Gary come to stay.'

'Is there so much planning to do?'

'I thought we could organise some interesting places to go and things to do while they're here.'

'I'd better think about getting the spare room ready, too.'

'Don't worry about that. I'll get Alan to help me with a bit of furniture-shifting. It'll only take us an hour or so one evening. You won't have to do a thing.'

'Will you and Alan be able to manage the staircase? There's a tricky corner to negotiate at the top,' she said meekly.

'You could be right,' he said. 'I could bring over a rug, too,' he suggested.

'It would make the room look less spartan,' she conceded.

'And how about some pictures?' he asked, his face brightening.

155

But Kate wasn't prepared to go quite that far. 'Are we talking blown-up photos of powerful motorbikes?'

'Possibly.' But he was smiling. He knew he'd lost that particular argument a long time ago.

'I expect your friends would be just as happy with a simple bunch of flowers.'

'So that's all agreed. I'll go and shave and then we'll get out the maps.'

'And as for amusing your friends, we can take them round the colleges, can't we? That's what everyone wants to look at when they come here. And then a walk through Port Meadow and a visit to a riverside pub. Peacocks. Swans. A rustic bridge. All very picturesque.'

'I'm not sure that young Freddie is all that interested in old buildings,' said Jon.

'You haven't mentioned a young Freddie before.'

'Oh, did I forget to say that they're bringing their son with them?'

'I believe you did – forget, that is. How old is he?'

'Two, or thereabouts.'

'A toddler? I've no idea how to amuse a toddler!'

'I imagine his mother will know how to do that. And he's very bright, very advanced, they say. He plays the cello.'

'What!'

Jon laughed. 'It sounds bloody ridiculous, doesn't it? I don't suppose he's exactly a virtuoso yet.'

'I'll leave the plans for the weekend fluid, shall I?'

'Good idea.'

A picture of George Dolby, tieless and rumpled, introducing a small child to the joys of a trampoline slipped into her head. She wondered whether he still had her phone number, and whether he'd take the trouble to use it.

'Do you think they'd like to go down the river in a punt?' asked Jon.

'Much too dangerous for a young child,' replied Kate, managing to avoid pointing out that there would hardly be room for his cello.

'You could be right.' Now it was Jon's turn to be conciliatory, she noticed.

'Did I tell you that Roz phoned yesterday evening? She's off on her travels again, for a short trip this time. To Portugal.'

'She and Avril work pretty hard, especially for women their age. I imagine they need a holiday from time to time.'

'Yes – but don't let Roz hear you refer to her age like that. And I can't see her lying on a sandy beach with a bestseller for company, can you?'

'No. Are you starting to worry about her again?'

'She was so vague about her arrangements, and I never trust her when she's like that.'

'She's often vague about things when she talks to you: she only does it to wind you up.'

'Do you think so?'

'Your mother and I get on very well, and I think I can read her fairly accurately by now.'

Jon could say that, but over the past few years Roz had managed to get herself into a number of awkward, sometimes shady, occasionally life-threatening situations. Kate felt perfectly justified in worrying about her. But Jon was right that she could do nothing about it, so she left the subject.

'Whereabouts do you want to go looking for idyllic villages?' she asked.

'Shall we try north-west of here?'

'I'll get out the maps.'

Jon's office was south-east of the city. She could soon

persuade him that he didn't want such a long commute through rush-hour traffic, even if he did find what he was looking for.

On Monday, George phoned. On Wednesday, Blake Parker sent her an email. He must have Googled her and found her website to send a message through a contact form, she thought complacently. She replied to both of them that she was tied up all week, but perhaps she'd be free for lunch one day after that.

On Thursday, Sam Dolby rang.

'I'm off to the airport in the early hours, Kate, so I just called to say goodbye.'

Kate knew what he really wanted to say, so she wished him well on his trip then said, 'And don't worry about Kerri. I have her phone number and email and I'll get in touch in a few days' time. And if she's anxious at all while you're away, she knows how to contact me.'

'Thanks. I'll remind her about it. There have been a few more graffiti and phone calls. They seem to be picking on her.'

'Maybe it's just a coincidence. Why would they pick on Kerri?'

'Well, she does help Conor with the animals. In her own time, of course; it's not really part of her job.'

'That's because she's an animal-lover, surely? I can't believe they're singling her out for attention. They ought to approve of the poor girl rather than persecute her.'

'They don't see it that way: in their eyes, she's condoning the torture.'

'There's no arguing with fanatics.'

'I'm wondering if I should ditch the trip to China and stay here and look after her.' This last was said in a rush, as though making up his mind to do something he didn't want to.

'First of all, Sam, I don't see what you could do to help. I'm being frank here, but you can't stand over her with a shotgun, warding off the attackers. You can't even stop the phone calls and the graffiti.'

'I'm not quite useless!'

'You're not useless at all, but the way these people operate isn't straightforward, is it? It's difficult to see how anybody can guard against them. You go to China, Sam. I'm here, and you asked me to look after your friend for you, didn't you? I can do as much, or as little, as you. You can rely on me, surely, to do my best? And what about the people who are expecting you to turn up in China? Didn't you say it's a school? You can't let them down. Just go!'

If she was honest, she was more anxious to see him escape from his family ties and make his own decisions in life than fulfil his obligations to some unknown Chinese school, but she didn't think she need to remind Sam of this.

There was silence for some seconds at Sam's end of the phone. 'You're right: I should go. And we can keep in touch by email. I should be able to send and receive messages at least once a week.'

'Goodbye, Sam. Enjoy yourself. I'll see you next year.'

17

Look on the bright side, Kate told herself. By tomorrow evening they'll be gone.

She was standing at the open front door, a welcoming smile freezing on her face as she watched Gary and Susie Browne unpack an amount of luggage from the back of their double-parked Chelsea tractor that would surely be sufficient for a month-long expedition to the Himalayas. Much of it appeared to relate to the diminutive and vociferous person who was still strapped into his seat but who had a lot to say about the proceedings.

Susie Browne paused on the pavement, holding a small travelling bag in one hand, and gave instructions to the rear half of her husband protruding from the boot. Kate tried not to notice the cars that were starting to queue up behind them. A single blast of a horn was all that the long-suffering inhabitants of Jericho permitted themselves in order to draw attention to their presence.

Just behind Susie stood Jon, and as Kate watched, Susie turned her face up towards him and smiled, in a movement that appeared both familiar and intimate. Kate was telling herself not to be silly, they were old friends and of course they were familiar with one another, when Susie placed her free hand on Jon's arm and rested it there.

At that moment a red male face appeared from behind the

161

raised hatchback, took in the situation with the traffic, then disappeared again. Another couple of seconds and he had deposited a small travelling bed and bulging plastic bags of what was presumably essential equipment for Freddie next to the five suitcases on the pavement, and climbed back into the driving seat. Kate took the opportunity to run forward and press a visitor's parking permit into his hand through the open window, while Jon gently removed Susie's hand from his sleeve and hopped up into the passenger seat, saying, 'I'd better show you where to find a place to park, Gary.'

'What about Freddie?' called his wife.

'He wants to come with me,' replied Gary Browne, raising a hand in apology to the drivers he had blocked, then pulling away down the road in search of a parking space. From the back, a high voice screamed, 'Mummy!' while five other cars, released at last, followed in Gary's wake.

'Men!' exclaimed Susie Browne. She had a light, rather high-pitched voice, and a drawling accent that Kate associated with wealth. 'You can see that Jon just wanted a good look at the car, can't you? Those two will be talking traction control and compression ratios for the next hour now.'

Kate nodded in agreement. Susie turned just as friendly a smile on her as she had on Jon, which made Kate think that she had been mistaken about the intimacy between them. It would make for an unhappy weekend if she indulged in groundless jealousy, so she made her mind up to stop it immediately, however hard it proved to be.

From a distance, Susie Browne was good-looking. Close to, she was quite stunning. The fall of shining platinum hair, accurately cut in a short bob, was surely natural, the woman's profile as clean-cut as a marble bas-relief, and her figure even slimmer than Kate's own. Her eyes were a dark slate blue with long black lashes. Her clothes, noted Kate, suppressing another pang of envy, must have cost at least three times what she had paid for her own, while the diamonds on her left hand flashed opulently in the morning light.

As the four-by-four disappeared round the corner, both women gazed at the heap of luggage.

'My goodness!' said Susie. 'I hadn't realised just how much stuff we'd brought with us. You must think we've come to stay for a month! But don't worry, most of it belongs to Freddie.'

Kate struggled to find something reassuring to say, and hoped that Jon and Gary would soon return to give them a hand. 'Why don't we make a start at getting them inside,' she said.

'I think we should wait for the men,' said Susie, with the confidence of a woman whom men had always fallen over themselves to help. 'We can stand here and guard the cases until they return. Not that I'm implying this is a dodgy neighbourhood,' she added quickly, realising that her remark might have offended Kate.

'Is anywhere totally safe these days? Better not to put temptation in anyone's way,' said Kate, though privately she thought that no one could run far while lumbered with a hundredweight of leather suitcase, plus contents.

Susie, meanwhile, was looking at Kate's house with approval.

'I just love that Victorian brickwork,' she said as Gary reappeared. Jon was carrying Freddie on his shoulders and the toddler looked delighted to be up at such a height. As Jon reached the gate he swung Freddie, shrieking with pleasure, to the ground and handed him back to his father.

To Kate he said something that sounded like, 'Five point

seven Hemi V8 Overland,' with strong undertones of envy, but she had no idea what he was talking about.

Then he turned to Susie and said, 'Wonderful to see you, Susie! You're looking marvellous,' and Kate watched Susie's face light up with the compliment. Then Susie was hugging him, offering kisses that appeared a fraction warmer than was strictly necessary.

'Don't even think about lifting those bags, Susie,' Jon said, masterfully hefting two cases off the pavement with a grunt that showed they were even heavier than they looked. He staggered back through the gate towards the open front door. 'Come on inside and I'll show you where your room is.'

Eventually they were all indoors and the Brownes' luggage was stowed upstairs in what Kate was learning to call 'our' spare room. Though large and bright, with cream linen blinds and polished floorboards, it still had a spartan air about it, in spite of the large double bed that Jon had provided and the vase of cream-coloured flowers that Kate had placed on the windowsill.

Ten minutes later, the five of them were in the sitting room, taking stock of each other.

Gary's colour had calmed down from scarlet to a light tan, and Kate could see he was a pleasant-looking, good-humoured man in his forties who obviously adored his wife and child. Susie's hair and make-up had been renewed and she was now wearing something different, but equally pale, casual and elegant.

Freddie had stopped demanding his parents' attention and was drinking in his surroundings and examining the new people. He was, Kate noted, a very attractive child, with fair hair and delicate features like his mother's. Really, she could see little of Gary in him.

Returning her interest, Freddie flashed Kate such a radiant smile that she understood why his parents doted on him.

'Have you got everything you need?' she asked. One of those questions that expected the answer 'yes'.

'We're fine. It's a lovely room, thank you, Kate.'

'Now, what would you like to do about lunch?' Kate asked. 'I've prepared some salads and—'

Before she could finish, Susie said, 'Freddie eats only organic food. But don't worry, Kate, we've brought everything with us. If you can let me have a corner of the kitchen, I'll get his meal ready. But Gary and I eat anything at all. Well, except for peanuts, of course, and shellfish, and Gary won't eat any kind of offal. And he's suspicious about what goes into a sausage.' She laughed to show how ridiculous she thought he was being.

At the mention of food, Freddie chipped in with, 'Hungry, Mummy!'

'He usually eats at midday,' explained Gary, beaming at his son. 'It's important for children to eat at regular four-hourly intervals, you know.'

While Susie busied herself in the kitchen, Gary put up Freddie's travelling bed in the spare room, helped by Kate and Jon. 'You'll be close to Mummy and Daddy,' Gary told Freddie, who was watching him. 'You'll like that, won't you?'

'No.'

'He says that to everything at the moment; it's a phase he's going through,' explained Gary. 'He doesn't really mean it.' He turned to his son: 'You don't mean it when you say "no", do you?'

'No!' Then, looking puzzled at the laughter from the adults, he screwed up his face and let big round tears roll down his cheeks.

'I'd better get downstairs and see if Susie would like a hand,' said Kate, feeling sorry for Freddie. Was it good to tease a child like that? Still, if Susie had completed the preparations for his meal, he'd soon forget his tears and she'd be able to do something about food for the adults. Luckily she had bought no peanuts or shellfish, and she and Jon would soon hoover up any rogue sausages.

'Freddie and I will come with you,' said Gary, and picking up Freddie, he followed her downstairs.

'Nearly ready,' said Susie, smiling at her son. 'You can sit up at the table and you'll have your lunch in your own little bowl in a couple of shakes.'

When Gary had set up Freddie's chair and strapped him in to it, Susie gave him detailed instructions about unpacking the rest of their son's food and putting it away. When he had finished doing this, Gary took the plastic carrier bags and twisted each of them into a knot.

'Just my funny little habit,' he said. 'Ready for recycling, eh?'

One of the really appealing things about Freddie, Kate discovered that evening, was that his parents believed in a regular bedtime for him – one that was early enough for the adults to have a reasonable evening ahead of them not dominated by the demands of a toddler. Kate was relieved, because after her first good impression of him, Freddie's behaviour had deteriorated. Every time he did something (spit out his organic carrots, scream for the television to be turned on, bite his mother's leg) that made her think 'spoiled brat', Susie or Gary would say indulgently, 'It's because he's so intelligent, you see.' And Kate had to accept that she knew little about small children.

But at six thirty Susie placed a gentle hand on Freddie's head, ruffled his silky hair and said. 'Time for your bath, sweetie,' and Freddie, after only a token attempt at saying 'no', took her hand and was led away upstairs.

Once he was bathed and settled in bed, to Kate's surprise Susie came downstairs and asked her to say good night to him.

'Really?'

'Oh, yes. He's asking for you.'

And Kate felt absurdly proud at having scored a hit with Susie's son.

'Hello, Freddie,' she said tentatively as she entered the room. Only the reading lamp was on and it caught the shine on his smoky blond hair, leaving his face in shadow. He was snuggled drowsily under his quilt, but when he saw Kate he gave her one of his winning smiles.

'Do you want me to read you a story?' she asked, this being the only way she knew to amuse very small children.

'No fank you,' he said politely.

She walked across the room and crouched down by the bed. 'I'm glad you've come to stay with us, Freddie,' she said. Close to, he smelled of soap and talcum powder, and somehow sweetly of himself.

'Want a good night kiss,' he said.

She leant across and kissed the amazing silkiness of his cheek, and in return received a soft damp kiss on her own.

'Good night, Freddie,' she said.

As she walked quietly out of the room she thought, So that's why people have babies.

A little later they were all relaxing after one of Kate's most imaginative meals, enjoying an after-dinner drink, listening to music they'd enjoyed when they were twenty, and thinking about moving back into the sitting room. Gary, who improved greatly on acquaintance, was making them all laugh with his descriptions of a play he and Susie had seen the previous week, and Kate was thinking what a good mimic he was, and what a delightful couple he and Susie were when they weren't preoccupied with their child, and how pleasurable it was to be spending such an agreeable evening together with friends of Jon's.

'Did Susie mention the place we've acquired in France?' Gary asked them.

'Jon told me something about it,' said Kate.

'It certainly will be something when we've completed all the renovations,' said Gary.

'A rural hideaway?' suggested Jon.

'It's quite big, actually,' said Susie. 'A farmhouse and its outbuildings, plus a couple of cottages.'

'Four cottages, to be precise,' said Gary. 'The locals are accusing us of buying up the whole village!'

'You make it sound as though you've become lords of the manor,' said Jon.

'I like the sound of that!' said Susie. 'But seriously, it does mean that there's loads of room for our friends – no tripping over each other or anything like that. If you came down next summer you could have a whole cottage to yourselves. Though you could join us in the main house in the evenings, of course. We've found a marvellous man who comes in and cooks for us all.'

'Really great food. Should be a lot of fun,' said Gary. 'It's so quiet and secluded, and yet only a few minutes' run from the coast, and another ten miles to the bright lights. Do you enjoy gambling, Kate?'

'It's not something I've ever got hooked on.'

'You must give it a try. Nothing like it for the buzz, I've always found.'

'And there's the thought that at any moment you could really be in the big money,' put in Susie. 'It's such fun, Kate.'

'Sounds good to me,' said Jon.

Remembering someone (certainly not her mother) once telling her that you should only gamble when you could afford to lose, Kate wasn't so sure about the lure of the casino. Still, it seemed churlish to mention it at that moment.

'Do you do much sailing down there?' asked Jon, returning to his real love.

'Oh, yes!' said Susie. 'Gary's not so keen, but I've always loved boats. Don't you remember?' And in her enthusiasm she leant closer to Jon so that the fall of her hair threatened to brush his cheek.

'I believe there's a great yacht club at—' Gary started to say, but at that point they were interrupted by the insistent ringing of the phone.

Kate didn't recognise the number on the screen. 'I'll take it in the other room,' she murmured to Jon. He and the Brownes could carry on their conversation about sailing undisturbed.

She pressed the green button. 'Hello?'

'Is that Kate?'

'Yes.'

'Kate! You must help me!'

18

The voice at the other end of the phone was hysterical, and Kate couldn't identify whose it was.

'I'll help if I can, but who is this?' she asked.

'It's Kerri here.' The girl was sobbing now.

'What's happened? Are you all right?'

'No. No, really I'm not. I've just had a phone call.'

'OK, Kerri. I'll do what I can, but you must tell me about it as calmly as possible. Who phoned you?'

'I don't know! It's them. They're threatening me again.'

'Them?' She knew, of course, but she was trying to lower the emotional temperature.

'Those terrorists.'

'Remember that they can't harm you over the phone. What did they say?'

'It was another of their threats, Kate. They say I'm a criminal and they're coming to get me.' Her voice broke.

'It's going to be fine, Kerri. They're trying to scare you, that's all. It's all a bluff.' She hoped this was true, but whoever they were, they had certainly succeeded in upsetting Kerri.

'What makes you think they don't mean it?' Kerri's words were tumbling over each other. 'It might not be a bluff; it might be for real. They sent me a letter bomb, remember? You've got to come over right away. Please, Kate!'

'I really can't at the moment, Kerri. I've got people staying for the weekend. Aren't your housemates there?'

'No, they're all away except me. I'm on my own.' She was sobbing again.

Kate thought for a moment. 'Ring off, Kerri. Then phone for a taxi and come straight over here. I'll pay for it.'

'Would you really?'

'Yes, of course.'

'Shall I bring my sleeping bag?'

'No need. I have a fold-up bed and another spare duvet. Just bring your toothbrush and a change of clothes.'

'I'm being a nuisance, aren't I?' Her voice was that of a little girl.

'Certainly not. You ring for that taxi straight away. And I bet you haven't eaten, have you?'

'No. But it doesn't matter.'

'Of course it matters. There's plenty of food, including veggie options.' In Kate's experience there was nothing like a plate of food to put things into perspective.

'Oh, thanks, Kate. Sam said you'd help out if I needed it. But I wasn't sure you really would.' She had cheered up considerably in the past few seconds.

'I'll see you in about twenty minutes.'

Kate cut the connection and considered her options: the simplest was to put Kerri upstairs in her workroom. It wasn't as though she'd get any writing done while the house was full of people.

She wasn't sure how Kerri would take to Gary and Susie Browne, since they didn't have anything much in common, but maybe Kerri liked children: she would introduce her to Freddie in the morning.

Back in the sitting room she told the others: 'We have

another guest arriving.' And then she explained about Sam and Kerri.

'You say he's only been gone three days and already she's moving in with you?' said Gary. 'You want to watch it, Kate, or you'll have her for the full nine months.'

'I'm sure she'll return to her own place once her house-mates come home. I can't see her wanting to stay for long with oldies like Jon and me.'

'Oh, I don't know,' said Susie kindly. 'You're not very old really, and it's a nice house you have here, Kate. You've made it look great, considering: Victorian on the outside, but light, bright and modern on the inside, while keeping all the period features – I like that, it's really clever. And it's so convenient for the town centre. I expect Kerri will want to stay for ever! I bet it's heaps nicer than her place, and much more comfortable.'

'I'm glad you like it.' Kate found herself warming to Susie.

'What you ought to do,' said the other woman enthusiastic-ally, 'is to knock this ground floor into one big open-plan space. We all live in our kitchens these days, don't we? So you could have a sitting area, with an L-shaped sofa at this end, and a dining area over there, and I suppose you could put Jon's desk and stuff behind a screen or something, by the front window.'

'I'm not sure that Jon wants us to live here long enough to get all that done,' Kate said, less warmly than before, feeling more proprietorial than ever about her house.

'That's right, Kate,' said Gary. 'Don't let Susie boss you around. She'll completely redesign your home if you let her.'

'*You* appreciate my creative ideas, don't you, Jon?' and Susie turned her slate-blue eyes in his direction.

'Well, it would be up to Kate,' he said.

Kate stood up. 'I must get things ready for Kerri. She hasn't eaten this evening with all those threats coming down the phone, so I'd better put up the spare bed and then get together a plateful of comforting vegetarian food for her.'

'Pity Freddie ate all the ice cream,' said Gary. 'It helps in a crisis, don't you find?'

'Every time, but don't worry, I'm sure I have an emergency tub of chocolate swirl hidden at the back of the freezer.'

Jon followed her upstairs to her workroom.

'Do we really have to have this girl to stay? And Susie's right, she may never want to go back home again. We may be landed with her for months.'

'We have to have her, at least for tonight, because I promised Sam Dolby that I'd look after her. To be honest, I didn't think she'd get in touch at all: I'm only pleased she feels she can trust me.'

'It's ruined the evening.'

'No it hasn't. Susie and Gary are quite happy downstairs, drinking the very good wine that they brought with them. I can hear that they've moved back into the sitting room, so if I clear away our meal, Kerri can eat at the dining table. We haven't woken Freddie, and when I've made this room as inviting as I can, we'll go downstairs and enjoy the rest of the evening.'

Jon looked unconvinced, and at that moment Susie put her head round the door.

'I thought you might need a hand, Kate. Is there anything I can do? Oh, sorry, Jon, I didn't see you there.'

'Thanks, Susie. I can manage. Why don't you take Jon back downstairs and keep Gary amused?' Privately she thought they would be able to talk about old times and mutual friends without worrying about excluding her from their conversation.

'If you're sure,' Susie said. 'Come on, Jon,' and she laid her hand on Jon's arm and smiled up at him. As they returned to the sitting room, Kate made a note to book herself a manicure. A few moments later the conversation level from downstairs sounded positively buoyant.

Kate put the few loose papers on her desk away in a folder, replaced a couple of reference books on the shelves, and pushed her chair under the desk to make the room look less like an office. Then she fetched the fold-up bed from the cupboard under the stairs and bed linen from the airing cupboard. Five minutes later she had a convincing second spare bedroom. She looked around critically, then fetched another vase and removed a few stems from the arrangement she had put in the Brownes' room. When she had placed the vase of cream flowers and greenery on the desk, the room looked as inviting as she could make it at short notice.

She went downstairs and quickly cleared the dining table, stuffing leftover food into the fridge and the plates into the dishwasher, and putting together a platter of meat-free items for Kerri to choose from, arranging them carefully to look as attractive as possible. She glanced at her watch. The girl would be here in a few minutes. She just had time to go back into the sitting room and pour herself a glass of wine.

Jon needn't have worried about ruining the Brownes' evening: the three of them were obviously having a great time without Kate's presence.

Five minutes later Kerri arrived. Kate paid the taxi and led the way into the house. Kerri looked slighter than ever beneath her bulky backpack.

'What a big house you've got,' she said, pausing just inside the gate and gazing up at the decorative brickwork. 'Is it just the two of you living here?'

'Plus a couple of guests at the moment,' said Kate, who

hadn't found the house big at all once Jon moved in with her. 'Come upstairs and I'll show you where you'll be sleeping.'

'Wow, it's vast,' said Kerri when Kate opened the door to her workroom. 'Who lives in here?'

'It's where I write my books. I like plenty of empty space around me.'

'You're lucky to have this much room.'

Kate wanted to say that luck didn't come into it, but talent and years of hard work did, but this wouldn't be strictly true, since she had been given a sizeable lump of capital when she was eighteen, so she shut up.

'There's no wardrobe in this room, but I've put a reading lamp over there for you, and you'll find the bathroom a couple of doors down. You'll be sharing it with our other guests, the Brownes, but I'm sure you'll manage.'

'Oh, yeah. Course I will. I'm used to sharing.'

'I expect you're starving, aren't you? When did you last have something to eat?'

'Not since lunch.'

'Well, come downstairs as soon as you're ready,' said Kate, showing her where the bathroom was. 'You can eat at the dining table if you like, though maybe it's cosier in the kitchen,' she added as an afterthought.

'Kitchen, please,' said Kerri politely.

Kerri joined Kate in the kitchen a few minutes later and, skinny as she was, tucked enthusiastically into the food that Kate had set out for her.

'There's chocolate ice cream for pud, if you'd like it.'

'Yes please.'

'I might join you,' said Kate, who could rarely resist a bowl of chocolate ice cream.

Between them they made more than half a large tubful disappear. Kate would top up her emergency supplies tomorrow.

'I expect you think it's a bit of a cheek, turning up on your doorstep like this,' Kerri said as Kate poured her a glass of apple juice. 'But you were really kind to me at Sam's party, and I thought maybe you meant it when you said I could get in touch.'

'Of course I did.' Kate refilled her own glass with white wine and sat down again at the table.

'I wasn't enjoying it much,' confided Kerri. 'What with Sam's relations looking me over as though I had designs on him, and Conor suggesting I had something to do with the two bombs, I thought everyone hated me.'

'Nonsense!' said Kate robustly. 'And Sam's relations will behave exactly the same to anyone he ever takes home to meet them – there's nothing personal in it.'

'They want him to marry money, don't they?'

'Probably. But why do you think Sam's taken off to China? I think he's tired of having his life mapped out for him and wants to get free of them all while he makes his own decisions about his future.'

'Yeah. That's what he told me before he went.'

'So take no notice of the Dolbys. They're relatively harmless, anyway.'

'We're not thinking of getting married, Kate. I don't want you to get that idea. It's just that I don't see that what we do has anything to do with *them*.'

'Forget about them, Kerri. And I'm sure Conor was only trying to wind you up over the explosions. No one can imagine you have anything to do with either of them.'

'Someone let the bomber into the lab, though, didn't they?

And people are wondering who gave them our home addresses and phone numbers.'

'Well *I* don't think you had anything to do with it.'

'But it must have been one of us.'

It occurred to Kate that if Conor was so keen to accuse Kerri, it might be that he was the one who had something to hide. She'd raise the subject again when Kerri was feeling more at home.

'Why don't you let me pour you a glass of wine, or maybe you'd prefer a Coke, or beer, then you can come into the other room and meet Jon and our friends.'

'Coke, please.' Yes, she was just a kid really, and touchingly grateful for Kate's attention.

And so they joined the others in the sitting room. Kerri was wearing jeans and a cropped crop, blue this time rather than black, and her face and eyebrows still bore the marks of the letter bomb. She stood just inside the door, looking as shy as ever, and Kate was relieved that Susie immediately said, 'Come and sit here by me, Kerri. There's plenty of room on this sofa.' She gave Kerri one of her stunning smiles, and Kate heard her say, 'What's this we hear about threatening phone calls? Come and tell me about it, you poor thing.' And Kerri started to chat to her.

Kate tuned into the conversation between Jon and Gary, but they were talking about car engines, so she moved back to Kerri and Susie's side of the room.

'So, first you were actually there when the bomb went off at the lab, and then you mean to say that they actually sent you a letter bomb?' Susie's voice rose high in disbelief. 'You're lucky to be alive!'

'It was weird, really. I suppose I was still feeling nervous after the explosion at the lab, and somehow, just as I went to open it, I was like, "This could be a bomb!" and I threw it across the room. I was lucky. I lost part of my eyebrows and got this burn on my face. But it isn't serious and it could have been a lot worse. I was really scared at the time, though.'

'I bet you were! And now they're phoning you up with threats! I don't know how you can stand it.'

'It is creepy, wondering who hates you that much,' said Kerri.

'You poor thing! How on earth did they know where you lived?'

Kerri dropped her eyes. 'People seem to think that someone from the lab passed on our addresses and phone numbers.'

'But who would do that?'

Kerri mumbled, 'Some people think it might have been me.'

'Why on earth would they think that?'

'They know I'm not that keen on animal testing.'

'I can't believe anyone could be so cruel. After all, you're the one who was attacked.'

'Maybe the bombers are getting ready to do something worse, and this time I'll be well away from it. That's what they think.'

'Poor Kerri! Well, at least you're quite safe here with us. Kate's looking after you, isn't she?'

'Yeah. I didn't think I could eat anything, really, but I feel safe here, and that made me realise just how hungry I was.'

'And your boyfriend's gone off to China, Kate says?'

'Yes, he's away on his gap year but he told me I could call Kate if anything happened.'

Thank goodness Sam's message had got through to her. Kate had thought that Kerri hadn't really taken to her, but it seemed that she was wrong. And Susie was doing a great job in drawing her out. Just talking about her ordeal seemed to help: Kerri was relaxing by the minute.

Kate went out to the kitchen to open another bottle of wine, and after a minute Kerri joined her there.

'Your friend's being really nice, Kate, but would it be OK if I went up to my room now?'

'Of course. Anything else you need, Kerri, just let me know.'

When she had refilled the glasses, Kate sat down next to Susie again.

'Thanks for making Kerri feel at home, Susie. You did a great job. She's a lot calmer now and I think she'll get a good night's rest.'

Susie sipped her wine. 'What do you think about it, Kate?' she asked slowly.

'About the addresses, do you mean?'

'Yes. Someone must have passed them on, just as someone must have let the bomber into the lab, whether knowingly or not.'

'But surely not Kerri!'

'How well do you know her?'

'She's Sam's girlfriend!' replied Kate, as though this ended the argument.

'It could have been one of the others, I suppose,' said Susie, sounding unconvinced.

'My money's on Conor,' said Kate, then stopped. 'Of course, I have no reason to point the finger at him – or anyone else, if it comes to that.'

'Conor?' queried Susie.

'He's the lab technician,' said Kate. 'And he struck me as someone with a chip on his shoulder. But I met him only once . . .'

'Does he belong to the animal rights gang?' put in Gary.

'I really don't know.'

'On the fringe, perhaps?' suggested Susie.

'Even if he is, it doesn't mean he'd want to use force. And they do have a point, don't they?'

'Not in my opinion,' said Gary.

'It's the barmy fringe who get the movement a bad name,' said Susie, looking at him reprovingly.

'They take attention away from genuine interest in animal welfare,' said Jon.

'Oh, let's change the subject,' said Gary impatiently. 'We've had enough of it for one night, haven't we.'

Kate drank her wine and listened to the conversation between Gary and Jon, which Susie had now joined in. They had moved on to the subject of house-buying, on which Gary appeared to be an expert. Relaxing in her comfortable chair and sipping her wine, Kate let the words wash over her.

Just for the moment, she thought contentedly, everyone had a bed to go to, they were all bursting with good food, their glasses were full. Freddie was asleep. Kerri had opened up to Susie. Everything was sorted.

19

Next morning Kate saw that, as guests go, Kerri was really no trouble: she spent no more than ten minutes in the bathroom, she left no hairs in the basin; by nine o'clock she had folded up her bed and pushed it against the wall, with her duvet and pillow neatly on top so that Kate's workroom was hardly disturbed; she made herself toast and coffee for breakfast and cleared away her own plate and mug. She even offered to do the washing-up for Kate, until she was shown the dishwasher, which she proceeded to stack tidily with their dishes, just the way Kate had demonstrated.

When she had finished her self-imposed chores she came shyly into the sitting room and said, 'Thanks for putting the flowers in my room, Kate. They really made me feel like, welcome.'

'I'm glad you're enjoying them. And of course you're welcome here, Kerri: I'm so glad you took Sam's advice and rang me. I'd hate to think you might be sitting at home feeling miserable.'

'As long as you're sure.'

'Really, we like having you here.'

A little later, when Kerri helped Susie to feed Freddie his breakfast, Kate noticed that the child didn't whinge or try to manipulate her. He smiled. He ate his organic baby muesli without spitting any on to the floor. He drank down his warm organic milk, he asked politely for some orange juice. And afterwards he even sang a song that Kerri taught him, involving much jumping up and down and waving of arms by both of them.

She's only a kid herself, thought Kate again, as she watched them, down on their hands and knees pretending to be lions and tigers. Just a scared kid. And who could blame her for that? They set off an explosion at the lab where she works, they send her a letter bomb, and then they ring her at home and threaten her. On top of that, the awful Conor accuses her of colluding with them. It was enough to terrify anyone.

Obviously Sam was the best thing that had ever happened in her life, and just as she was feeling confident about their relationship, he'd left her, if only for nine months or so. Kate was a link with Sam's life outside the lab, so it was no surprise that Kerri wanted to stay here for a while. Once Susie and Gary left, she could move into the spare room if she wanted to. Kate would have her workroom back and everyone would be happy. Kerri could stay as long as she liked.

She suppressed the thought that life with Jon might be easier with a Kerri-shaped buffer in the house.

For his part, Jon was delighted that Kerri was such a hit with Susie and Freddie. At first he'd been irritated when Kate invited her over so readily the previous evening, feeling that she would get in the way of his plan.

But now he felt that, on the contrary, she showed his friends in a better light than before. Kate would never be impressed by the amount of money the Brownes had in their bank account, their opulent holiday home in France, or how successful they were in their careers. But she did appreciate how kind they were being to Kerri, and how, in return, Kerri was blossoming in the light of their attention.

Later that morning they all went for a walk across Port Meadow, where Kerri introduced Freddie to cows and horses and persuaded him that they weren't at all intimidating. Then they both took their shoes and socks off and splashed around in the shallow water of the river until it was time to amble on to the pub, where they ate lunch in the open air, and the peacocks screeched against the background of the tumbling water.

The sun shone and the air was balmy.

Jon and Kate chatted to Gary; Kerri and Susie seemed like old friends as they kept Freddie amused, and when she listened in to their conversation Kate heard Kerri opening up to Susie about the work she was doing at the lab, her dreams for the future, and her hopes for a university education. Certainly, thought Kate, Susie could show the younger girl the heights that could be reached with brains and determination.

In their separate ways, they were all well contented with the way the day had turned out.

After lunch, Kate and Gary walked briskly back to Cleveland Road to collect the Overlander and drive back to pick up the others, who had walked quite far enough and were waiting in the pub for a lift back to Jericho.

'I can't see how people manage with a small car when they have children,' Gary said to Kate as they climbed into the vehicle. 'Susie drives a Toyota in town but I don't know how she fits in all Freddie's gear. Have you seen how much we tote around for him?'

'And I imagine a cello's tricky to fit into a modest car.'

'It's a very small cello,' he replied, smiling, 'and I'm not sure how long it will take before Susie notices he's never going to be a virtuoso.'

Kate was glad that Freddie appeared to have one parent at least who didn't take his accomplishments too seriously. 'You all seem to have settled back in London again pretty quickly,' she commented, as they sat in a queue of traffic in the Woodstock Road. 'After Brussels, I mean.'

'We were only over there for fifteen months, and once we were home we slotted back into our old lives no problem.'

'You sound very organised.'

'It was luck as much as planning. Susie took three months' maternity leave before Brussels, and she was able to be a full-time wife and mother while we were there, which is what we both wanted for Freddie: give him a good start in life.'

'Sounds ideal,' said Kate. So it appeared that even Susie took time out from work when she had a new baby.

'Mind you,' continued Gary, 'I think it's taken a bit longer for her to get used to the routine since we got back. At lot happened while we were away which didn't help her confidence. It's been good for her to meet up with old friends like Jon – and to meet you, of course. This weekend was just what she needed.'

'Don't you get down to Provence? It sounds like the ideal place to relax.'

'Not as much as I'd like. We're not encouraged to take more than three weeks' vacation a year, but we fly down for a long weekend from time to time. Roll on early retirement, I say!'

'Really? I'd have thought you'd be bored after a very short time.'

'I have plenty of plans of my own I'd like to develop,' said Gary. Then, as though nervous that they might be overheard, he added, 'Though I'm very happy where I am, of course. And

I wouldn't want to be without my company benefits, let alone my salary.'

'It's good to have a financial cushion if you're going to be self-employed,' said Kate, reflecting that Gary's financial cushion was likely to be substantially larger than her own. And she'd need more savings than she had at the moment if she went along with Jon's ideas about starting a family.

'You've gone very silent,' remarked Gary. 'Jon been pushing you to have children, has he?'

'How did you know?'

'Well, he's reached that age, and I can see you've had a disagreement about something or other.'

'Oh, it's not really—'

'No need to go into details, Kate, but it's not difficult to read the body language. Pity, because I can see you two are made for each other.'

'And what's your advice?' asked Kate, gratified that Gary thought that she and Jon were, after all, well suited.

'Ah, here we go,' said Gary, as the traffic started to move forwards and they reached the turning to Wolvercote. 'I'll just say that Freddie's the best thing that's happened to me, and I know that Susie feels exactly the same; in fact if anything she's even more devoted to him. And she holds down a well-paid and responsible job in the company, Kate, so I'm sure you'd be able to combine your writing with bringing up a kid, if that's what you're worried about.'

Kate wasn't quite so sure about her ability to multi-task. Susie had a job waiting for her when she wanted to return to work, and she could afford plenty of help at home by the sound of it.

They had reached the pub car park and pulled into a free space at the far end, but Gary made no move to leave the car.

'I can see it might not be so easy for you,' he said. 'Working from home as you do. No, it wouldn't be easy at all, with a baby needing attention every few hours, or a toddler scribbling all over your newly printed manuscript.'

'And no guarantee that anyone would remember who I was when I finally produced a new manuscript.'

Later, Kate felt quite disappointed when the Brownes started to pack up their gear – which no longer looked at all unreasonable given the requirements of a small child.

Kerri, too, seemed sad that they were leaving. Susie had shown so much interest in her, and she had really taken to Freddie. With their help the memory of the threatening phone calls was fading.

As the Brownes were walking out to their car, Freddie insisted on being swung up into the air and on to Jon's shoulders, and then he gave Kate another of his soft, wet kisses when he said goodbye.

'And say "thank you" to Kate,' urged Susie.

'Fank you,' said Freddie.

Then Freddie was strapped snugly into his toddler seat, Susie gave Jon a farewell kiss that seemed to Kate to go on for a little too long, and at last the Brownes were off, with Kate, Jon and Kerri waving them goodbye and promising to visit them next summer in France.

When the three of them went back inside, the house felt quite empty and unnaturally quiet.

'Shall I help you with the laundry?' asked Kerri.

'We could take their duvet cover and sheets down to the machine, I suppose.'

'And after that I should be getting back to my place.'

'You don't have to do that unless you really want to, Kerri.'

You're very welcome to stay for a bit longer.'

'Mel and Lynne will be home this evening. I could cook something for our supper so it's ready for when they get back. They've been very kind looking after me since the accident, and it's time I did something for them in return.'

'If you're sure. Just as long as you know you can stay here as long as you like. We've enjoyed having you.' In fact, she was going to miss Kerri's undemanding company, she found.

'Thanks. I liked your friends, and Freddie's a great little kid once he forgets he's supposed to be a genius all the time.'

Which was a pretty accurate estimate of the situation, in Kate's opinion.

'I'll give you a lift back to the Cowley Road,' she said.

'I can get a bus, no problem.'

'I'm sure you can, but I'd like to give you a lift. OK?' She knew she sounded impatient, and she remembered how Susie had been so tolerant with Kerri and had made friends with her so easily. She had been positively motherly, Kate thought – something she herself seemed unable to achieve. Jon didn't seem to realise that there was more to parenthood than he had ever considered. She just wasn't a natural at it.

Kerri was silent as Kate started the engine and switched on the indicator. Then, 'There's something I wanted to ask you about,' she said suddenly.

'Yes?' Kate cut the engine and waited for Kerri to go on. There was a feeling of tension in the car and she sensed that what Kerri had to say was important.

'Maybe I shouldn't say anything. It's not as though I *know*, after all.'

'Know what?' prompted Kate.

'It's about Conor.' She stopped again.

'Yes?'

189

'On the day of the lab explosion. It was lunchtime and the demonstrators were standing outside and that man Razer was making a speech, saying how evil we were and that. Conor got fed up of it after a while and left the roof. He said he was going out for a smoke. That's what he said when we asked him where he'd been.'

'Right.'

'But he could have smoked on the roof. In fact he took a packet out of his jeans pocket, but it was empty.'

'Maybe he went out to buy more.' This didn't seem like strange behaviour to Kate.

'He didn't have time. And he stopped to chat to one of the demonstrators.'

'So?'

'Afterwards, when we asked him about it, he denied it, and then refused to say any more.'

'Maybe you were mistaken. Maybe he went back towards St Giles and bought some cigarettes.'

'We all saw him. We agreed it was him. He and this demonstrator were arguing about something and then when he joined us afterwards he said he'd been out at the back, having a smoke.'

Kerri was getting worked up and Kate said soothingly, 'It's OK, Kerri. You've told me about it now, and I'll keep it in mind.'

'You like working out puzzles, don't you?'

'Can't resist them.'

'You like working out what people are thinking, and why they do what they do. I've seen you.'

'I didn't realise I was that obvious.'

'No, you're not. But I like watching people too, so I saw what you were doing.'

190

'Well . . .' said Kate, disconcerted. She switched on the car engine again, the indicator blinked, and she pulled away.

When she turned off the Cowley Road, Kerri said, 'You can drop me at the corner,' but Kate drove the extra fifty yards and stopped opposite the house Kerri indicated. She watched her as she walked away, the size of the rucksack making her look even more like a skinny kid as she crossed the road and disappeared through the front door.

Later that evening Kate telephoned just to make sure that Mel and Lynne had turned up as expected. Kerri assured her they had, sounding more cheerful than Kate had ever heard her. Then she sent an email to Sam, telling him what had happened and what a successful weekend they had spent together. There were no real problems, she told him; it was just that Kerri was feeling a bit lonely. Nothing for him to worry about.

On her way to bed she looked in at her newly vacated workroom. Tomorrow she would get down to serious work on her proposal for a new novel. It was several weeks since she had spoken to her agent, Estelle Livingstone, and she hadn't heard from her editor, Neil Orson, either. But ideas were starting to buzz around her brain, and she was sure she could turn at least one of them into a bestselling book.

Jon was sitting up in bed reading when she entered the bedroom. His narrow black-framed glasses made him look older and more serious than usual.

'That was a pretty good weekend, don't you think?' he said.

'I thought your friends were great company. And Susie certainly went out of her way to make Kerri feel at home.'

'Kerri got on really well with Freddie too, didn't she?'

'That was a bit of a surprise.'

'Not really. He's a very likeable child. And bright with it.'

191

'He's OK, but I thought he was a bit of a pain when he first turned up, even if he is a whizz at the cello.'

'Why do you always have to be so over-critical, Kate?'

'Oh, come on! What about when he threw a tantrum when he was politely asked to eat his carrots?'

'That's just normal behaviour for a child his age.'

'I didn't realise you were an expert.'

No, she thought. We have to stop right here. What are we quarrelling about? Freddie isn't our child, so we don't have to worry whether he throws a tantrum or not. We certainly don't have to care whether he eats his carrots or practises his scales.

'But maybe you're right,' she continued in a calculatedly soft tone of voice. 'We all had a good time today on Port Meadow.'

'Yes, I suppose we did.'

Jon had gone all huffy on her.

'And I agree that Freddie can be a lovable child sometimes.'

'I'm glad you think so.'

'And we have that lovely invitation to spend time at their place in France,' she said.

'That was very kind of them.'

'So what's wrong?'

'Wrong?'

'You're angry about something.'

'I just wish you wouldn't take against small children like that.'

'I don't take against them. Once or twice I felt quite fond of Freddie. It's just that I don't have a natural affinity with toddlers, not like Kerri.'

'It wouldn't be like that if you had one of your own. You'd feel quite different then.'

There followed what Kate tried hard not to describe to herself as a pregnant pause.

'But suppose I felt just the same as I did with Freddie, or worse, even. Suppose I didn't like the child and it didn't like me. We'd be stuck with each other for at least eighteen years, not just a weekend. Now that really would be a tragedy.'

'You're being impossible.'

And he put down his book, switched off the light on his side of the bed and turned his back on Kate. What a pity, she thought, that such a good day had to end like this.

Driving back to London, Gary and Susie were also talking over their weekend while Freddie slept.

'That turned out better than I expected,' said Gary.

'I told you you'd like Jon and Kate. And their little friend was quite interesting when you got to know her.'

'You were right that it made a break from London.'

'I suppose so.'

'What's up? I thought you were enjoying yourself.'

'I don't see why Kate had to be so boringly possessive over Jon. He obviously wanted to spend time with me, but she refused to see it. He won't stick around for long if she clings like that.'

Gary laughed. 'You're just hacked off because he no longer fancies you the way he used to.'

'Gary!'

'Oh, come on, Susie! You've been hoping you could show him just what he's been missing since you two broke up. Admit it, you don't like to think that there's someone out there who got away.'

Susie laughed. 'You know me too well,' she said. 'I don't like to let go of any of my possessions, do I?'

'It's not such a bad fault. And neither do I, if it comes to that.' He reached out a hand and patted her thigh.

'Jon and I were good mates, though. I wouldn't want to lose that, even if he has found himself a new girlfriend.'

'It's obvious there's one thing he does envy you.'

'Freddie?'

'Exactly. And I think those two are in the middle of a major row about having children.'

'Really? I missed that.' Susie had perked up.

'In their usual polite, restrained way, of course.' And he patted her thigh once more.

Susie laughed again. 'You're right, as always. I certainly won the jackpot when I fell for you, Gary.'

They continued in contented silence for a mile or two, and as their speed reached ninety-five, Susie said complacently, 'I wouldn't fancy driving back to London in that scruffy little car of Kate's.'

'This is the safest way to transport a child,' agreed Gary.

'Nothing but the best is good enough for Freddie,' said Susie.

'And when he goes to school, he'll be getting the best education money can buy,' added Gary.

'You've done your sums?'

'Don't I always?'

'I bet Kate and Jon haven't thought how much a child is going to cost them,' said Susie.

'I don't suppose they've got the funds. It'll be state schools and caravan holidays for their kid, if they have one.'

'They're not exactly poor,' said Susie, trying to be fair.

'And they'll never be rich.'

'Watch it,' said Susie. 'Those lorries are blocking all three lanes.'

Gary flashed his lights and then accelerated past as the offending vehicle lumbered out of his way.

'Tell me,' he said, as he cruised down the outside lane, 'what was so interesting about the scrawny girl who turned up on Saturday night? I couldn't see why you were spending so much time with her.'

'She's called Kerri,' said Susie. 'And she was telling me about her work.'

'She's just a temporary lab assistant, isn't she? What's so fascinating about that?'

'Apparently she's a bright young spark on a bursary, working for a hot-shot biologist in a research lab.'

'Yeah?'

'And she was telling me how their lab was going to conquer the world's worst neurological diseases with its latest research.'

'Did she know what she was talking about?'

'Seemed like it.'

'And was she telling the truth?'

'I thought she was quite painfully honest.'

'What did she say, exactly?'

'You don't want to hear the details of cell biology, do you?'

Behind them, Freddie started to whimper in his sleep and Susie twisted round to look at him.

'Is he all right?' asked Gary.

'Yes. But it might be a good idea to stop at the next service station. I saw a sign just now saying it's seven miles away.'

'What did you learn about the work at Kerri's lab, though?' persisted Gary.

'That she has a dishy boss called Dr Blake Parker—'

'Ah . . .'

'That they're being targeted by animal rights thugs.'

'They need to strengthen their security, then.'

'And that one of her colleagues must be passing low-grade information on to an extremist group.'

'Did she reckon this is affecting their work at all?'

'It must be, but she believes they're miles ahead of everyone else in the field and it won't matter in the long run.'

'I think you've—'

But at that moment there was a sleepy wail from the back of the car, followed by an urgent request from Freddie for his potty.

'Another two miles,' said Gary. 'Don't you worry, Freddie. Daddy will get you there in time.' And his foot jabbed the accelerator.

'Do hurry up,' Susie urged her husband as their speed rose over the hundred mark. 'I don't want him ruining the upholstery.'

20

In her workroom early the next morning, Kate looked complacently at the substantial shelf of books, all of which had her name on the spine. *My babies.* That was the way she thought of them, and she was sure that she'd always be fonder – and prouder – of them than she could ever be of a child like Freddie. (Or even a child who was much nicer than Freddie – more like Jon and her, for example.)

And then she remembered the softness of his cheek and the sweet, clean smell of drowsy toddler.

Books, she told herself. Not babies. Let Jon think about producing babies if he wants; today it's your job to come up with a strong idea for a new book. She seated herself at her desk and switched on the computer.

A contemporary setting? Or a historical one? She could enter whatever world she wished, though she had to admit that her knowledge of many historical periods was hazy. Modern, then. Or how about the recent past? Shouldn't there be a vogue for the 1950s by now? The 1970s – the decade that style forgot, or so she had heard?

The computer had finally stopped flashing its LEDs and whirring, and now presented her with a blank screen. She tentatively typed a few words and then started to play around with some ideas. She had covered a couple of pages when she was interrupted by the telephone.

'Kate?'

'That's right.'

'Blake here. Blake Parker.'

'Hi, Blake.' She was so wrapped up in her thoughts that she hardly remembered who he was. Oh, yes. At Sam's birthday party, and afterwards in a punt on the river. Kerri's boss. Not the type to forgive you for forgetting him so quickly.

Blake was saying, 'If you remember, you mentioned that you might be free one day this week, and I wondered whether you'd like to meet up for a drink after work?'

'What sort of time were you thinking of?'

'I'm flexible. How about six?'

Kate did a quick calculation involving the time Jon normally left work, the evening he usually played squash with a colleague, and the likely density of traffic on the A34. 'I could manage Thursday,' she said.

'Thursday it is, then. Six o'clock?'

'Fine.'

'Shall we make it the bar of the Randolph?'

'I don't believe I've ever been there,' said Kate, then realised that Blake's partner and their friends, not to mention Jon and Kate's friends, probably never went there either, which was possibly why he'd chosen it.

'Well, if you don't mind the gossip, we could go somewhere livelier,' said Blake.

'Not that we have anything to hide,' said Kate. 'But let's make it the Randolph.'

There was a pause.

'You sound busy; I'd better leave you to get on with your work,' he said.

'Thanks.' She tried not to sound impatient, but she couldn't wait to get back to what she'd been doing. Before she did so, she reflected that it would be a good opportunity to quiz Blake Parker about the possibility that someone other than Kerry had passed on the addresses and phone numbers of his staff to members of an extremist group. And he might have up-to-date information for her about the explosion at the lab. She could explain her interest by invoking the promise she had made to Sam about looking after Kerri. No one could accuse her of idle interest in the affair.

When he'd rung off, she settled back with her pages of notes. Another hour's work and she felt ready to phone her agent. Estelle had a disconcerting habit of forgetting who Kate was if she wasn't reminded of her existence from time to time, so she dialled her number.

'Hello, sweetie. How's it going?' Estelle sounded distracted, and Kate had the impression that, as she feared, her agent was having difficulty in remembering whether she was due for a new contract or whether she had recently delivered a manuscript. She'd better give her some helpful hints.

'I thought I'd try out a couple of ideas on you, Estelle. It must be time to ask Neil for a new contract.'

'Neil? Neil Orson, do you mean?'

'Yes. He is my editor,' she prompted, since Estelle had probably forgotten this detail, too. 'At Foreword Publishing.'

'Is he? Well, I'm not at all sure what the future holds for Mr Orson. Everything's fluid at Foreword these days. All the talk is of restructuring.'

'Restructuring? I didn't know about that.' Kate wasn't entirely sure what it meant, but it had the ominous sound of other, more familiar, euphemisms, like 'downsizing' and 'outsourcing'.

'Nothing for you to worry about, Kate. It really won't impinge on you and your work at all. But I'd heard a rumour that Neil would like to move on to Penguin, or perhaps take over one of Macmillan's imprints. I believe he's not happy with the way he's been stagnating at Foreword.'

'I wouldn't call it stagnating exactly. He's only been with them for a couple of years and he's had some notable successes in that time. And personally I've always got on with him very well.'

'They haven't promoted him though, have they? It might have something to do with the unpleasantness he was involved in when he first joined them.'

'That was hardly his fault!'

'Mud sticks, though. I think you should hold fire with your proposal and wait until we know exactly who's going to be handling your work. They've just recruited a very bright young woman, a lawyer, who's been making a name for herself in the States. She might be just the person to move your career forward.'

It sounded as though the knives were out at Foreword, thought Kate. But Estelle would know what was happening at least as soon as anyone else, and she could rely on her canny judgement.

'Anyway, Kate,' said Estelle bracingly, 'I have much more exciting things on my mind at the moment. Did I tell you I was getting married?'

'Well, no, Estelle, I don't believe you did. I hope you'll be very happy.'

'I must send you an invitation,' and Kate heard the sound of biro scratching on paper – doubtless her name, or something resembling it, was being added to one of Estelle's famous lists.

'Do I know your fiancé?' asked Kate tentatively.

'I'm not sure.' It almost sounded as though Estelle herself

was searching for his name among the host of rich, strong and often unreliable men that she had dated over the past decade.

'Peter. It's Peter I'm marrying,' she announced, as though making up her mind at last. 'I believe you may have met him.'

'Is he the one who gave you a pot of geraniums?'

'That's him. Peter Hume,' she added triumphantly. Maybe Kate wasn't the only person whose details she forgot as soon as they were out of sight. 'Though he's been rather more magnanimous with his presents since then, I'm pleased to say.' Estelle purred the words as though remembering the feel of cashmere against her skin and the sound of cash registers.

I bet he came up with something extravagant, or he wouldn't have lasted, thought Kate. And by her calculations, he'd lasted for two years, even if there were occasional blips during that time.

'Now, Kate, let me give you the date, and you can put it in your diary. Have you got a man around at the moment? Would you like his name on the invitation as well?'

'Jon Kenrick. We've been living together since the beginning of the year.'

'Oh, yes. Tall, dark and serious.'

'That's the one. Do you have a wedding list somewhere, by the way?'

'Harvey Nicks.'

Of course. 'Shall I email you the notes I've made about the new book?'

'Forget about your book proposal for the moment. Get back to me in a couple of months' time, why don't you? I'm sure everything will have settled down by then.'

Really, thought Kate, when she had put the phone down, it could be time to look for a new agent. But then again, she and Estelle had been together for ten years or more, and even if she was only a faint blip on Estelle's radar, she didn't fancy starting again with someone new.

She looked again at the two proposals she'd come up with and wondered which book she should actually write; she would have welcomed Estelle's opinion. Infuriating as she was, Estelle was capable of handing out useful advice, though this time her mind was understandably elsewhere.

The phone rang again, postponing her decision.

'Kate? It's Neil Orson.'

'Neil, I was just thinking about you. It's ages since we've spoken.'

'I was wondering how things were going with you. Have you got any ideas about the next book you want to write for me?'

So much for Estelle's gloom! Neil sounded as solidly ensconced at Foreword as ever. Kate agreed to email her notes to him, and they arranged a time the following day when they could discuss her ideas. Once she'd put the phone down, she sent her file across to him. Then she thought she might as well print out a copy for herself. It always helped to see words on paper, rather than on the screen, she found.

Two pages in, the printer jammed. Kate switched it off, removed the back and yanked at the sheets caught around the roller. They tore. She pulled out a few rags of paper but then could do no more to free the rest of her notes.

That was the trouble with inkjet printers: they didn't last long. After a couple of years' heavy use they chewed up a perfectly good manuscript. But she didn't feel like dismantling the machine now and covering herself with more printing ink. She'd deal with it tomorrow.

After she'd cleaned all the black ink off her fingers, Kate leant back in her chair and swung round in idle semicircles while she contemplated the rest of her working day. There was no point in getting on with either of her proposed books until she had discussed them with Neil, so the day was her own. She could start with a long walk through Port Meadow and on into Wytham Woods.

At which point in her planning process the phone rang.

'Hi, Kate. It's George here. Your phone was engaged for so long that I thought it must be out of order.'

'I've been holding fruitful conversations with my agent and editor,' said Kate virtuously. 'About the book I'm going to write next.'

'Well in that case, you're definitely in need of a break,' said George.

'What sort of break were you thinking of?'

'Lunch? We agreed we might meet for lunch one day, didn't we? This seems like an excellent opportunity.'

'Shouldn't you be working?'

'They do allow me time in which to eat. And as it happens, today's lunch hour might just stretch to three, since some dreary committee meeting has been cancelled.' George sounded particularly happy about this.

'I was about to set off for a walk across Port Meadow.'

'Then why don't we meet at the White Hart?'

Kate was grateful he hadn't suggested the pub where they had eaten lunch on Sunday, and she agreed to meet him there.

'I'd better get going if I'm to be on time. It's several miles away.'

'Don't worry. I'll be waiting, even if you're late. And do you still like a glass of Sauvignon Blanc at the end of your exertions?'

Kate confirmed that yes, she still did, though a Viognier, a Torrontés or a Pinot Grigio would be equally welcome.

As soon as she had disconnected, the phone rang yet again and she pressed the green button, expecting George to say that he had changed his mind.

It was Roz. 'Just to let you know, Kate, that I'm off tomorrow.'

'Off?'

'Don't say you're losing your short-term memory already,' said her mother. 'Portugal, remember?'

'Of course. Sorry, my mind was elsewhere.'

'I'll be gone at least three weeks, Kate, perhaps a little longer. I'll send you an email to let you know when I'm coming back.'

'Fine. Would you like me to keep an eye on your place?'

'If you would. Since the Freemans tried to burn it down, I do occasionally worry about things.'

'No problem. And have you got an address in Portugal?'

'Not yet. But I'll be picking up my emails, so you can always get in touch that way.'

'You're being very mysterious.'

'Not at all. I just have very fluid plans. It will make a nice change from my normally highly structured life.'

'And work's going well, is it?' asked Kate, probing gently.

'Very well. Very profitably, in fact.'

'But you don't want me to keep an eye on any of your projects while you're away?'

'I don't think it's exactly in your area of expertise, is it, Kate?'

'Probably not,' said Kate, deflated.

'Well, I have to ring off now. I still have plenty to do before I leave.'

'Oh, yes. Me too,' said Kate, hoping that this would make her mother a little curious. But since there was no reaction from Roz, she added, 'Would you like me to drive you to the airport?'

'But you say you're busy. I wouldn't want to interrupt your work.'

'Of course I can find time for that!'

'As a matter of fact, there's no need. I've already booked a taxi.' And Roz said, 'Goodbye, Kate,' as calmly as ever, and disconnected.

21

For a long time afterwards, Kate looked back on her lunch with George at the White Hart with nostalgia as the last good thing to happen before the hammer blows began to fall.

It was a fine, warm autumn day and it was still possible to sit outside in the sun, enjoying a glass of wine in the company of an old friend, before the weather turned cold and stormy and they started to think of thick coats and log fires.

She had forgotten how amusing George could be. Or maybe it was just that she had forgotten how conventional she had found him when they were living together, whereas today there was the added excitement of sitting here chatting to another man while Jon remained in the dark about their meeting. She knew it was childish, but it still added something to the lunch.

'So, how did you enjoy the party?' he asked.

'I thought it was a great success. A really good send-off for young Sam. And I enjoyed meeting his colleagues from the lab.'

'Like dear little Kerri?'

'Don't you like her?'

'The trouble with Kerri is that there's so little to dislike, don't you find?'

'She's shy, that's all.'

'She has no personality.'

'Sam seems to think she has.'

'He'll forget her soon enough, now he's away from Oxford.'

'At least we both agree that's a good move.'

'Yes.'

'You haven't any real basis for disliking Kerri, have you?'

'You sound as though you have.'

'Certainly not. She stayed with me at the weekend and I'm growing to like her a lot.'

'There is a rumour.'

Kate's heart sank. 'Go on.'

'The word is that someone must have helped the bomber, and again that someone – presumably the same someone – passed on a list of home addresses.'

'And have they named Kerri?'

'The general consensus is that it's one of the young, junior members of staff, since they have less to lose, and that it's also someone who's sympathetic to the animal rights movement.'

'That could be Sam or Conor. Or Lucy, or Eric, or Greg, if it comes to that.'

'Quite right. But it could be Kerri, too, and I don't like to think that Sam might be involved with a criminal.'

'You can't have it both ways. Either she's a colourless young woman, lacking in personality, or else she's a clever, scheming terrorist. I wouldn't have thought she could be both.'

The waitress arrived at this moment to take their order, and they quickly decided what they were going to eat.

'You weren't overwhelmed by the number of ageing Dolbys at the party?' asked George, when the waitress had left.

Kate was glad they'd dropped the subject of Kerri. 'It was

good to see so much family support for Sam,' she said diplomatically.

George laughed. 'I know you too well, Kate. You found them a nightmare.'

'I thought you did sterling work keeping their plates filled and amusing them with your small talk.'

'I didn't do so badly, did I?'

'And you were marvellous with the children, too.'

'Now that part I enjoyed, even though all the old aunts ganged up on me and told me that it was time I produced little Dolbys of my own.'

'And why haven't you?'

George pulled a clown's face for her. 'How could you ask, when the one and only woman in the world—'

'Rubbish, George.'

'Perhaps. Perhaps I just haven't wanted children till now. Emma and Sam have been populating Oxford with intelligent and good-looking sprogs, so I thought my efforts would be superfluous.'

'But. I can definitely hear a "but" in there.'

'But now I believe I would like one or two of my own. Three, even.'

It seemed as though everyone she knew wanted to produce children. She glanced at George. He didn't want her to be the mother of his offspring, did he? He must know by now how hopeless she'd be at it. Deep into writing Chapter Four, she would leave the infants entirely to their own devices. Cats, now they were a different proposition altogether. As she thought about the suitability of cats as opposed to children, George's voice intruded on her thoughts.

'Kate, you don't have to frown like that. I only asked whether you'd like another glass of wine.'

'Oh, sorry, George. No thanks. But tell me, did the aunts have any suggestions about who you should choose to be mother to the little Dolbys?'

'You know perfectly well that they did.'

'I can imagine that they warned you against considering the frivolous novelist, however lovely she looked in her new green dress.'

'One of them mentioned your dress, another commented on your hair – I do like the colour today, by the way – and a third mentioned the calculating set of your face.'

'Then it's just as well there are none of them in this pub, sitting over there, sipping their gin and taking notes.'

'Their spies will be reporting back to them this afternoon, I'm sure.'

They were both smiling, but Kate knew there was more than a small grain of truth in what George was saying.

When they'd finished their meal it would be time to get back to Jericho. But as Kate walked across Port Meadow she found she was more cheerful than she had been for some weeks.

It was turning out to be one of those weeks when Kate and Jon spent little time together. It wasn't that they'd planned it that way, or that they were avoiding one another; it was simply that they were busy with their own affairs.

If Kate was honest with herself, it was true that they were avoiding several subjects on which recently they had been failing to agree: buying a house (and selling Kate's, naturally); having, or not having, children. Commitment, that was what it all came down to.

By Thursday she was glad that Jon was playing squash with a colleague and she was meeting Blake Parker at the Randolph. There was an atmosphere of mild disapproval in the house whenever Jon was at home that was wearing her down. It had peaked a couple of evenings ago when she had mentioned, casually, that she was replacing her printer and wondered whether to get a laser rather than an inkjet next time.

'That sounds expensive,' said Jon.

She wanted to say that it was her money and what she did with it was her business and no one else's. 'Inkjet cartridges cost a fortune,' she said reasonably. 'A mono laser printer would pay for itself in a few months.'

Jon drew his breath in through his teeth in the way that always set her nerves on edge. 'I suppose it's your decision,' he said, in a voice that told her that he thought it was very much his decision too.

At ten past six there weren't many people in the bar, and she saw Blake sitting at a table in the opposite corner. He lifted a hand in greeting as she went to join him.

'You know, for the past five minutes I've been wondering whether you were going to make it,' he said.

'But I'm barely ten minutes late.'

'You could have changed your mind.'

So Blake was more insecure than he appeared. 'You think I'd have left you sitting here, drinking by yourself all evening?'

'I thought there'd be a call to my mobile at about twenty past, telling me that something had happened to prevent you leaving the house.'

'I'd be more inventive than that. Given twenty minutes I could come up with a really credible story that would have you begging me not to come out on such a tragic evening.'

'Yes, I believe you could. Now, what would you like to drink?'

For the few minutes that he was standing at the bar, Kate

pondered whether he really was quite as lacking in self-confidence as he was making out, or whether it was his way of eliciting sympathy from a woman. She hadn't reached a conclusion when he returned with two glasses of white wine and a bowl of olives.

'You guessed I'm an addict,' said Kate, helping herself. The olives were small, pitted Greek ones dressed with herbs and oil.

'I was actually being quite selfish,' said Blake, taking a couple too.

He appeared to recollect something and took out his mobile, so that she expected him to make a call. But he switched it off and returned it to his pocket. Kate didn't follow suit: she thought it unlikely that Jon would ring her. Blake's partner, she remembered, had phoned him at Sam's party, so maybe she was in the habit of checking up on him all the time. He saw Kate noticing and said, 'I've had another tough day. I can't face any more aggro just now.'

'That's the problem with a mobile phone: people expect you to be available twenty-four seven.'

'Marianne does, certainly.'

'Your partner?'

'For the moment. I'm not sure how much longer I can stand it. If I can't account for every moment of my time, I'm in the shit when I get home.'

'And this evening?'

'I'm working. Hadn't you noticed?' And he grinned.

Maybe Marianne had every reason not to trust him.

'I can see what you're thinking,' he went on, 'and yes, I enjoy the company of a good-looking woman. But I'd be less likely to stray if Marianne didn't get so hysterical over every stray glance.'

'She's the highly strung type?' asked Kate, wondering

whether Marianne was actually unhinged. Supposing she'd been jealous of young Kerri: would she be unhinged enough to send her a letter bomb to warn her away from Blake?

'Highly strung. Oversensitive. You name it. Part of the trouble is that she works from home, which means she doesn't get out and meet enough people. She should socialise more. She broods on things.' He was silent for a few moments before adding, 'But you don't want to talk about Marianne, do you?' And if Kate wanted to hear more about how jealous she was, she could hardly tell him so.

'I had your young Kerri to stay at the weekend,' she said. 'She was under stress too.'

'I didn't realise the two of you were friends.'

'We weren't, but Sam asked me to keep an eye on her while he's away. And she's still getting threatening phone calls, so I told her to come over to my place.'

'That was kind of you,' he said drily. 'I wouldn't have thought you'd have much in common.'

'I've known Sam a long time. I didn't want him to cancel his trip to China because he was worried about what was happening to Kerri.'

'She won't be working in the lab much longer. I think she has about three weeks left of her time with us. Once she's away from Oxford, the activists should leave her alone.'

'Have you discovered how they managed to find out her home address?'

'No. And she's not the only one. Just about all the staff have been harassed at home.'

'I imagine you've checked out those who escaped the attacks?'

'Very discreetly, yes. And I'd be glad if you didn't pass that on – people are jumpy enough as it is.'

'Is this kind of thing happening a lot in the university?'

'Sporadically. But this time it's like our lab is being targeted for some reason.'

'Jealousy, do you think?'

For the first time, Blake smiled. 'Personal or professional?'

'I was thinking of the professional variety, but I suppose it could be personal.'

'Both seem unlikely. And why attack all of us if the grudge is against only one?'

'Maybe it's a question of coincidence. A list of addresses and phone numbers of your staff happened to fall into their hands, and so they used them. They could have been anybody's.'

'I can't think it was just an accident. And if the list included Sam and Kerri, then it must have been a recent one. Kerri's only been with us for the last five weeks and Sam just a couple of weeks earlier.'

'In that case—'

'In that case I'd better check who's had access to our personnel records, hadn't I?'

'Sounds like a good idea. And . . .'

'Yes. What is it?'

'I just wondered whether you'd heard the rumour that it was Kerri who was too friendly with the animal activists.'

'Yes, I had. I wasn't going to mention it, though. It could just as easily be Conor, or even Sam.'

'Or Greg. Or Lucy.'

'And I don't think it's any of them.'

'Who, then?'

'I don't know. But I don't want to believe it's someone I know and trust, someone who's been working for me.'

'But it seems the most likely.'

'I'd prefer it if you didn't pass this rumour on, OK? The

214

company that provides most of our funding has got hold of the same idea, and I don't want there to be a witch hunt. And I certainly don't want Kerri to be victimised.'

'Like I said, I promised Sam I'd look out for her, so you can count on me. Speaking of which, there's one thing that's bothering me.'

'Yes?'

'Don't you think things are going to escalate if you don't do anything about them pretty soon?'

'How do you mean?' Blake was sounding bored.

'I don't think these people and their nasty tricks are going to go away. I think they'll only increase in confidence until eventually something really serious happens.'

'I'm sure you're exaggerating.'

'Someone will get hurt, believe me.'

'You're overdramatising. This stuff's been going on for years. We've learned to live with it. And now let's change the subject, shall we?' He took another couple of olives as though marking the end of the conversation. 'I know hardly anything about you, Kate. Why don't you fill me in.'

Kate, too, speared another olive. 'There's not much to tell. Novelists lead dull lives, stuck in front of a computer screen trying to think of the next sentence.'

'So tell me about your, what – partner?'

'Jon? Well,' she said slowly, not wanting to talk about him to another man in his absence. 'We've been living together since January. We got tired of the travelling back and forth and he moved down from London so that we could be under the same roof.'

'So it's serious?'

There was the smallest pause before Kate replied. 'Yes, it is.'

'And successful?'

'Pretty well.' Kate was aware that she wasn't being as enthusiastic as she might be about her life with Jon.

'I see.'

'And what about you?'

'Marianne and me, you mean? We've been together for nearly three years.' He drank some of his beer as though giving himself time to consider his reply. 'The first two years were wonderful, but it's been falling apart for the past few months. You probably heard her on the phone?'

'Well . . .'

'Don't worry. Everyone knows. Everyone's heard her screaming down a phone at me at some time or other.' He spoke lightly but she could tell that he was affected by her behaviour.

'So why do you stay?'

'Cowardice, mostly. And habit. And then again, I'm still fond of her.'

'I see.'

'I don't mean that I'm in love with her, but after three years you can't just walk out on someone for no reason.'

'It sounds as though there might be several reasons to leave.'

'Can you imagine the size of the row if I told her I was going?'

'Scary, certainly, and probably involving a lot of loud shouting down telephones. And I suppose that you'd have to go through the gruesome business of separating out your possessions and arguing about CDs.'

'You sound as though you've been through it yourself.'

'Yes.' With George Dolby, as it happened, but she wasn't going to go into details like that with Blake. And to give George his due, he hadn't really argued about possessions. 'Though I still had my own place I could return to.'

'Actually, I have my own house, but it happens to be where Marianne's living.'

'And she hasn't a place of her own?'

'No. She walked out of a marriage to join me.'

'So she has quite an investment in your relationship. And you have a feeling of responsibility.'

'You think I should stay, don't you?'

'Maybe things would be easier if you made a decision one way or the other. She must know that you're in two minds about your future with her.'

'It might be simpler if things weren't so tricky at work. I just can't take on any more hassles at the moment.'

'It's more than the animal rights crowd, isn't it?'

'At Sam's party I was cornered by one of the technical people from the company who are funding our research.'

'What was he doing there?'

'He's a friend of Sam's dad, it seems. He took the opportunity – off the record, naturally – to tell me it was time we came up with some convincing results from our work.'

'And can you?'

'We need more time.'

'And, presumably, money.'

'Exactly. I'm sure that Jim was being pressured by his own boss about it. It comes down to the fact that if we can announce some spectacular breakthrough, then their company's share price will go up dramatically.'

'And if you can't, then it will creep downwards.'

'I imagine so. But that shouldn't be my concern! And I don't care about the dividend they pay to their shareholders, either. I can't allow their profits to influence our results.'

'It's a tough old world,' said Kate. She glanced at her watch.

'Would you like to eat before you go home?' Blake asked.

'I imagine that Marianne would take very badly to that idea.'

'Marianne has an evening class on Thursdays. And Jon?'

'Jon's playing squash and he won't be home for another hour and a half, but I still think I should be getting home.'

'Can we meet again? I promise to be in a better mood next time.'

'Perhaps.'

'Shall I give you a ring next Thursday?'

'Yes. But it's possible the answer will be no.'

When she left the Randolph, Kate pulled the collar of her jacket up against the chill of the evening. When the rain started to bucket down, driven into her face by the brisk wind, she wished she'd worn something more substantial. She put her head down and hurried along the glistening streets as the streetlamps lit up in the premature darkness. It wasn't far to her house, but it gave her a chance to think over what Blake had told her about the attack on the lab. He had brushed aside her suggestion that it might be due to personal jealousy, but if someone wanted revenge, what better way of getting at Blake Parker would there be than attacking his lab, and even getting it closed down for lack of funds? She knew from the intense way he spoke that the lab was the most important thing in his life and its closure would mean the destruction of his career.

Could he really have pissed someone off so throughly that they would do that to him? Yet if Blake was, unknown to his partner, meeting Kate for a drink, how many other women had he chatted up and invited out over the past year? She could hardly believe that she was the first. And from the sound of her voice over the phone, Marianne was deeply suspicious of Blake, and also pretty angry.

But she couldn't have sent a letter bomb to Kerri, surely? Kerri was a most unlikely *femme fatale*, and it was equally unlikely that Marianne knew how to construct such a weapon.

Now she was making assumptions that weren't necessarily justified. For all she knew, Marianne was a qualified explosives expert as well as a translator. (Though in that case it would have crossed Blake's mind that she was the one who had sent the lethal letter to Kerri.) She had seen Kerri with Sam at his party, and with Susie and Gary at Cleveland Road at the weekend, and she had thought her a rather immature young woman, and devoted to Sam. But who was to say what she was like when she was alone with, say, Blake, and no longer had the beady eyes of the whole Dolby clan upon her?

On the other hand, the letter bomb had been an amateurish affair that had caused little damage: probably there were websites where even a tyro could learn how to construct one.

And what about the other women she'd met at the party? Candra had looked quite put out when Blake had paid attention to Kate. And Lucy had made it clear that she was keen on him too. Maybe the man had been chatting up every reasonably attractive woman he came into contact with. Any one of them might want to take her revenge.

Yes, but like *that*?

It would be interesting to know who hadn't been on the receiving end of the attacks, but if the culprit was one of Blake's group, they'd have enough intelligence, surely, to make sure that they too suffered some form of persecution.

All this was not just idle speculation, she told herself as she turned the corner into Cleveland Road. If she and Blake were to continue to meet for a drink after work on Thursdays, then she needed to know what she was letting herself in for.

Well, if she arrived home and found graffiti all over her

front door, threatening messages on her answering machine and strange knobbly envelopes on her doormat, she'd know her suspicion of Marianne – or one of Blake's other women – was justified. She had to smile at how she had let her imagination run riot.

As soon as his key entered the lock, Blake heard rapid, angry footsteps approaching down the hall. For a moment he thought of turning and escaping. But where to? And anyway, as he had told Kate, this was his house and he had no intention of abandoning it to Marianne.

'Hello, darling!' he called as he took the first step inside.

'Don't fucking "darling" me!' shrieked Marianne. 'Where have you been?'

'Just for a beer with a couple of the lads,' he said.

She sniffed the air. 'That's not beer, it's wine,' she said.

'Rubbish,' he said. 'I told you. I stopped off at the Lamb for a pint with Greg and Jim.'

Marianne sniffed again. 'Then either Jim or Greg has taken to using a flowery aftershave. Kenzo, I'd say.'

'Must have been Greg. Anything for supper?' asked Blake optimistically.

'Don't talk to me about fucking supper,' said Marianne.

That would be a no then. But Blake kept the thought to himself.

'Your turn for the bedtime story tonight, isn't it?' asked Susie.

'Has he been waiting for me?'

'Of course. He loves it when it's your turn.'

'We both enjoy it,' said Gary fondly. 'Remind me what I'm supposed to be reading.'

Susie frowned in concentration. 'It's the one on his bedside table, with a picture of a fair-haired boy on the cover.'

Gary reckoned that Susie hadn't been paying attention when it was her turn to read last night, her mind wandering to the next day's assignment. But she'd have been as entertaining as ever, naturally: Freddie wouldn't have noticed anything. Just because Susie was a career woman didn't mean that her son ever missed out on quality time with her.

But Gary wouldn't let his mind wander for a moment. He loved the whole experience of tucking in the sweet-smelling, silky-haired wonder that was his son, hearing him laugh at the jokes, or shriek with delight when he was scared, his small hand clutching Gary's arm for reassurance. This was the best part of Gary's day. It reminded him why he was working such long hours for their future.

Freddie was already snuggled under his duvet when Gary found the book and opened it at the marker.

'From the beginning,' ordered Freddie sleepily. 'And do all the animal voices.'

Gary read, adding in the sound effects and the various voices that Freddie loved so much, but after only a couple of minutes, Freddie's eyes drooped closed, and he slept.

'That's the way,' said Gary softly. 'You keep it up, Freddie. You need to know your own mind and then demand whatever you want. Most people aren't aware of their dreams, but you won't be like that. You'll stride out and grab the moon out of the sky for yourself, won't you? You won't wait for someone to come and offer you a tiny piece of it. You'll want the whole shebang, just for yourself.'

Freddie's sleeping face twitched in a smile.

'You understand it all, don't you?' said his father.

22

Blake came knocking on Kate's door late the next morning.

'Kate! I have to come in. Let me in!'

Taken aback by his drawn face, she led the way down to the kitchen. As always, it seemed the right place to deal with emergencies, and by the look of him, Blake was in shock.

'Coffee? Tea?' she asked. 'Or brandy, maybe?'

'Coffee,' he said, sitting down at the kitchen table. 'Please,' he added as an afterthought.

'What's happened?' she asked as she put the kettle to boil and spooned coffee into the press.

'I can't believe it. I can't take it in.' He looked at her then, and made an effort at a boyish smile that came out all wrong. 'You're looking great this morning. So normal.'

Kate dismissed his automatic chat-up line. 'Milk? Sugar?' she asked briskly.

'Black. Two sugars.' He seemed unwilling to begin his story. She put chocolate biscuits out on a plate and pushed them towards him. He took one absentmindedly and sank his teeth into it as though biting off the head of a small defenceless animal.

Kate set mugs on the table, waited a scant thirty seconds for the coffee to brew, then poured it out.

'Now,' she said, pushing one of the mugs in front of him, 'tell me what this is all about.'

'Kerri's dead.'

They both sat in silence for a minute while Kate took in what he was saying. The words chimed in her head, over and over, but she wanted to tell him that he must be mistaken, that it wasn't possible. Kerri was a young woman, not yet twenty, how could she possibly be dead? She shook her head. 'No,' she said. 'No. I don't believe it.'

After a silence, Blake continued. 'I'm sorry. I shouldn't have blurted it out like that, but it was a shock to me too. To everyone. I somehow thought that if I told you, you'd be able to deny it, tell me that it wasn't so. Ridiculous, aren't I?'

'What happened?' she asked.

'It was a traffic accident,' he said eventually. 'A hit-and-run, close to where she was living. You know what foul weather it was last night?'

'Yes,' said Kate, remembering the driving rain and gusting wind as she walked home from the Randolph.

'Kerri and Conor and some of their friends had gone out for a burger and then to the pub – it's something they do every Thursday, apparently. They separated afterwards and Kerri walked home on her own. It wasn't far. Not more than about ten minutes' walk, and it's not as if she was drunk or anything. The girl had been drinking Coke.'

'Yes,' said Kate. 'That's what she drank when she was at my place. She's just a kid still, I thought.'

Blake continued as though she hadn't spoken. 'It happened only fifty yards or so from the house she shared with her mates.' He paused, unwilling to go on.

'Tell me about it.'

'No one knows exactly. But I'll tell you what the policeman told me: she must have been walking in the road. Or crossing

224

the road, perhaps. Who knows? She was off the pavement and she got hit by a car, and the car just drove away.'

'The driver didn't stop?'

'No. The bastard just drove straight on. He hit her. He must have known he'd hit someone. How can you not know something like that?'

'No. You're right. He must have known. And he must have been driving fast.'

'Yes, must have been. Fifty or sixty, maybe. I don't know how much they'll learn about it, what with the torrential rain and the traffic that passed that way before the police got to the scene.'

'Do you think they'll find him?'

'If he was callous enough to drive straight off, he's not likely to walk into a police station and give himself up, is he? And he'll have been through a car wash by now, removing any signs that the rain didn't rinse off. Or it could have been a kid in a stolen car. He'd just have driven it into a country lane, parked it in a field and set fire to it. No evidence left.'

'So he'll get away with it?'

'What do you think?' Blake sounded bitter. 'And no one saw anything. It's quiet round there at ten at night. It was pissing down with rain. Who would be out? There wasn't even a dog-walker abroad in that weather.'

'Who found her?'

'A neighbour. He arrived home, parked his car, got out and nearly fell over her on the pavement.'

'I thought you said—'

'She didn't die immediately. No. She lay there on the road, by herself, dying. But she managed to crawl, to drag herself, God knows how with her injuries, halfway on to the pavement.'

'That's horrible! Are they sure that's what happened?'

'They know where she was when she was hit. In spite of the rain there were still traces of blood in the road, but she was dead when she was found. That's what they say. The man who found her phoned for an ambulance, but there was nothing the paramedics could do by then.'

'Yes. I see.' His face was even paler than before. She said, 'Drink your coffee, Blake.'

'Where the fuck does it leave us?' he asked.

'Us?'

'The lab. The group. It's one more piece of bad publicity, isn't it? One more indication that we're dogged by bad luck. We're losers.'

Was this Blake's main concern? Kate looked at him and wondered just how well she knew this man.

'Thanks for coming round to tell me about her,' she said slowly. 'But to be honest, I still don't understand why. I met her for the first time at Sam's party. I know she was staying here last weekend, but I had other friends here too and, really, I didn't know her all that well. What do you want me to do?'

'I was hoping you could let Sam know about it.'

'Me?'

'You're in touch with him, aren't you? You told me he'd asked you to keep an eye on her.'

'You want me—'

'To tell him what's happened, yes. You said you'd known him for a long time. He was an old friend, you said.' There was a note of pleading in his voice: the last thing Blake wanted to do was to have to speak to Sam and tell him that his girlfriend was dead. Kate didn't want to do it either. Sam had relied on both of them to look after Kerri and they'd let him down. But how could they have prevented it? It was an accident, a horrible accident.

She started going over in her mind what she would say to him. How could she break those dreadful details?

'I only have his email address,' she said. 'He's in some remote rural village.' She thought for a moment. 'I wonder if his mother knows of some other way of reaching him.'

'Can I leave that to you?'

'I suppose so. Yes. Yes, of course. I'll get on to it straight away. But what about Kerri's parents?'

'That was something else I was going to ask you about. No one seems to know anything about them. She'd fallen out with them and hadn't spoken to them for over a year; that's all her housemates could tell the police. They knew about her work at the lab and they knew my name because Kerri had spoken about me. And I believe the police have contacted Conor too, but he didn't know much either. Poor lad, he's in a dreadful state. He kept repeating, "If only I'd walked her home."'

'What could he have done? He might have been injured, or even killed too.'

'He doesn't see it that way. He's going over to talk to her housemates later, and I suppose it might help him to come to terms with what's happened. But he feels so guilty and I think he wants her friends to keep telling him it wasn't his fault. I tried to send him home, but he said he'd rather work and keep his mind occupied. I'll make sure he'll takes the afternoon off, though.'

'Of course it wasn't his fault. I hope he'll be able to see that eventually.'

'Everyone here at the lab wishes they could do something, but it's difficult to know what to suggest. Inadequate as we are, we appear to be the only family Kerri had.'

'I'll get on to Emma. I can't just send Sam an email with news like this. Someone has to speak to him. Face to face, I mean. Not just some impersonal electronic message.'

'Can I leave that with you?'

'Yes, Blake. Yes, of course. What are you going to do now?'

'I have to get back to work. We can't stop now, of all times. We don't forget her, but we have to carry on the work to which she made a useful contribution.' It sounded almost as though Blake was rehearsing the words he would speak at Kerri's funeral. He stood up.

'Will you be all right?' she asked.

'Who knows? But I have to try.'

'And . . .' She didn't know how to go on. 'And what about the funeral?' she finished in a rush.

'I don't even know what her religion was. Or if she was a believer at all. She must have someone, Kate. No one can go through the world for nearly twenty years without impinging on some other human beings, surely?'

'In the twenty-first century it's all too possible.'

'Maybe her housemates will know more about her.'

'Yes, maybe. As a matter of fact, I have remembered one thing she said about her home. She remarked on how big this house was, how large the rooms.'

'So she came from a small cottage or a council flat. That doesn't get us much further.'

'In Didcot. That's what she told me. I had the impression it was a council estate or maybe a housing association flat.'

'I'll pass it on. The policeman who called at the lab left me his phone number in case I thought of anything useful to tell him.'

'What's Kerri's surname? I don't even know that.'

'Ashton. It might be possible to trace her family, as it's not a very common name.'

'That's if her family share the same surname.'

'We could start by looking for Ashtons in the phone book, I suppose.' Blake didn't sound convinced, and now he turned and moved towards the door.

'Just one more thing,' said Kate.

'Yes?'

'After the explosion at the lab and the letter bomb addressed to Kerri, not to mention the phone calls and so on, has no one thought that this "accident" might be connected to all that?'

'Not an accident at all, you're suggesting?'

'I'd have thought someone might at least have considered the possibility.'

'But does it fit in with the other incidents?'

'Yes. I think it does. Of course it's much worse than those others, but you could see it as a progression of violent acts.'

'I'm not sure the police have as much imagination as you, Kate.'

'You're laughing at me.'

'No. But I'm not taking you entirely seriously, either.'

They had reached the front door and now Kate held it open for Blake.

'And why should Conor feel so guilty?' she asked. 'Any of Kerri's friends might have walked home with her. He wasn't the only one to leave her at the end of the road. It seems out of proportion.'

'I don't think I like what you're suggesting,' said Blake, frowning. 'But thanks for listening, Kate. It's been good to talk the situation over with someone like you, even if I don't agree with your wilder conclusions.'

'Wild! I think I've been entirely logical,' interrupted Kate.

'I can see I'll have to go to her house and speak to her friends. Maybe there's something in her room that will tell us more about where we can find her family and who we can contact.'

'OK. You can leave it to me to speak to Sam.'

'And you'll keep me posted?'

'Yes, of course.'

When she'd watched him walk swiftly up the road towards Walton Street, Kate went back to the kitchen and poured herself the remains of the coffee. If Blake needed someone to talk to, why hadn't he chosen Marianne? Or Candra, or Greg or Eric, if it came to that? And why had he dismissed her speculation out of hand? It seemed like a simple progression to her: abusive phone calls, graffiti, letter bomb, explosion, murder. Was she really the only one to believe there was more to Kerri's death than met the eye?

And Blake hadn't understood that Conor might be feeling guilty about something other than leaving a friend to walk a few yards on her own. Supposing he'd been the one to pass on addresses and phone numbers to the animal activists? He might have thought they would do little more than make some unpleasant phone calls, or scrawl insulting messages on a wall or two. But if they had gone a lot further than that, using the information he had given them, wouldn't he feel terrible about it? Maybe he knew that one of his friends was a psychopath and that he'd passed on the information that had caused Kerri to die.

She tasted the coffee, pulled a face, and put it in the microwave to heat up. Bitter dregs, she thought. How appropriate.

Upstairs, in front of her computer, she considered the problem of breaking the news to Sam. If she got it wrong, he'd be back on the next plane, and she still felt that would be a bad idea: at this stage in his life, Sam needed to get away from his family, and she didn't see Emma and Sam Senior managing to cough up the return fare a second time. And there was nothing he could do here in Oxford. Nothing was going to bring Kerri back.

When she rang Emma, she found she had to compete with even more background noise than usual, which made her task no easier.

'I was wondering whether you knew—' she began, but Emma interrupted her.

'Get down, Jack! I told you not to do that!'

'I'm sure Jack's not really ill,' she said into the telephone. 'He's just jealous of all the attention that Geraldine and Lucas are getting. You'll have to go to your room if you can't behave!' And Kate assumed that this last remark was addressed to Jack rather than to her. 'Kate, is this call really important? I'm rather in the middle of things here.'

'Yes, it is, Emma.' Better get straight to the point rather than pussyfoot around it. 'Kerri's dead. Killed in a hit-and-run accident.'

'Oh, the poor girl!' Emma's attention was fully on her.

'Yes, it is terrible. And her boss, Blake Parker, has contacted me because he knows I'm a friend of Sam's. We have to let him know, Emma.'

'I suppose we do.' Emma sounded far from certain, and the background squeals were coming closer again. Kate spoke quickly before she lost Emma to the flood of children.

'I have his email address, but do you have a more direct way of getting hold of him? A phone number, for example?'

'You want to phone him?'

'I thought you might want to do it.'

'Oh, no. I have far too much on my hands at the moment, Kate. I'm sure it would be better coming from you.' Emma's voice was drifting away again. Kate wanted to yell, 'You're his mother!' but she knew that once they hit sixteen or so, Emma's children ceased to hold a central position in her universe. Tris, Jack and Flora were the children now, and Geraldine and Lucas, too.

'Do you have a number?' She was shouting to compete with the childish voices calling out to Emma.

'No. He told me he wouldn't be able to use his mobile. I just have the email address. You'll have to use that. And Kate, you will impress on him that he should stay in China, won't you? There's nothing he can do if he comes back to England, and really, I'm not sure where I'd fit him in, the house is so full.' A loud wail came from the background. 'All right, darling, I'll be with you right away.'

And at that point Kate realised she would get no more sense out of Emma that morning. She said goodbye, went upstairs to her computer and started to compose an email.

She had typed 'Hi Sam,' then deleted it as being too upbeat, and put 'Dear Sam' instead, when Emma rang back.

'It's possible that his friend Ben can get in touch with Sam sooner than you and I can,' she said. 'I didn't really listen to what Sam was saying, I'm afraid, but it was something about messaging – whatever that might mean.'

'Do you have a number for Ben?'

'Yes. Here it is. Ben Fryer. This is the number at his parents' place, so there should be someone there.' And she gave Kate an Oxford number.

But when Kate rang, she reached only an answering machine. She left a message asking Ben to call back. Some hours later, when she was thinking she should give up waiting for his call and send her email anyway, the phone finally rang.

'Kate Ivory? It's Ben Fryer. You left me a message.'

Kate explained why she had rung.

'Kerri? You mean she's dead?'

'I'm afraid so.'

'Sam will be gutted.'

'I know. That's why I wondered whether you had a more direct way of communicating. It seems so heartless just to send an email.'

'I'll log on and see if he's online too, so's we can chat, but it's pretty late over there, and he's way out in the sticks so he only checks his gmail every few days.'

'I hadn't even thought about the time difference.'

'They're seven hours ahead of us till the clocks go back. So it's nearly midnight where Sam is.'

'And what's gmail?'

There was a pause as Ben considered how to explain everyday technology to someone as old as Kate. 'Like email, only better if you're off travelling, since it's web-based. And you can form a group and chat to your mates.'

'But you'd both need to be online at the same time?'

'Yeah.'

'Didn't he take a mobile phone?'

'He said he wanted to immerse himself in the local culture and not anchor himself to his old life. To be honest, I think he was afraid his family might be on at him every day unless he cut himself off.'

'He's succeeded there, I should say. I'd better send him the email after all.'

'Thanks for letting me know about it, Kate. If I do get through to him, he and I can talk about her if that's what he wants.'

Kate opened her email program and returned to her message. She put a read receipt request on it so that she would know whether Sam had received it OK. Then she thought for a moment.

'Dear Sam,' she started. 'I'm afraid I have some very bad news . . .'

23

The next morning, Kate was still preoccupied with Kerri's death. She went out for a walk in the morning to clear her head, but she still didn't feel like eating much at lunchtime. By half past one she was sitting at her computer, opening the folder of ideas for her new book. It was time to push everything out of her mind. She needed to concentrate on developing her notes into something specific if she was going to convince Estelle and Neil that the book was going to be publishable. But however hard she tried to focus on her invented characters and their actions, she found herself once more running through the sequence of events preceding Kerri's death. And it was Kerri's real-life friends and colleagues, and their stories, that were preoccupying her mind as she stared at the screen.

Explosion, letter bomb, hit-and-run, she found herself typing. *Sam, Kerri, Conor.* Was there a more complex relationship than she'd originally thought between the three of them? When she'd met Conor at Sam's party, her impression had been that he was a joker, someone who'd wind the others up just for the hell of it. She'd thought, too, that he was keen on Kerri – not that Kerri noticed anyone else when Sam was around. And then Kerri had mentioned his odd behaviour on the day of the explosion at the lab, so it seemed to Kate that he was worth investigating.

Investigating? What did she think she was doing!

Phone calls, graffiti, hit-and-run, she typed, ignoring her own sensible advice to leave well alone. *Blake, Greg, Candra.* It was all very well toughing it out the way Blake had encouraged them to do, but if he'd taken more notice of the early warnings, perhaps Kerri would still be alive.

And what about rogue animal rights protesters, if it came to that? Where did Razer and his followers come in to it? Everyone assumed that they were behind the other attacks, so weren't they the logical suspects in Kerri's death? But why should they pick on someone junior like Kerri? If this was one of Kate's stories, someone else would have taken advantage of their activities, using them as a cover for Kerri's murder. Even if the police suspected it was more than a careless, drunken accident, they would assume that the extremists were responsible for her death.

Blake, Marianne. Underneath *Razer*, she added their names to her list. *A wandering eye,* she wrote next to Blake's name. And *a jealous woman* next to Marianne's. She would have pounced on this as a promising idea for a story, but the problem with real life was that you couldn't just make it up as you went along.

As she was considering jealousy as a motive, she pictured Kerri, quiet and slightly built, surrounded by a crowd of tall and bossy Dolbys, their red hair shining in the sun, their confident vowels and crisp consonants drowning out the young woman's words. Another promising idea for a story, Kate conceded, but would George or his brother, or even one of the formidable Dolby aunts, be capable of deliberately driving a car at someone?

Kate imagined the prim face of Sam's great-aunt, fiercely

set in concentration, urging on her Ford Prefect to a mighty twenty-five miles an hour.

Again, nice idea, she thought, and added the name to her list. Then she quickly turned back to the notes for Neil Orson that she was supposed to be working on. Fifteen minutes later she scowled at the screen: if she was going to write another paragraph as boring as that, she might as well break off now and go and do something useful.

Kate walked along the same route she had taken in the car when she had given Kerri a lift home. She found herself looking at the shops in the Cowley Road with a different eye, imagining Kerri coming out of Tesco with a couple of carrier bags, then crossing the road, just as she was doing, and eventually turning away from the crowded main road into a car-lined side street. Kerri would have noticed the turning leaves and the fading flowers, just as she did. She'd have spoken to the friendly cat basking on the wall and smiled at the toddler in his buggy as his mother pushed past on the narrow pavement.

When she reached the corner where Kerri had asked to be dropped off, Kate paused. This must have been it: the stretch of road where Kerri had started to cross, and the car – she imagined something bulky and menacing, with darkened windows. And what about the driver? Was he alone in the car, or was he now sharing his secret with a companion?

A red car puttered past, its door panel dented and mud-spattered, loud music escaping through the open window, four young people inside. Students, thought Kate. She couldn't imagine the cheerful-looking driver, seeing a pedestrian in the road, pushing his foot down on the accelerator. In her head she ran through the list she had made earlier: she couldn't imagine any of them doing it.

She crossed the road and walked a little further on, recognising the house where she had dropped Kerri off such a short time ago. The door was ajar and from the interior she heard the subdued buzz of conversation. She pushed the door open and walked in.

The conversation was coming from the room to her right, but straight ahead, at the end of the hall, lay the kitchen. This door, too, was open and a slim young woman with fair hair and wearing faded jeans was pouring water from a kettle into half a dozen mugs on the table.

'Can I give you a hand with those?' asked Kate.

'The coffees? Oh, yes. Cheers.'

'I'm Kate, by the way.' She had found a tray and was placing the mugs on it.

'Lynne,' said the coffee-maker. 'Would you like me to make you one too?'

'Please.'

'Pass over the clean mug on the shelf behind you.'

Kate did as she was told. 'We haven't met before, but Kerri mentioned you,' she said. The Sunday when she had returned to her own place, she had said that two of her housemates were Mel and Lynne.

'And you're the one she stayed with when the rest of us were away for the weekend.'

'Yes. Shall I take these coffees in?'

'Yeah. I wonder if I should find some food. Conor's looking hungry.'

'I'd have thought you had enough to do.'

'It's good to feel I'm useful,' said Lynne. 'It's better than sitting around feeling like shit.' She broke off, opening a cupboard door. 'Oh, great. I've found some crisps. Don't know who bought them, but I'm sure she'll understand.' She poured crisps into a couple of bowls and then led Kate into the room at the front of the house where Kerri's friends had congregated.

'This is Kate,' said Lynne, putting the crisps on a table and handing round mugs of coffee. 'Another of Kerri's friends,' she added.

Everyone in the room was young, sitting squashed up on the sofa or cross-legged on the floor, clumped together for protection, it seemed, and there was a subdued chorus of 'hi's as they looked at Kate.

'Have the police contacted Kerri's family yet?' she asked Lynne.

'They contacted them all right. And Kerri's sister and her mum were straight round here this morning. Not that she stayed long.' From the tightening of Lynne's expression, Kate inferred that Kerri's family hadn't been popular visitors.

'She just marched in and out again, taking all Kerri's stuff with her.' It was Conor speaking.

Noticing him for the first time, Kate looked across the room to where he sat, hunched up in the corner. His face was pale and puffy, as though he had been shedding tears for his friend's death.

'Not quite all her stuff,' said Lynne, trying hard to be fair.

'She never even offered us anything to remember her by,' said Conor, his voice thick.

'We'll remember her all right,' said another young woman, one of those on the sofa. 'Kerri's mother can't take that away, can she?'

'It was when she said that Kerri had brought it all on herself that I really disliked her,' said Lynne.

'What did she mean by that?' asked Conor.

'She wanted Kerri to spend her life stacking shelves at Asda, like she did. She shouted at her every time she picked up a book: "How much you going to earn with your A levels?"'

'And her sister was no better. She picked over Kerri's clothes, grumbling that they wouldn't fit her.'

'Fat cow,' said Conor.

'Maybe they were more upset than they were showing,' suggested Kate.

'Don't you believe it!'

'Kerri was right to walk out of a family like that,' put in one of the others.

'Her mum hardly said a word to any of us, Mel,' said Conor, still deep in misery. 'I tried to talk to her. I wanted to explain what happened that night, tell her it wasn't my fault. But she wouldn't listen.'

'Coffee, Conor?' Lynne's voice was falsely bright, as though she'd had too much of Conor's relentless self-pity for one day. Kate could see she was longing to suggest he take his empty mug back to the kitchen and then walk himself home.

'Hi, Conor,' said Kate. She wondered if she could find herself a place next to him. There were one or two things she wanted to ask him about. It wasn't rational, maybe, but she had the strong feeling that Kerri had been relying on her to find out what Conor had been up to – still was, for all she knew. Kerri had been right to point out that Kate enjoyed puzzles, and she'd understood that it had nothing to do with crosswords or sudoku.

Conor looked blank for a moment, then he said, 'Oh, yeah. Hi, Kate. Didn't expect to see you here.'

It was an unpromising start, but Kate made her way over to where he was sitting and settled herself down next to him.

'How's it going, Conor?' she asked, sounding as sympathetic as she knew how.

'It's bloody awful.'

'Kerri's mother doesn't sound as though she helped the situation.'

'I told her it wasn't my fault,' said Conor again, and Kate had the impression he'd been repeating the same phrase all day.

'Why should anyone think it was?' she asked, interested in how he'd reply.

'We were all out at the pub, like always on a Friday night. It's not far from the Cowley Road, is it? I mean, you wouldn't think anything would happen in a couple of hundred yards.'

'I suppose it was dark,' said Kate doubtfully.

'There are street lights,' said Conor defensively. 'And it was too early for the drunks to be leaving the pubs. "G'night, Kerri," I said to her. "Want me to walk you home?" But she wasn't having any. So you can't blame me for what happened, can you?'

'Who's doing the blaming, apart from Kerri's mother?'

'Everyone,' he said, and she heard again the unattractive note of self-pity in his voice. 'I expect they blame me for the letter bomb, too,' he added morosely.

'But it's not as though you had anything to do with the animal rights activists, did you, Conor?'

'Who's saying I did?'

'I heard you were arguing with some mates of yours on the march when the lab was attacked.'

'He's no mate of mine,' said Conor. 'Who told you he was?'

'Someone was having a go at you, they said.'

'"They" should keep their noses out of my business. And what's it to you, anyway?'

241

'I'm just interested. I like to think that Kerri was my friend too.'

'Pity you weren't here when her mother and sister were clearing out her stuff.'

'Have they really taken everything?'

'Most of it. I was hoping I could have the glass paperweight to remember her by, but they've certainly nicked that,' he said bitterly.

'I suppose they're allowed, since they're her nearest relations.'

'They could of asked us,' said Conor.

'Would you mind if I had a look at her room?' asked Kate. There wasn't much chance of finding anything of interest if her mother and sister had really stripped it bare, but it was worth a try. And anyway, she wanted to see what Kerri's room looked like. It would tell her something about the young woman who had been so close to Sam Dolby.

'I suppose so.' He looked at her sharply, as though he was about to argue with her, then changed his mind and called to Lynne. 'OK if we go up to Kerri's room for a bit?'

'Yeah, I suppose. Don't you go taking anything, though.'

'I wouldn't do that!' he protested. 'And there's nothing left to nick, is there?'

Lynne scowled.

So Conor wasn't popular with Kerri's housemates.

'Come on, then,' he said to Kate, scrambling to his feet and walking through the open door without checking that she was following him.

'Keep an eye on him,' muttered Mel as Kate left the room in his wake.

They were right: there wasn't much to see. The walls shone brilliant blue in the autumn sunlight, dotted with scabs of Blu

Tack where Kerri had presumably fixed her posters. The small bookcase held only a couple of textbooks, which Kerri's mother must have left behind as being of no interest to anyone else. The mattress on the bed was covered in an old grey blanket, the single pillow flattened and stained. There were no clothes on the hanging rail in the corner, just a washed-out T-shirt flung over the back of the chair by the desk. On the desk lay an A4 pad with only a couple of sheets remaining, a ballpoint pen, an old electricity bill and a flyer from a local shop. Kate stared around disconsolately. They'd taken away her duvet, as well as anything else in the room that might have spoken of the real Kerri.

She picked up the ballpoint and started to write idly on the pad, not even knowing what she wanted to say, but the pen was empty and no words appeared. All she could do now was to pick up the crumpled T-shirt, sniff at it – there was nothing but a faint smell of detergent – and fold it carefully before replacing it on the chair seat.

'I've seen enough,' she said to Conor, turning to leave.

'What?'

Conor was standing by the desk with his back to her, and now he turned, looking as shifty as ever, and led the way out of the room and down the stairs.

Kate called goodbye to the others and left the house, wondering what, if anything, she had learnt there, apart from the fact that Kerri was right to have moved away from her family.

24

Jon was working late that evening, so when the phone rang at around eight, Kate expected to hear his voice telling her he was just leaving the office and would be home in twenty minutes. Instead, a different male voice said, 'Kate, I said I'd keep you up to date with what's happening,' and for a moment she couldn't place who it was.

'It's Blake,' prompted the caller as she failed to respond.

'Oh, of course. Has anything new turned up?'

It had taken her a while after leaving Kerri's place to put everything she'd seen to one side and concentrate at last on the work she was supposed to be doing for Neil Orson. She wasn't sure she wanted to be dragged back into the real world, but as Blake spoke, she felt her interest re-awakening.

'The police have managed to contact Kerri's family,' he said.

'Yes, I gathered that when I went round to her place this morning. Not that her mother and sister were popular with her housemates.'

'I called in there myself this afternoon and they told me about it. Difficult to believe people can be that callous, isn't it?'

'Have you heard any more details? Have the police traced the car that hit her?'

'No, I'm afraid not. I don't think they have much to go on.'

'They have to find him soon. He mustn't get away with it.'

'Yes, but that's not why I phoned you. Kate, something cropped up this morning that I wanted to tell you about. I found it disturbing, but I don't want it generally known about for the present.'

'What?'

'You'll keep it to yourself, won't you?'

'Of course.'

'When Lynne took me upstairs to look at Kerri's room she said there was nothing there, that Kerri's mother and sister had stripped it bare. And it's true that the room was nearly empty – just an old T-shirt on the chair and a couple of things lying on the table she used as a desk: an old electricity bill and an A4 pad, and underneath them a thin manila folder. When I opened it I found a printout of the names and addresses of everyone in the group.'

'All the people who work in the lab?' Kate felt cold suddenly.

'Exactly that.' Blake sounded grim.

'So what are you saying?' she asked.

'Oh, come on! What do *you* think it means?'

'It makes it look as though she was behind all the stuff that's been happening.'

'You sound as if you're doubtful.'

'I am.'

'Don't you think she was capable of doing it?'

'Could she spray graffiti, make abusive phone calls, blow herself up, do you mean? No, of course not. It's a ridiculous idea. There must be some other simple explanation.' Even as she spoke, two possibilities came into her head.

'I'm not saying she did it all herself, but maybe she passed the personal details on to friends of hers who *were* activists.

We've always thought it was one of the younger members of staff, and Kerri was a likely candidate. Maybe she didn't realise what she was doing; maybe she thought she'd do something to help them. What do we know about her, except that she was bright enough to win a bursary to come and work with us for eight weeks this summer? Maybe she applied simply in order to pass information on to the bastards who are trying to undermine our work. She was an animal-lover and a vegetarian, after all.'

'Oh, yes. Very dangerous people, vegetarians.'

'You think I'm jumping to conclusions?'

'I can see it looks bad, but I can't believe that Kerri would knowingly do something that might harm another human being – or an animal, if it came to that.'

'That's the impression she gave everyone, but it needs explaining, don't you think?'

When Blake had rung off, Kate wondered why she hadn't told him that the folder hadn't been on the desk when she had been in the room earlier. The simplest explanation of the presence of that manila folder on Kerri's desk was that someone had placed it there. There were two people she knew about who were in a position to do such a thing, and one of them was Blake himself. She couldn't think why he would have done it, but just how well did she know Blake Parker anyway?

The other person seemed, on the face of it, more likely. It made her so angry to think that someone had deliberately tried to frame Kerri for the attacks on the lab that she decided to go straight out and confront the person concerned.

She made a quick phone call, consulted a street map, grabbed her jacket and set off.

* * *

Kate found herself in a narrow street of terraced houses, most of which appeared to be divided into bedsits. Their mean front plots grew only bicycles and dustbins, their paintwork was scabbed and peeling, weeds pushed up through their cement paths.

She stopped outside one of the most depressing houses and read the handwritten names on the row of bells at the side of the door. She rang, waited a few seconds then rang again, more insistently. From somewhere at the back of the house she heard a door open and steps approach. Finally the door opened.

'Hi, Conor,' she said. 'OK if I come in?'

'What you doing here?'

'I want to talk to you.'

'How d'you know where I live?'

'I asked.'

She took a step towards him and he looked uncertain what to do, then shrugged and led the way down an uncarpeted passage to a room that smelled of cheap burgers and chips. He indicated the only chair, seated himself on the bed and stared at Kate, then pulled a packet of cigarettes out of his pocket and lit one for himself without offering the packet to his guest.

'What's this all about?' he asked when the silence had stretched too far.

'Why did you leave a folder of names and addresses on the desk in Kerri's room?'

'I don't know what you're talking about!'

'Don't waste my time, Conor. We both know that you put something down on her desk when we were in her room, and now I hear that a folder of info about the lab staff has turned up, shoved under the pad and the electricity bill.'

'It wasn't me!'

'There was nothing there when I looked. And shortly afterwards, there was. How do you explain it?'

'I dunno. Must of been one of those girls she shared with. They *would* blame me. They've always had it in for me.'

'But they don't work at the lab. You do.'

The silence stretched out again.

'I didn't let them keep it. They just had a quick look and gave it back.'

'They?'

'A mate of mine.'

'The one who was on the march? The one you were arguing with?'

'Just a mate.'

'"A quick look" was enough, though, wasn't it? What did he do? Take a photocopy? Then make abusive phone calls and send the letter bomb to Kerri?'

'It wasn't serious. No one got hurt.'

'That was a matter of luck! I want to know just who this mate of yours is, Conor.'

'Why're you so nosy? Who gave you the right to walk in here and ask all these questions?'

'I'm a friend of Sam Dolby's, and a friend of Kerri's. If you're a friend of the person who killed her, or if you try to blame her for something *you* did, I'm going to walk in wherever I like and ask questions till I find out the truth.'

'You're fucking stupid, you are. Don't you know by now who you're dealing with? You'll be on their list as soon as I tell them you were round here.'

'Then I'll know who tipped them off, won't I? And the police will be in here, turning over your room, finding whatever you have hidden that you wouldn't want them knowing about. Apart from lists of names and addresses, what else have you got, Conor?'

'It wasn't my fault. They made me do it,' he said sulkily, giving up the pretence.

'I expect they did,' she said, trying not to show how she disliked his self-pity. 'What was it, blackmail?'

Conor stubbed out his cigarette in an old saucer full of fag-ends, then lit another, drawing in a lungful of smoke while he thought about his answer. 'They're not people you argue with,' he said.

'So who are they, Conor?'

'I can't tell you.'

'Then I'll have to go to the police with what I know.'

Conor laughed, sounding genuinely amused at what she'd said.

'I'll deny knowing anything about it,' he said. 'Don't you know there's far worse than the police?'

'What can they do?' Though she knew from experience this was a stupid question.

'I don't want a petrol bomb through my letter box, do I?'

She didn't think she'd get any more from Conor, so she stood up to leave. It might be worth trying one more question, though.

'Do you know who killed her, Conor?'

'Kerri? They're all saying it was an accident.'

'Is that what you believe?'

'Most likely some rat-arsed twelve-year-olds, nicked a car and then went out looking for a bit of fun.'

'They'd have ditched the car half a mile away and it would have been found by now.'

'Or they'd have set fire to it in a field so's there was no evidence to link them to the hit-and-run.' He stared at her defiantly, gripping his cigarette between thumb and index finger.

'What about your friends? Do you think they did it?' she asked.

'I don't know nothing about it,' said Conor. 'But I'd guess it ain't their style.' And this time he too stood up, indicating that the conversation was over. 'You'll have to go now.' And he added, 'I'm expecting some mates.'

She didn't believe him, but she left the room and walked to the front door, turning when she'd opened it to see him still standing there, drawing on his cigarette, watching her with his eyes half closed.

'Don't come back!' he shouted as she closed the door behind her.

As she made her way home, Kate thought about what he'd told her. He was right: there was little point in passing the information on to the police. Conor would simply deny that he had placed the folder on Kerri's desk, and would point out that any number of people had been in the house and could have put it there – one of them being Blake Parker, naturally.

But she was sure now that it was Conor who had passed on the names and addresses to the activists, and she would tell Blake so. She was inclined to believe Conor when he said he didn't think the same group had killed Kerri, but it sounded as though he was on the fringes, and didn't know everything they'd been up to.

She wondered about discussing what she'd learned with Jon when he got back from work, but she could already see the expression of disapproval on his face. He would point out that she was dealing with violent people and putting herself needlessly in danger. I survived, didn't I, she told herself.

25

Next morning, Kate was woken up by the ringing of the telephone rather than the bleating of her alarm. Ten to six, she noticed blearily as she reached the kitchen. This had better not be a wrong number, she thought as she answered.

'Kate Ivory.'

'It sounds like I woke you up.' Sam Dolby.

'That's OK, Sam, I was hoping you'd be able to ring.'

'I have a mobile.'

'Good.' Kate made a note to ask him for the number before he rang off.

'I can't believe it yet,' he said. 'Please tell me all you know about how it happened.'

Kate gave him the information that Blake had passed on to her, as succinctly as she could. Should she tell him how Kerri hadn't died immediately, but had dragged herself halfway on to the pavement before being found by a neighbour? But while she was giving him the facts as gently as she could, Sam broke in.

'You mean she was crawling away, bleeding and injured?'

'We think that's what must have happened.'

'And no one helped her? Christ! Didn't anyone see?'

'It was a dark, blustery evening and it was raining, so the streets were empty.'

'But the bastard who did it must have seen her.'

'It's likely he realised he'd hit someone, yes.'

'Are they looking for him? Have they any ideas about who it was?'

'No one saw what happened, I'm afraid. It could have been a kid in a stolen car, or someone with no tax and insurance who didn't want to be questioned by the police. There were no witnesses.' She didn't tell him about her conversation with Conor. It was Conor's fault that Kerri had received the letter bomb, but Sam still thought of him as a friend and this didn't seem the moment to disillusion him.

'Maybe. But they're questioning the animal activists, the ones who were picketing the lab, aren't they? And what about the man who sent Kerri the letter bomb; haven't they found him yet, either?'

'Not as far as I know.'

'You've got to go and talk to the police, Kate. Persuade them this wasn't an accident.'

'Now, I'm not sure—'

'After all that's been happening, this had to be deliberate, surely? If it had been an accident, the driver would have stopped. Were there signs that he'd braked, even?'

'I know that the rain had washed some of the evidence away.'

'You're saying that no one's doing anything! I'll have to come back to England and tell the police to treat it as murder. I should come back, shouldn't I, Kate?'

'I'm not sure you could tell the police any more than Blake and Kerri's friends have done. We're all doing our best, Sam.'

'She'd want me to come back, though.'

'But is it what *you* really want to do?'

'I guess there are arrangements to make, but I'm not much

on funerals,' he said doubtfully. 'Do you think I should come back and help organise something?'

'Kerri's mother and sister came to the house she shared with Mel and Lynne and picked up her stuff, so they do know what's happened. I expect they'll want to arrange things their way. They're her next-of-kin, after all.'

'I should be there.'

'Can you afford your return fare?'

'Not really. Well, not at all, actually.'

'You could plan a memorial service for all her friends, when you get back to England next year.'

'That might work,' he said. Then he added fiercely, 'But I don't want her murderer to get away with it.'

There was a pause while Kate thought about it. 'You want me to see the police and tell them what I know?' Not that she knew very much. And she certainly wasn't as convinced as Sam that Kerri had been murdered.

'Would you do that?'

Kate thought about Sam's birthday party and his flocks of Dolby relations all waiting to squawk their directives on how he should live his life. If she promised to help him, there was a good chance he wouldn't come back until his nine months were up.

'I'll do my best,' she said, inwardly sighing at the thought of putting aside her research.

'I'll have to go now. My credits must be nearly used up.'

'Before you go, give me the number.'

Sam did so, then he added awkwardly, 'You won't pass it on to Emma, will you?'

'Wouldn't dream of it.'

'I'll make sure I check my emails as often as I can too. Thanks for what you're doing.'

As Kate prepared to ring off, he added, 'You will make sure her death's investigated properly, somehow or other, won't you? You can contact Blake. I'm sure he'll feel the same way.'

'Sure, Sam. Leave it to me.'

Shit. She didn't think she could convince the police that Kerri's death was deliberate. And she didn't much want to contact Blake again at the moment either. She'd have to pass on what she knew about Conor, and she didn't want to do that. She didn't like the man, but there was something to be pitied there, too.

There was no point in going back to bed, so Kate made herself a pot of coffee and thought over the conversation. She'd ring Blake, she supposed, but first she'd get in touch with Sam's mother. She'd have to wait until after nine, when most of her children would be at school, before dialling Emma's number.

Eventually she heard the alarm go off upstairs and a few minutes later Jon appeared in the kitchen.

'What was the phone call at that unearthly hour?' he asked.

'Young Sam. He's read my message about Kerri and wanted more details. Poor lad wasn't thinking straight or he'd have remembered the time difference.'

Jon sliced bread and put it in the toaster, then poured himself a coffee.

'From the expression of deep and troubled thought on your face, he's also asked you to perform some tricky task for him.'

'He won't believe her death was an accident.'

'It will take time for it to sink in; it always does.'

'He wants me to persuade the police to treat it as murder.'

'And will you?'

'I'll give them a ring and find out what, if anything, is happening.'

Jon spread marmalade on his toast before replying. 'It's a natural reaction to the death of someone so young: he needs someone to blame. But please, Kate, don't get involved. If there are suspicious circumstances, the police will look into it, believe me.'

'I'm not arguing; I know you're right. But if I don't at least go through the motions, Sam's going to get on the next plane home.'

'So?'

'Then he'll never get away from that stuffy family of his.'

'I don't see Emma as stuffy.'

'Maybe, but you didn't see all the great-aunts and distant cousins at his party.'

Jon continued to go through his morning routine in his usual unhurried, efficient way, leaving Kate to stare gloomily at her cooling coffee and wonder whether to make herself another round of toast. She was interrupted a few minutes later by Jon, holding a pair of jeans.

'Kate, what have you done to my jeans?'

'Put them through the washing machine, by the look of it.'

'They've shrunk. You must have washed them too hot.'

She looked from the jeans to Jon and wondered what to say. She hadn't noticed it happening, but now she could see that he had put on weight. There was a belt of fat round his waist that hadn't been there six months ago. It wasn't enough to make a fuss about, but certainly enough to stop a man from breathing if he wore those jeans.

'Sorry about that,' she said. 'Maybe it's time to buy a new pair.'

When Jon had left the house, she showered and dressed and did her usual fifteen minutes' housework before retiring to her workroom. She opened a book, read a few pages, made some desultory notes, but it was impossible to concentrate on her work, she found.

Just after nine she dialled Emma's number.

'Is it urgent, Kate? I'm rather in the middle of things at the moment.'

You always are, Emma, thought Kate. 'I've just been talking on the phone to Sam,' she began.

'Sam? But he's still eating his breakfast. He hasn't been on the phone.'

'The other Sam.' Had Emma forgotten her son's existence so quickly?

'In China?'

'That's the one.'

'I didn't know he had a phone,' said Emma sharply.

'He hasn't. It belongs to a friend,' improvised Kate. 'Look, Emma, I emailed him about Kerri, and so he rang me back. He's very upset, naturally, and I thought it might be a good idea if you contacted him.'

'I don't see what I could do, Kate. And I'm really busy at the moment. Jenny's taken a turn for the worse and we're going to have to get some help for her. She needs a team of carers, really. You can't believe how difficult it is to get anyone in authority to act when it's a case of someone in their early forties.'

'I'm sure. But about Sam . . .'

'You've coped beautifully, haven't you, Kate? Sam's not flying home or anything silly like that, is he?'

'No, but I still think he needs someone . . .'

'I'll try to send him a message this evening. I ought to let him know I'm sorry about Kerri's death, in any case. She was quite a sweet little thing, really, though I don't suppose the relationship would have lasted much longer. They didn't have much in common. But you know she even offered to give me a hand with Lucas and Geraldine. She said she was very fond of children, and that has to be a recommendation, doesn't it?'

'She was certainly wonderful with young Freddie,' said Kate.

'Freddie?'

'The toddler belonging to friends of Jon's.' There, she was doing it again: Susie and Gary hadn't yet become 'friends of ours'.

'I'm sorry about Sam's girlfriend, of course I am, but the most useful thing I can do at the moment is look after Geraldine and Lucas, and try to keep them from fretting about their mother. Bob really can't cope on his own, poor love, let alone look after the children as well. He seems quite confused himself about what's happening to them all.'

From the distance sounded the wail of a child demanding attention, and Emma put in hurriedly, 'Kate, I really have to go now. I'm sure you'll do everything that's needed for Sam.'

And Kate was left feeling she hadn't perhaps put Sam's case as strongly as she might have done. But could anything break through to Emma at the moment? Probably not.

She decided to get the call to Blake out of the way before starting on her own work.

'Do you have a few minutes to talk?' she asked him.

'Not really. I have someone new joining the group this morning and I can't leave her to her own devices. Can we meet after work for a drink again?'

'Same place?'

'Yes, why not?'

'Can you make it a bit earlier this time?'

'Five thirty?'

'That would be good.'

'I'll have to get back to the lab afterwards. Since Greg and I spent so much of our time last week fine-tuning our begging letter, we now have a load of real work to catch up with.'

'I won't keep you long: I won't be able to stay more than half an hour myself, in any case.'

'I was nearly forgetting your friend.'

Kate ignored this. 'Goodbye, Blake.'

The next one to phone her was Jon.

'Kate, I forgot to mention I'd be late this evening.'

'You mean you didn't even put it in the diary?' she said, mock-disapproving.

'Uh, well, no, I don't think I did.'

'Will you be eating out, too?'

'It's a working evening, half a dozen of us, throwing around some new ideas, doing a brain storming session, seeing what comes out of it, and I expect we'll order in some sandwiches or something when we get hungry.'

Kate thought they were more likely to order in pizza, or Chinese. Plenty of spring rolls and fried rice, no doubt. No wonder Jon was beginning to put on weight.

'Don't wait up for me,' he said. 'We'll be finishing late, and I'll try not to disturb you when I come in.'

'Don't work too hard,' she said cheerfully. 'I'll see you much later, then.'

Again she found that she felt quite pleased to be spending time on her own – or rather, she remembered, in the company of another man, at least for half an hour or so. The only thing that seemed a little odd was the way Jon had given her so much unnecessary explanation as to why he was going to be late. Was this perhaps one of the oldest and most reliable of excuses: 'I'm working late at the office, dear.'

No, not Jon. He wouldn't do anything like that.

An email pinged into her inbox: it was the reply from Neil Orson about her proposals. She was pleased to see that he had chosen the one she privately preferred, though it meant doing more research than usual. She spent some time with Google, then started to make a list of books to order from the library, but an image of Jon with another woman imposed itself on the page. What did she look like? What was her name?

Stop it, Kate, she told herself. Was this how Blake and Marianne had started to fall apart?

'I want Daddy!'

'Yes, I know you want Daddy to read you a story, but you've got Mummy tonight.' Susie still sounded kind and reassuring, but this was the fifth time in one evening that Freddie had cried for his father's attention.

'Why?'

'Daddy's working, earning lots of lovely money, so Mummy's here at home with you.'

Even though she was working longer hours and taking on more responsibility again, Susie was doing more than her fair share at looking after Freddie. She wasn't going to miss out on this, the most rewarding stage in his life so far. Freddie would just have to get used to seeing less of Gary. He was a wonderful father, after all, when he was at home, and Freddie shouldn't get greedy. And the extra money they were both bringing in was a great help in furthering their long-term ambitions.

'Sometimes Mummy will be here, sometimes Daddy. That'll be fun, won't it?'

'No,' said Freddie.

'Of course it will,' said Susie firmly. 'Now then, you can choose which story you want me to read. And if you're very good, I'll read you two.'

'This one,' said Freddie promptly, pointing at a familiar book with a bright red cover.

Susie's heart sank. Not the talking tractor again! Maybe they should have made it plainer to Kate and Jon just how time- and energy-consuming being a parent was.

26

When she left the house to meet Blake at the Randolph, Kate's appearance attracted rather more attention from her neighbours than she was used to. It was true that she had taken more care than normal with her hair and make-up, her skirt was shorter than those she had been wearing in the past six months, her jacket cut a little closer, her earrings longer and more colourful.

Patrick, who lived next door, was coming out of his front door as she passed, and joined her by the gate. She hadn't seen either of her neighbours on that side recently and so she paused to exchange a few words.

'Love the lip gloss, sweetie. You should wear it more often,' he said, examining her appearance with the eye of a connoisseur. His own eye shadow was a silvery shade of plum this evening, and his long eyelashes were heavily mascaraed, which surprised Kate as he usually kept his more exotic outfits and make-up for the privacy of the home he shared with Brad, his partner.

'You look pretty good yourself,' she replied.

'Hope you're not planning to walk far in those heels, though,' added Patrick. 'I wouldn't attempt more than about ten metres in them myself.'

'You could be right,' said Kate, looking down at her elegantly shod feet. 'You think I should change them for something more sensible?'

'No, don't do that! Phone for a taxi.'

'Excellent advice,' and Kate took out her mobile and dialled accordingly. 'Ten minutes,' she told Patrick. 'I may as well go back indoors.'

'Come round to our place,' he said. 'Brad's out this evening, the slut, and I was just aiming to make him a teeny bit jealous by going out on the pull myself. You can bring me up to speed on the local gossip while we wait for your taxi.'

It was Brad rather than Patrick who was Kate's friend, and she didn't like to hear him slagged off like this, but she followed Patrick inside. They seated themselves by the bay window so that they could see when Kate's taxi arrived.

The room, as usual, was immaculate. 'You've redecorated, haven't you?' she asked.

'I like to change the decor every couple of years. It cheers me up.'

Now that she looked at him, Kate could see that Patrick's face was sad under the make-up.

'Are you and Brad going through a bad patch?'

'Have been for a couple of months now,' said Patrick dolefully.

'I'm sorry to hear that. You know I'm fond of both of you – and I thought you were such a happy couple.'

'We have been for the past five years, but nothing lasts for ever, does it? It's the longest relationship I've ever been in.'

'But what about Brad? He's devoted to you.'

'Do you really think so?' Patrick brightened a little. 'I thought he was beginning to wander away from hearth and home.'

'I'm sure he wouldn't really go off with someone else. And look at your house: you've both invested a heap of money and made it so beautiful. You can't give up on each other now.'

'Dear Kate. Making the best of it. Holding on to the positive view. But things don't happen just because you want them to, however hard you wish for it.' He switched back to the vivacious manner and brash voice of a moment ago: 'But what about *you*?'

'Nothing to report, Patrick.'

'Said a tad too quickly, sweetie. And where are you going, all tarted up like that and not a sign of the gorgeous Jon?'

'This ancient thing?' she said, indicating her jacket. 'I'm meeting an old friend for a drink. Jon's working late, so he won't miss me.'

'Working late? Meeting an old friend? Sounds like the beginning of the end to me,' said Patrick.

They stared at one another for a minute, taking in all the possibilities.

'Take no notice of me,' said Patrick. 'What do I know?' The garish make-up and mournful expression transformed his fine-boned face into a clown's.

Kate was about to ask him to tell her more, but at that moment a taxi drew up outside her house and she quickly thanked Patrick for his hospitality and left. Sitting in the taxi on the short journey to the Randolph she told herself that Patrick was upset over his relationship with Brad and was putting his insecurities on to Kate and Jon. She was shocked at his appearance, though, so far from the understated elegance he used to display when going out clubbing with his partner.

As for Kate and Jon, they might be going through a mildly sticky patch at the moment, but it was nothing to worry about, nothing serious enough to make them split up. Doubtless tomorrow, or next week, Brad and Patrick would be walking down the road hand-in-hand once more, and Kate and Jon would be ... what? House-hunting? Turning the spare room into a nursery?

In the Randolph bar, Blake was sitting at the same table as last time, staring gloomily into a nearly-empty beer glass, looking as though he had been there since Thursday.

'Well, you're looking very nice this evening,' he said when she joined him, which was a little lower-key than Patrick's comments earlier, but still welcome. 'What would you like to drink?'

Kate opted for her usual white wine.

When he had brought it back to the table, together with another pint for himself, Blake asked, 'So what's come up? What was it you wanted to talk about?'

He was looking tired, Kate saw, and making an effort to sound cheerful, so she tried to keep her story as brief as possible.

'I've spoken to Sam and told him everything I know about Kerri's death, but he's refusing to believe it was an accident. He's sure that the people who sent her the letter bomb are responsible. And he wants us, you and me, to go to the police and persuade them he's right. He believes that you'd agree with him and that you and I could act together to get the case treated as murder.'

'Poor Sam,' was all Blake said. 'If he's right, the police would be doing more, surely? If they've found nothing so far to indicate it was murder, they're not going to take our word for it, not unless we can produce some new evidence – and we can't.'

'No. But it's quite a coincidence, isn't it? First the members of the lab are targeted in their own homes by animal rights activists, next Kerri opens a letter bomb which could have seriously injured her. And then, a couple of weeks later, she's killed by a hit-and-run driver. If you were Sam, you'd believe all those events were connected, wouldn't you?'

266

'He loved her. He can't believe she's gone. He wants to believe that someone was responsible.'

'Well someone was! He's right about that.' Kate's voice was loud enough to cause heads to turn in their direction.

'So you want us to go to the police and tell them what we suspect? Had it occurred to you that if Kerri was killed deliberately, then there's a murderer out there? And who would that be, do you think? Can you think of any reason why anyone would want to kill her, and do you know any person who hated her so much that he climbed into his car and hunted her down, then put his foot on the accelerator and slammed into her, driving off afterwards without even verifying he'd killed her outright?'

'Put like that . . .'

'It's not like the graffiti, is it, where this unknown man would creep out in the early hours wearing dark clothes and spray obscenities on a wall while no one was looking? It isn't even like ringing up and telling people they're murderers, or putting a device in a Jiffy bag and sending it through the post. This was close and intimate.'

'Not quite,' Kate interrupted. 'He – and why are we assuming it was a man? – was safe inside his car. He didn't have to speak to Kerri, or touch her.'

'But a car is a very personal space. Yes, it insulates you from the outside world to a certain extent, it's womblike and it keeps you safe, but it would be like projecting a part of yourself at another human being in order to kill her.'

'I see that it would be impossible for you or me, or any normal human being, to run someone down deliberately. But this wouldn't be a normal human being, would it?'

'Suppose this person was threatening someone you loved, though. Then you'd do it.'

267

'I don't think so.'

'I could,' said Blake. 'It would be like punching someone who was attacking your partner. In this case the fist would be heavy, fast and made of metal.'

'I don't see it.'

'Years ago, before my father handed me the keys to his car and we set off for my very first driving lesson, he told me, "Always remember that a car is a lethal weapon, and drive accordingly." I expect most fathers say the same thing, and it's an idea that sticks. If a figure looms up in front of you on a dark, wet night, you automatically wrench the wheel round and jam your foot on the brake. But suppose you saw the face of someone you hated. What then?'

'Who would hate Kerri? And the driver would have to be a psychopath.'

'Or someone who loved obsessively. And someone who planned carefully in advance,' said Blake. 'He would have to take into account Kerri's way of life: her friends, her habits. He'd find out where she lives, of course, how she travels to work, what she does in the evenings – and how she always goes out with her friends after work on Thursdays. And he'd need to know when she is likely to be alone.'

'But I still don't believe that anyone would go to so much trouble to kill *Kerri*. I'm finding it difficult to imagine, and everything you say is bringing me round to your original point of view: it has to be an accident.'

'Difficult, but not impossible,' said Blake slowly. 'How would you feel if you found out that your Jon was having it off with another woman?'

'Furious. I'd throw all his belongings out on to the pavement and tell him to leave.'

'You wouldn't want to do something violent?'

'That's about as violent as I get.' She might have added that Jon was bigger and stronger than her, and very fit. 'And I can't see Kerri having it off with someone else. She loved Sam, and she needed him, too. She wouldn't risk the relationship even if she were tempted, I'm sure of it.'

'So there you are: we're stuck with the fact that Sam is mistaken.' Blake sat back, pleased to have finally won the argument.

'We can't leave it at that. You haven't mentioned the animal rights group that has been causing all the trouble. Don't you think that one of them might be our murderer?'

'It's a big step from chanting and heckling to murder.'

'I'm not sure I agree. I've seen them marching through town and I saw close-ups of their faces on television. They looked capable of any violence – as long as it was towards human beings. And full of the kind of hatred you were talking about.'

'You're not going to let it drop, are you?'

'I might if it weren't for Sam,' said Kate. 'And the fact that I promised I'd look out for Kerri. I didn't do a very good job, did I?'

'There's nothing you could have done. Look, I'll tell you what I'll do: tomorrow morning I'll ring the young constable who's dealing with the case and put it to him that there may be more to Kerri's death than appeared at first.'

'Do you need me to back you up?'

'I don't see what you could add at the moment.'

'True.'

'And then there's the fact that Kerri had a list of staff details,' said Blake. 'Do you want me to hand that piece of information over to the police, too? I know we were saying that she probably passed them on without realising what she was doing, but we don't know that, do we? She could have been in much deeper with that group. Or she could have fallen out with them. I doubt they'd be forgiving over that.'

Kate thought a moment. Then she said, 'I wasn't going to tell you this unless I really had to, but I can't let you go on thinking it was Kerri who passed on the addresses.'

'Who do you think it was, then?'

'Conor. I was pretty sure it was him, so I went to see him and he admitted it.'

'I should have known! He tried to frame Kerri, did he?'

'Yes. He was clumsy over it, though, and that's what made me sure it was him.'

'You're not telling me all you know, even now, are you?'

'There's no point. You can't prove it was Conor, and he's going to deny everything he told me.'

'I can fire him.'

'I think he's the one who's got himself deep into something he underestimated. He's weak, not evil.'

'I'm not sure I agree with you. I don't want him around in my lab after this.'

'Why don't you try giving him a second chance?'

'He's good with animals,' said Blake, weakening.

Kate didn't push the point: Blake would have to make up his own mind. So far she had hardly touched her wine, but now she drank some of it as though to take a step back from their unsatisfying conversation. Blake was already halfway through his beer.

'We could leave this depressing subject now, if you like, and pretend we're simply two people having a pleasant drink together one evening after work,' he said into the silence.

'So how was your day, dear?' asked Kate sweetly.

'Bloody awful. How about yours?'

'Interrupted by phone calls every twenty minutes.'

'Maybe we're not very good at this game,' said Blake, only half joking.

'It's just that we need practice.' Kate looked at her watch. 'I don't want to hurry you away, but didn't you say you had to get back to work?'

'Yes, but no. I got through all I could at the lab this afternoon. There's no point in returning now. But I imagine that you'll need to get home soon.'

'In fact, no. Jon's working late—' She was interrupted by laughter from Blake.

'Not that old chestnut!'

'It has to be true sometimes, doesn't it? And what about Marianne?' she put in quickly to divert him from her own situation. 'Isn't she expecting you home any minute? Or did you tell her . . .?' She raised her eyebrows and waited for a reply.

'It's just possible that I mentioned that I had a pile of work to finish this evening,' he conceded.

'There you are!'

'Not quite,' he pointed out. 'I'm not doing what I said: I'm not exactly working at the moment, am I? I'm sitting having a drink with a very attractive woman wearing provocative shoes.'

'I'm glad you noticed them,' said Kate. 'I wouldn't like to have suffered in vain.'

Blake leaned closer. 'I would guess that Jon rang you this afternoon to say he'd be working late, and you, instead of putting on the polite jacket and jeans that you would normally wear for a meeting like this, decided to tart yourself up, just to show him that you didn't care. Am I right?'

'There may be a grain of truth in what you say.'

'You bet there is.'

Kate drank the rest of her wine. If she was honest, the conversation that she and Blake were engaging in could only be described as flirting. And if she and Jon were thinking seriously about buying a house together and having babies, surely she shouldn't be flirting with another man, let alone enjoying herself?

'Now, the most important fact to have come out of that sparring match,' said Blake, 'is that neither of us has to hurry home to dinner. In fact, if we do we'll be sitting at a lonely kitchen table, eating cold beans on leathery toast. So what about treating ourselves to a decent meal instead?'

Kate was strongly tempted. She couldn't say that she had to get home to feed her cat. Since Susanna died, she didn't even have that excuse.

'It's a bit early, isn't it?' she said.

Blake glanced at his watch. 'True. But if I get us another drink, I'm sure the time will pass quite pleasantly until we stroll through town and choose ourselves a restaurant.'

'Good idea,' she said. 'Though, as you remarked earlier, these aren't ideal strolling shoes.'

As Blake squeezed a lemon wedge over a heap of glistening golden whitebait, he said casually, 'I'm not actually married, you know.'

Kate put down her soup spoon. 'But you're living with someone.'

'You think I'm being dishonest?'

'I think you're unhappy.' And she continued eating her soup.

Blake had joined her in drinking white wine with his meal, and now he gulped down half a glassful.

'I'm as much of a coward as the next man when it comes to ending a relationship,' he admitted.

Blake forked in whitebait, avoiding the look in their dead pinhead eyes.

They both concentrated on their food in silence.

'You say that someone new's joined the department?' Kate asked eventually, as the silence lasted a little too long.

'Another imposition,' said Blake gloomily.

'By whom?'

'"By whom?"' Blake mimicked. 'Trust an author to be so bloody pernickety.'

'So who's thrust their favoured man into your group?' she said, refusing to get riled.

'Our fucking sponsors. The big uglies. The ones who write the cheques. Who else?'

'Why should they do that?'

'To be fair, they have several projects on the go in Oxford: promising pieces of research that they've put money into – not as much money as they're feeding into our group, but important all the same. And they've sent this young woman down to look around and familiarise herself with the projects – and report back, naturally. But most of her time is spent in our lab, and everyone's feeling the strain. After the explosion, she's naturally interested to see whether we're falling behind – and how much money it's going to cost them to catch up. As a result, we're all on our best behaviour, looking earnest, coming in early, working late. You know how it goes.'

'I'm seeing a nasty little person with pebble lenses in her black-rimmed specs who wears a grey suit and does nothing but spy on your staff and tap away at her laptop all day.'

'Then you'd be very far from the truth. She's good to look at, and apparently competent at her job. But at coffee break—'

'You mean you all have coffee together?'

'It's a way of making sure we talk to each other at least once a day. Not such a good idea this morning, as it happens. Everyone was telling their animal rights horror story. The phone calls, the graffiti, the excrement on the hall carpet.'

'Just as well for her to know what she's letting herself in for if she's going to be spending time in the Oxford Science Area.'

'But you could see how they were laying it on thick, glorying in the drama. They can be very childish sometimes – I suppose it's a way of letting off steam. But this morning they were exaggerating and inventing scary stuff, and she was getting upset. Candra was objecting, of course, but she's so uptight that they wind her up whenever they can. And then that little shit Conor—'

At that moment Blake's mobile trilled and he fished in his pocket to find it.

'Marianne,' he grunted when he'd glanced at the screen.

Kate gave up all thoughts of a sticky toffee pudding and pulled out her own phone to call a taxi to take her home without crippling her feet.

Blake was still speaking into his phone, quietly but intensely, while she worked out how much she owed for her half of the meal, added enough for a moderate tip, and found the correct money in her purse.

Kate left the restaurant to wait on the pavement for her taxi. She didn't want to listen in on yet another of Blake and Marianne's spats.

In the back of the cab, she thought over what Blake had said during the evening, and didn't much like it.

What did she expect? She had wanted to convince him that Kerri had been murdered, but when he presented her with a realistic description of her death, she rejected the idea. She knew that underneath all her demands for Kerri's death to be taken seriously, she was really hoping that Blake's police constable would tell him that there was no chance the killing was deliberate, so they could forget about it.

Nevertheless, she was left with niggling doubts. And unlike Blake, she couldn't dismiss the animal rights people. If it came to that, she couldn't dismiss Blake himself, though why he would want to kill anyone, let alone Kerri, she couldn't imagine.

27

Candra Gupta was as disciplined over how she spent her evenings as she was in every other aspect of her life.

She prepared a light but nourishing meal, and drank no more than two small glasses of wine with it, 'for her health', as she told herself. She cleared up afterwards so that it looked as though the kitchen had never been used.

She checked the *Radio Times* to see if there was anything worth watching later on. She washed her underwear by hand in the basin and hung the garments up to dry on the shower rail in the bathroom.

There was no dusting or hoovering to do, since she dealt with these chores first thing in the morning, before leaving for work. She made a conscious effort to relax by making herself a pot of organic white tea, and then she stitched at her embroidery while listening to a concert on Radio 3.

At ten she switched on the television to watch the news. At ten forty she showered, cleaned her teeth and changed into her pyjamas to watch ten minutes of *Newsnight* before going to bed.

She sat up reading a biography of Charlotte Brontë for twenty minutes before checking the alarm was set for six fifteen, switching off her bedside light and settling down with her eyes closed. Within seven minutes she was asleep.

Two hours later, most unusually, she was awake. She

scrabbled for the light switch and looked at the clock – ten past one. Something had woken her. Something was outside her window, making a racket. A cat, she concluded, and closed her eyes. Cats had been getting into the dustbins for some time now, knocking them over, strewing their contents all over the grass, making a dreadful mess, and a smell, too. She had even been grumbling about it at work, but no one took her seriously. If anything, they laughed at her, she remembered, hurt.

The English were a filthy race, she thought viciously, then pulled herself up. She too was English, after all. Or British Asian, which was a different and in many ways superior thing to be.

By now she was fully awake. It was impossible to sleep. The cat was scrabbling around by the dustbins, sounding as though it had tipped at least one of them over, and was now joined by its friends, or rather by other cats competing to share its prize.

Candra waited for a moment, hoping that someone else would hear the noise and do something about it, but it was no good. People had no sense of social duty any more, and in any case, hers was the nearest flat, since the couple on the floor below were away for the week. She was probably the only one disturbed by the noise. If she was going to get any more sleep that night, she would have to do something about it herself.

She found her slippers (under the chair where she left them every night), her dressing gown (hanging on the door), and a small torch (next to the fuse box in the hall). She drew back one of the bedroom curtains and peered out to see if there was anything visible, but it was a dark night and the light from her window didn't reach far. As though mocking her, one of the cats yowled out of the darkness.

Candra dropped the curtain and went downstairs. Outside,

a brisk wind was blowing a tin can around, making the clattering sound she had heard earlier, and she switched on her torch to see where it was.

Behind her, the timer in the stairwell switched off the hall light. Candra pointed her torch beam towards the dustbins. She could see no cats, but she moved forward to where a tin can glinted on the ground. As she bent over to grasp it, she barely sensed the figure moving out of the shadows behind her, until it spoke.

'We need to talk. There's stuff you need to understand, OK?'

'Who are you?' Candra's voice quavered, and she made an effort to control it.

'That doesn't matter. But you've got to change your ideas, change what you're planning to do, or . . .'

'Or what?' Candra's courage was returning and her voice was firmer.

'It's all comes down to point of view. If you come round to our point of view, nothing unpleasant will happen.'

28

Next morning, as Jon was leaving for work, the post arrived, earlier than usual. He returned to the kitchen, handing Kate a postcard.

'It's from Roz,' he said, glancing at the back.

On one side there was a coloured picture of Porto's picturesque old quarter. On the other, a message that read: 'Having a lovely time. Weather warm, skies blue, food excellent. Love, Roz.'

No news. No hotel address, Kate noted. No contact number. Still, that was Roz for you. Every now and then she liked to go off on her own, reappearing eventually, all too often with a new and unsuitable man in tow.

'Don't worry about her. She knows how to look after herself well enough after all these years,' said Jon, conveniently forgetting the time recently when Roz had been taken in by con artists and nearly lost her life. Then, when there was no response from Kate, 'Well, I'll be off then. Oh, and there's another letter here, addressed to both of us. Could you deal with it?'

Kate said vaguely, 'Oh, right. See you later,' while she continued to stare at the postcard as though she could force it to yield up more information. The trouble was that it was bringing back memories of the times when she was still in her teens and Roz had disappeared, staying away for years. All she'd had then had been an occasional postcard, always from a different place, with the briefest of uninformative messages written on the back.

The sound of the front door closing reminded her that it was time to stop living in the past. With Jon out of the house she must start work herself if she was to get her research done within the time she had set.

She did register, briefly, that she and Jon were less communicative than ever these days. She hadn't told him about meeting Blake at the Randolph, and he hadn't told her anything about his evening, either. Was her relationship with Jon as rocky as Blake and Patrick were hinting? Or was it just that they no longer needed to share every small detail of their lives?

Before going upstairs she opened another item of post and found herself staring at an old-fashioned invitation, engraved in black copperplate on thick white card. Mr and Mrs Matthew Livingstone were inviting Kate Ivory and Jon Kenrick to attend the marriage of their daughter Estelle to Peter Hume, and to join them at the reception afterwards. Estelle had parents, Kate noted with awe. Would her father, Matthew Livingstone, resemble Victor Frankenstein? Would Estelle's mother be even more formidable than her daughter?

The wedding was to take place in six weeks' time at a church in a Buckinghamshire village, and afterwards there would be a reception at a country hotel with a proper sit-down lunch. Definitely posh. And Estelle would doubtless be marching down the aisle in boned, strapless white satin with a floating veil and an assertive bouquet. Did Peter Hume realise what he was letting himself in for?

Well, the first task on her list for the morning would be to write an acceptance. There was no way she was going to miss this, the performance of the year. And Jon would be present too, even if she had to force him to cancel a date with a boat.

And she'd need to buy herself a hat.

It was getting to be a regular occurrence that Kate's morning was interrupted by phone calls and unexpected visitors, and this one was no exception. First there was a phone call from Neil Orson, discussing her proposal. Then Emma phoned, belatedly, to ask if Sam had left any message for her and to ask Kate to tell her son that she hoped he was looking after himself properly. Kate promised to pass the message on, though thinking privately that she'd edit his mother's words before doing so, and told her that Sam sent his love, which she was sure he would have done if he'd remembered.

'I'm sorry I'm not being more supportive,' Emma said, in a rare moment of self-criticism. 'Jenny's illness is so aggressive, none of the doctors are committing themselves to a precise diagnosis, and any practical help for her is so painfully slow in materialising that I'm having to run her household as well as my own. And as for Bob . . . Well, I have this feeling that he may crack under the strain and just walk away from his family. Apart from hurting Jenny, he'd never forgive himself later for abandoning her when she has so little time left. You see why I can't spare much energy for Sam at the moment, don't you, Kate?'

'I don't see that there's much that any of us could do for him really. You've got quite enough on your plate, Emma, so you concentrate on Jenny and the children.'

'Thanks, Kate.' Emma sounded relieved, though normally she had little faith in her friend's practical abilities. 'And I should be taking more notice of Abigail, I know that too. But

I just haven't got the strength to spare to argue with her. She's taller than me now, and can be very dominating.'

'I noticed she'd grown.' And not only in height, thought Kate. 'I can't help you there, though, Emma. You'll just have to believe that she's sensible enough to avoid doing anything stupid.'

Fat chance, she thought. Abigail and Eric are probably at it like knives every evening, then smoking a post-coital spliff, sprawling across his rumpled duvet. But that thought wouldn't make Emma feel any happier in her current situation, so she kept it to herself.

She managed to get some work done, and was thinking about going out for a walk after lunch when Blake rang.

'Have you heard the news?' he began abruptly.

'What news?'

'It's happened again,' he said. 'Kate, it looks like Sam got it right after all.'

'What? I don't understand what you're talking about.'

'Can we meet?'

'Now? I was just going out for a walk.'

'You can walk any time. This is urgent.'

Apparently she had no choice. 'You'd better come round to my place then.' And she gave him the address.

'See you in five.'

Kate looked at the clock: a quarter to two. Blake sounded terrible, so maybe it was an occasion for some medicinal booze. She found brandy and whisky and a couple of glasses, then took a half-full bottle of Pinot Gris out of the fridge. You couldn't leave a man to drink on his own, after all.

Blake, as he had promised, was there 'in five'.

'Better put the bike round the back,' she said, opening the

side gate to show him the way. They entered the house through the french windows into the sitting room.

'Nice place,' he said admiringly.

'I like it,' she said, wondering when he was going to get to the point. 'Shall we sit in here rather than the kitchen?'

'Sure.'

'Brandy or whisky?' She could see now that he looked awful: the lines on his face deeper, his anxiety exaggerated, his skin with a greyish tinge.

'Whisky, dash of water,' he replied, and followed her out to the kitchen, watching as she poured his then splashed white wine into a small glass for herself. 'You might find you need something stronger when you've heard what I have to say.'

'Before we start, would you like me to get you something to eat?'

'Couldn't face it.'

'OK. Let me know if you'd like a sandwich later.'

They sat with their drinks on Kate's deep, comfortable sofas, arranged facing each other to make for easy conversation.

Blake scrabbled in his jacket pocket, taking out a packet of cigarettes and a lighter. 'Do you mind?' he asked.

'I'll find you an ashtray,' she replied, not having the heart to tell him she hated the smell of cigarette smoke.

'I've given up really,' he said. 'At least I thought I had.'

Returning, Kate handed him a saucer that she had once used for cat food.

'Thanks,' he said, lighting up.

'Now, tell me what's happened,' she said when he'd swallowed half his generous measure of Jon's favourite single malt and drawn deeply on his cigarette.

'It's Candra Gupta,' he said baldly. 'She's dead.' He looked around him at the normality of Kate's room. 'You know, just for a couple of minutes there I managed to forget about it.'

'How did it happen?'

'There was a lot of blood, but I think she was shot.'

'You're the one who found her?'

'Yes.'

'Shouldn't you be giving a statement, or helping the police with their enquiries or whatever it is one's supposed to do at times like these?'

'I'm not a suspect! At least, I hope I'm not. I've given my statement, I've answered all their questions. And I'd say that Candra must have been dead for several hours, by the look of . . .' He stopped, not wanting to go into it. 'For the moment I'm free to spend time drinking whisky with a friend and filling my lungs with smoke. I'm sure they'll want to ask more when they've found out exactly how she died.'

'Are you sure it wasn't an accident?' asked Kate.

'Pretty sure.'

'And could she have done it herself, do you think?'

'Again, I doubt it.'

'It's just that the alternative is so horrible to contemplate.'

'I suppose the police will have the answers to those questions in the next day or so.'

'They know where you are?'

'No. I didn't bother to tell anyone. I just wanted to get away from the lab. If they really want me they can ring my mobile.' He pulled it out of his pocket and looked at it. 'Though I appear to have switched it off. Luckily.' He leant back against a cushion and closed his eyes for a moment.

'Shouldn't you be offering support to your staff?' suggested Kate.

'I've done what I can, but just for the moment I need to talk about what's gone down to the one person who knows the story so far and the people involved, but who can't possibly have had anything to do with it. Do you know what it's like to wonder about everyone you know. "Are you a murderer?" That's what I'm asking myself all the time.'

'Are you saying that you suspect someone in your group?'

'I'm starting to think that only someone in our group would have the necessary knowledge.' He stubbed out his cigarette and lit another one immediately, without even noticing what he was doing.

'Knowledge of what?'

'Candra. Where she lived, what she did, how it affected the group. You know she was our statistician?'

'You mentioned it when we first met at Sam's party, but I'm not sure I understand exactly what she did.'

'To put it at its simplest, she was the one who interpreted the results we were getting from our experiments. As you probably gathered, Candra was a scrupulously, even irritatingly, honest person. And she was particular over details. There was no way she would massage the results to give a sunnier view of what we were achieving.'

'I'd always assumed that was the way all scientists worked, all the time.'

Blake laughed humourlessly. 'Maybe. In a more innocent time. These days you'd better come up with what your pay-masters want or you'll find yourself out on the street, out of a job. And unemployable, of course.'

'I can see that Candra with her old-fashioned attitudes might be unpopular in some quarters. But surely not within the group? Not with the head of your department?'

'Things are changing. Of course, the pharma has always

had its own man – or woman – to look at what we were doing.'

'Pharma?' queried Kate.

'Pharmaceutical company. There have been arguments about how results might be presented. It's a bit like having the accountants in, I suppose, and it used to be a man called Joe Greenham taking a good look at our results. He knew who paid his salary, of course, and what he was supposed to find, but he was a straightforward enough man and we could trust him, at least up to a point.'

'And you're saying that honesty is no longer popular.'

'What's the point in being scrupulously honest if it brings your work, however important, to a halt – and for good? Once a group, with all its specialist skills and habit of working together, is broken up, there's no hope of getting the scattered members back together. They move on. Our work *is* important, I really believe that. And given a little time, we'll make major contributions in our field.'

'Another whisky?'

'Please.'

She had asked because he looked as though he needed it. Presumably he wasn't often brought face-to-face with the realities of his situation at the lab, on top of finding Candra dead like that. And Kate imagined he hadn't entered a career in science in order to compromise his principles so blatantly. There seemed to be no longer a clear right and wrong, just shades of grey through which someone like Blake had to find his path.

He was leaning back with his eyes closed once again while she poured him another drink, adding just the splash of water he had asked for. Her own glass of wine was still full.

'I know this sounds crass, but her death is really inconvenient at the moment,' he said wearily. 'I needed her to work on the results so that I can put a report in to LDPharma, and now it's going to be at least three months before we'll get a replacement for her. Three months! We could be virtually closed down by then, firing staff, digging around, looking for new funding.'

'Are all your colleagues at the pharma as mercenary as that? There must be some of them who think the way you do.'

'There are a couple of people I could contact, I suppose,' said Blake doubtfully. 'I could try to get them on my side. I'll make a phone call, see if I can drum up support.

He stared into his whisky as though the answers were in the golden liquid.

'Where did you find her?' asked Kate.

Once more he fished out his cigarettes and lit a fresh one, though there was still a long stub smouldering in the saucer. 'She and I had a meeting scheduled for nine o'clock to discuss the latest batch of results. She's usually in by eight, and I get to my office soon after, so I was surprised when she didn't appear at the time we'd agreed. As you can imagine, she's never late.' He breathed out a long plume of smoke. 'I went looking for her, but no one had seen her that morning. And she hadn't rung in sick. At that point I started to feel uneasy. Of course, there could have been half a dozen explanations for her absence, but none that fitted in with her character. Candra was simply incapable of letting people down. If there was a family emergency, say, she would have phoned in to tell me about it.'

'Yes.' Kate remembered the woman at Sam's party. She remembered, too, how jealously Candra had watched Blake's every movement. Even if she'd been the most careless person in the group, she wouldn't have passed up the chance of a meeting alone with him, not unless something serious had happened to prevent her.

'She lives in Headington, so I climbed on my bike and cycled up there. God, I wish I hadn't!' He gulped down most of the second glass of whisky and Kate wondered whether she should have watered it down while he wasn't looking. If the police wanted to talk to him again, they wouldn't be impressed by his condition.

'Shall I make us some coffee?' she asked. Even though she wanted to hear his story, part of her shrank from learning the details.

'You think I should sober up?' He gave her a smile that was more of a grimace. 'I don't think so. I'm getting nicely insulated from reality thanks to your friend's whisky. And by the way, I see I've taken quite a sizeable amount out of it. I'll drop off a replacement bottle before he's due back home.'

Kate made herself a coffee and then rejoined Blake by the window. He carried on with his story as though she hadn't left.

'To begin with I rang the outside bell at her block of flats. Normally she'd use the entryphone to ask who was there and then buzz me in, but this time there was no reply. I pressed the button that lets in tradesmen and went into the entrance hall. But when I walked upstairs and rang her doorbell, there was still no reply. I peered through the letter box but could see nothing. There was that feeling, you know, something about the quality of the silence, that told me that the flat was empty, and so I went back downstairs and took a look outside.

'At the back of the flats there's a utility area: rotary clothes driers, dustbins, all nicely landscaped and out of sight of anyone coming to the front. And it was there that I found her, lying on a patch of grass by the dustbins.' He shuddered.

Yes, thought Kate, it was an especially inappropriate place

for someone as neat and particular as Candra to end her life.

'She was in her pyjamas and dressing gown. One of her slippers had fallen off.'

Kate thought of Candra, so well groomed, so carefully dressed.

'There was a lot of blood and ... other matter,' added Blake. 'I wouldn't have known straight away that it was Candra unless I'd been looking for her.'

'Have you any idea when it happened?'

'It must have been some time before I found her. The policeman who took my statement asked about my movements last night as well as this morning. Maybe that's routine,' he added, and then fell silent.

Kate waited. He was finding it hard to go over it again. He stubbed out his cigarette before he continued.

'I didn't even like her that much,' he said. 'She could be a real pain sometimes, and the others used to wind her up just to watch her uptight reaction. I knew she hated to be called "Candy", but I did it just to tease. We could have been kinder, we really could.'

'It's normal to feel like that after a death,' said Kate.

'Sometimes we're right to feel that way.'

'Do you believe Candra's death was down to the activists – and Kerri's, too?'

'It would be too much of a coincidence, don't you think, if someone else had killed her? First there was the harassment, then Kerri, and now Candra.'

'It all seems a little too convenient to me,' said Kate slowly.

'But the obvious answer is so often right, isn't it? Most criminals aren't all that bright, or cunning, in spite of all the fiction that's written around them.'

'Maybe.'

'And if it wasn't the animal rights thugs, then who was it?'

'I believe that if we knew *why* she was killed we'd be closer to knowing *who* killed her. And Kerri, too. Don't forget Kerri, will you?'

'I'd have thought it was obvious: Candra was killed because of her job, because of us, simply because she worked at the lab. Anyone who works here, or who is associated in any way with us, is fair game as far as that shower is concerned.'

'And Kerri?'

'The same. She often helped Conor look after the animals. She reckoned that they should be as comfortable and happy as possible during their short lives.'

'And that made her a collaborator?'

'That's the twisted way their minds work,' he said bitterly. 'And it's probable they simply wanted to close us down. They knew that if they made enough trouble for us, our funding would dry up. We're an investment for LDPharma, not a charity.'

He looked at his watch and stood up.

'I can't hide away any longer, can I? I'll have to get back to the lab. But I'll drop that bottle of whisky off as soon as I can.'

Kate went with him to collect his bike from the back garden. He gave her a hug and said, 'Thanks for listening, Kate.'

It's not good enough, thought Kate, when she returned to the kitchen. As she emptied her untouched wine down the sink and washed their glasses, she was thinking over what Blake had said. It seemed as though she, Blake and Sam were the only ones who saw the connection between the various attacks. With the lab explosion blamed on nameless extremists, and Kerri's death labelled an accident, the police might think that

Candra's murder is connected to something in her personal life.

Outside the kitchen window another apple thumped to the grass, dislodged by the autumn temperature and the rising wind. It was time to go and shake an apple tree of her own, thought Kate. Who knew what might fall out of it?

First, though, she needed to make a phone call.

29

Kate kept her thumb on the bell until she heard the door at the end of the passage open and the unwilling footsteps approach.

As the front door opened, she removed her thumb and stuck her foot in the gap.

'Hi, Conor.'

'What you doing here? How d'you know I'd be at home?'

'I gather you called in sick this morning. Would that be because of Candra?'

'What?' He looked genuinely puzzled.

'Or perhaps you haven't heard what happened to her.'

'I don't know what you're on about.'

'Let me in and I'll explain.' She pushed against the door and it opened wider, allowing her to enter the narrow passageway. Conor slouched down to his room, seeming not to care whether she followed or not.

Conor's room was thick with a fug of cigarette smoke and dirty laundry, but Kate sat down on the same chair as before and ignored it.

'What's up with Candra, then?' Conor asked.

'She's been murdered.'

'What!'

'Her body was found this morning. It looks as though she's been shot.'

Conor sat on the bed, staring at her, trying to take in what he was hearing.

'It's going too far, Conor. You have to tell me who these people are.'

'What people—'

'Don't pretend you don't understand. You know I'm talking about the animal rights crowd. Or, more specifically, the group who have a list of names and addresses of the people who work at Blake's lab. The ones who tried to blow the place up, who sent a letter bomb to Kerri and then ran her over. The ones who've now murdered Candra. The police may have been stupid enough to put Kerri's death down as an accident, but they're not going to brush away Candra's, are they? Not if your friends have used a gun this time.'

Conor's mouth opened and closed a few times, then he said, 'You've got it wrong. It can't of been them.'

'Just give me their name, Conor. An address and phone number would be useful, also the names of anyone you know who's a member. And a website address, maybe?'

'What you going to do? Stomp round and accuse them of murder? If you're right, you'll be next on their list.'

'Just give me the details.' *I'll think about what I'll do with them once I'm out of here*, she thought.

'Mad bitch,' said Conor, but he found a scrap of paper and a biro and wrote something down for her nevertheless. 'Here you go,' he said, passing the paper across. 'And don't come bothering me again.'

Kate stuffed the paper into her pocket and stood up to leave.

'Thank you, Conor,' she said. 'I'll do just that.'

In the street, she looked at what he'd written.

A-Skwod, she read. With a name like that, they didn't sound like a group to be taken seriously, but you never knew. She'd do some digging when she got back to her computer.

On her way back to the main road, she walked past a small playground. She would have taken no notice of the group of teenagers gathered by the swings if her eye hadn't been caught by a familiar mop of red hair. One of the Dolbys? Yes. She saw it was Abi, draped over a youth who was definitely not Eric. She might have thought this was none of her business, but she could see they were smoking, and the unmistakable tang of weed reached her nostrils. Abi and her friend were sharing a spliff, and liberal as Sam and Emma were, Kate didn't think they'd approve of the idea. They might consider that Abi should be safely tucked up in her school library, too.

Forget it, she told herself. She had plenty of other things to concentrate on at the moment, and Emma could do without another child to worry about.

Kate knew that the first thing she had to do when she reached home was to contact Sam about Candra's death. He was powerless to do anything from so far away, but even so, he had a right to know.

She made a quick calculation: it was very late in China but she would try him on his mobile anyway. He picked up after two rings, as though he'd been waiting for her call.

'Sorry to be bringing more bad news, Sam,' she said. And she told him about Candra.

'They'll have to take Kerri's death seriously now, won't they?' he said, when he'd taken it in.

'I hope so.'

'And they'll have to look at the animal rights activists

too. Those thugs have been threatening direct action for weeks now and no one seems to have done anything to stop them.'

'Do you know anything about a group who call themselves the A-Skwod?' she asked.

'I've never heard of them,' he said. 'Are they new?'

'Could be. I'm trying to find out about them, but they're not advertising what they do anywhere I'm likely to look,' said Kate. 'So far the moderates have managed to hold up work on the new research block, but they haven't stopped it from going ahead, have they? Perhaps A-Skwod believe in direct action, of the illegal kind.'

'Keep looking, Kate.'

Kate wondered whether she'd achieve more than the police could with their resources, but she promised nevertheless. 'I'll email again when I have some news,' she said.

When she'd rung off, she thought she might as well look up the A-Skwod on the internet.

To her surprise, she found that they did in fact have their own website, even if badly designed and poorly written. There were one or two names mentioned, though these were obvious pseudonyms, like Labwrecker and RatsWiskers, but most of the content consisted of the usual anti-science polemic.

They did, however, have a logo: an oval frame enclosing the simple outline of a monkey's face with 'A-Skwod' across the top and, in smaller letters, 'Remember Henry' underneath. It looked familiar: some of the placards carried by marchers on the day of the lab explosion had featured the logo, she was pretty sure. Well, that connected the group to the march, but it didn't get her much further than that. And since anyone could download the logo from the website and use it on a banner, or even a T-shirt, it didn't tie LabWrecker – whoever he might be – into any of the violence, though his name gave a clue to his intentions.

And what about the time and place of Candra's death? Why would she have gone outside in her pyjamas? And why was she over by the dustbins? If the killer had come prepared to shoot her, why didn't he do so as soon as she opened the outside door?

It all spoke to Kate of premeditation, of planning, and of cold-blooded murder, not the hot-headed action of a fanatic. If LabWrecker or one of his fellow-members was responsible, they weren't ordinary thugs, that was clear.

The ideas were chasing themselves around in her head and she decided to go out for half an hour to clear them out.

She ambled towards St Giles, staring into every shop window to try to replace the disturbing images of Candra with something more frivolous. Little Clarendon Street usually provided sights distracting enough for the most dedicated window-shopper, but today nothing was working.

As she came out on to the wide, tree-lined road just at the point where it divided into two, Woodstock Road to the left and Banbury Road to the right, she glanced across to St Giles church in the centre. A footpath led through the churchyard which many people took when crossing from the Science Area to the western side of the road. A couple of students, backpacks slung over their shoulders, walked briskly, deep in conversation. Behind them, more slowly, came a man pushing a bike, also immersed in conversation with his companion, a slender woman with a platinum blond bob.

The woman was walking on his right, so that Kate couldn't make her out clearly enough to be sure who she was, but she could recognise now that the man was Blake Parker. Before she could get close enough to confirm her suspicion that it was Susie Browne he was talking to, the pair turned to their right and walked away up the Woodstock Road. A couple of vans and a double-decker bus blocked Kate's view, and the lights were against her as she waited to cross the road.

By the time the traffic had cleared, Blake and his companion were some way up the Woodstock Road, turning into a side street. Kate strode out, trying to catch them up, but as she approached the corner, she paused. They had stopped next to a parked car and the woman was climbing into the driving seat. Kate's view was still partially obscured by Blake and she hardly liked to come up and peer over his shoulder at the woman he was with.

The car drove towards Kate, the light reflecting off the windscreen so that Kate still couldn't see the woman's face properly. And yet she was sure it was Susie Browne, in the Chelsea tractor in which the Brownes had driven down to Oxford.

How odd. But of course there was no reason why Blake should have mentioned Susie Browne's name, since he was unaware that she and Kate knew one another.

But what about Jon? If Susie was on his doorstep, she was sure he would know about it. And if he did, why hadn't he mentioned it? Kate was trying to convince herself that their relationship was nothing but an old friendship, but if it was so innocent, surely he would have told her Susie was in town.

Her next problem was to decide whether she was going to mention what she had seen and ask for an explanation. It was, of course, the only thing to do. For the first time, she felt sympathy for Blake and his dilemma with Marianne. It would be so much easier to pretend nothing was happening and then hope that it, whatever 'it' was, would just go away.

But Jon wasn't Blake, or anything like him, and Kate could rest secure in the belief that nothing was going on between the two of them.

When Jon came in that evening he stood at the door to the sitting room, his nostrils twitching.

'Someone's been smoking,' he said.

'What?' queried Kate, who had left the glass doors open for the past two hours and washed up the saucer Blake had used as an ashtray. 'Surely not?'

Jon looked at the bottle of whisky which Blake had brought round as promised.

'I didn't realise we still had a full one of these,' he said.

'I wouldn't know,' said Kate.

Jon went to the kitchen, frowning slightly, and she heard the sound of cupboards opening as he collected the ingredients for that evening's supper.

'Shall I pour you a glass of wine?' she asked, hoping to improve the atmosphere.

'I see there's already a bottle of white open in the fridge,' he said pointedly.

'No, I haven't taken to solitary drinking,' she replied. 'A friend called round at lunchtime and was in need of a listening ear and a glass of plonk.'

'Why is it your friends only come to see you when their lives are falling apart?'

'That's unfair—' she started to say, but they were interrupted by the ringing of Jon's mobile.

He glanced at the screen, looked surprised, and said, 'Hi, Susie.'

The soft voice spoke for some time before he said, 'I don't think she knows any more than you do, but I'll pass your message on.'

'What was that about?' asked Kate when he had hung up.

'Susie was ringing to thank you for a wonderful weekend,' he began.

'That's kind of her, but she's already written me a thank-you note,' said Kate.

'And secondly,' he continued, 'she was very upset to hear about Kerri. She really took to the girl, if you remember, and she wondered if you'd heard any more about how she died and whether the police are any nearer to finding out who was responsible.'

'The police still think it was a hit-and-run,' said Kate, not wanting to fill Jon in on the latest news. She had no wish to discuss Candra's death after her gruelling session with Blake. 'Apart from Sam, I don't think anyone seriously believes it was a deliberate act. And as far as I know, they're no nearer finding the person responsible. The best guess is that it was a joy-riding kid.'

'Yes, that's what I told her,' said Jon, and choosing the largest chef's knife, he turned back to the onion placed in the centre of the chopping board and reduced it to tiny fragments with an enviously fluent action of his strong wrist.

After dinner, which was, as usual when Jon was doing the cooking, excellent, he left Kate loading the dishwasher, picked up his jacket and said, 'I'm just going out for a while.'

'Really? Shall I come with you?'

'I'm meeting a colleague from work. We'll be talking shop,' he said briefly.

Kate heard the front door close and wondered what he and Susie (for she was sure that it was Susie that Jon was

302

meeting) had to talk about that she wasn't invited to hear.

Putting Jon out of her mind, she returned to her workroom and her computer to make up for some of the time she'd spent on her investigation during the day.

Much later, her draft of Chapter One was interrupted by the sound of Jon's footsteps on the stairs. She glanced at her watch: it was later than she'd thought. A moment later her workroom door opened and Jon's head appeared.

'Are you coming to bed?' he asked.

'In a minute. I'm just finishing off the chapter,' she said.

When he'd gone, she sat staring at her blank screen, again seeing Candra's body sprawled by the dustbins.

Next morning, having walked for some way along by the river and through Christ Church Meadow, Kate decided that the only way to stop herself from inventing ridiculous dramas about Jon and Susie would be to phone Blake Parker.

He answered immediately with his name.

'Kate Ivory here. Look, Blake, I know this sounds odd, but do you think you could tell me the name of the woman you were talking to in St Giles's churchyard yesterday – the woman with platinum blond hair?'

'You have had your spies out, then!'

'I just need to know her name. You saw her to her car. She was driving a four-by-four.' She couldn't keep the disapproval out of her voice.

'It was a Freelander HSE Td4.'

'What?'

'You asked about her motor.'

'I don't care about her bloody motor.'

'OK. Don't get all uptight on me. If it's so important to you, her name's Susannah Browne and she's the expert sent down from London by our chief funder to check on how we're earning the money they've given us.'

'Is she staying long?'

'Originally, no.' Blake sounded amused at her interest in Susie. 'Like I said, she was down here taking a look at all LDPharma's various interests in Oxford, and she was pissing us off by spending the bulk of her time with our unit. But with Candra's death and the mess it left us in, she's turned out to be invaluable. She has all the right qualifications to take over Candra's work and write the report on the latest batch of results. If she's as good as I think she is, we'll get our next tranche of funding, no problem.'

'Well, that's good news.'

'So what's your interest in our Mrs Browne?'

'Oh, it happens that she's a friend of Jon's. She was staying with us just a couple of weeks ago, so I was surprised to see her back in Oxford so soon. It's odd she hasn't been in touch to let us know she's here.'

'The poor woman hasn't had a minute to call her own. She's here to work, after all, and I don't suppose she's thought about socialising. I imagine she spends any spare time she gets on the phone to her devoted husband and charming small child.'

'I'm sure you're right. Thanks, Blake.'

'Though there is one thing.'

'Yes?'

'Nearly every time her phone rings, she looks at the number and pulls a face.'

'So? Maybe it's her bank manager.'

'I doubt he's much of a threat to the Brownes. But as a matter of fact, she told me that she was being pursued by an old boyfriend who wouldn't take no for an answer.'

'It could have been anyone, couldn't it? I'm sure there must have been many men in her past, and I'm sure several of them would want to keep in touch.' She could hear herself banging on about Susie, but she couldn't stop.

'Of course.'

'I'm sure she wasn't referring to Jon.'

'Most unlikely.'

'Right.'

'I'm glad we've got that straight,' he said, amused. 'Now, do you think we can meet up again for a drink, Kate?'

'Why not?' she replied.

30

Kate needed to speak to Emma again, to keep her up to speed with what was happening at the lab, though the last thing she wanted to do was give her more bad news.

'Is it important?' Emma sounded as harassed as ever when she answered the phone.

'Afraid so, Emma.' And Kate told her as briefly and unemotionally as possible about Candra's death.

'I thought you'd want to know,' she added. 'After all, Sam knew her quite well, even if they weren't close friends. And he might mention it when he gets in touch, so it's as well for you to be prepared.'

'*If* he gets in touch,' said Emma. 'You seem to know far more about him than I do at the moment.'

'We didn't want to bother you, knowing how much you had on your plate.'

'You're right.' Emma sighed. 'Things are increasingly difficult with Jenny and her family. I can't seem able to get through to people how urgently she needs help.'

'And meanwhile you're taking on all the responsibility.'

'I shall surprise you one of these days by taking a week off and spending it entirely on myself.'

'Good idea!'

'Have I told you about Abigail?'

'No.'

'Twice this last week she's stayed out until the early hours of the morning. And she won't give me any proper explanation of where she's been and what she's been doing. She's suddenly turned so stroppy and confrontational, Kate, I can't get any sense out of her.'

'Is she still seeing Eric?'

'No, thank goodness.' Emma didn't sound as certain as her words suggested. 'Mind you, she's gadding about more than ever, and I'm not sure where or who with.'

Unfortunately, Kate could imagine all too well what Abigail had been doing, but she didn't think this was the moment to tell Emma. 'She could have fallen in with a dodgy crowd. Have you tried talking to her about it?'

'You've found something out, Kate. I can tell. What is it? What do you know?'

'I'm not investigating any of your children!' Kate protested.

'Please tell me what you know.'

There was no arguing with Emma when she was in this mood, so Kate told her what she'd seen on her way home from speaking to Conor.

'Who were they?' demanded Emma.

'I've no idea. Just ordinary-looking teenagers.'

'Yobs, you mean?'

Kate didn't reply.

'What time was this, by the way?'

'Half past two, three o'clock, maybe.'

'She's cutting school.'

'It's possible.'

'I shall certainly speak to her when she gets in.'

Kate hoped Emma wouldn't tell Abi who had grassed her up (as Abi would probably put it).

'Have I got it all wrong, Kate?'

'What in particular?' asked Kate, mystified.

'The children. Once they get to fourteen or so, I like to treat them as friends. I hoped that I'd brought them up with the right principles and now I feel I can rely on them to lead decent lives. But maybe I'm wrong. Maybe I should keep prying into their affairs and telling them how to behave. What do you think?'

'Me? I know nothing about children, Emma. I wouldn't dream of giving advice to you, of all people.'

'I seem to have forgotten entirely what it's like to be young,' said Emma wistfully. 'I don't think you've ever lost the knack.'

'Really, Emma, you have children that anyone would be proud of. Just trust your gut instinct, as usual.'

'Gut instinct?' she said doubtfully. 'I'll try to remember what that feels like. Thank you, Kate.'

George contacted her next, suggesting lunch. This time they arranged to meet at a pub closer to his office.

'Sorry I can't manage a longer lunch break,' he said. 'I have to be back in an hour, but I'd like your views on a couple of matters.'

'Sounds intriguing,' she said a little later, biting into her chicken sandwich as they enjoyed the autumn sunshine in the pub's tiny garden. 'What's it about?'

'To begin with, I gather that you and I are in agreement about young Sam: he shouldn't come back from China until his nine months are up. So I thought I'd better do something about arranging Kerri's funeral, as no one else seemed prepared to take it over. I've met the two members of her family who bothered to turn up in Oxford, but frankly I can understand why she left home and why she didn't keep in touch with them. When they reached the point of suggesting that Kerri had only received what was coming to her, I stopped trying to involve them in the arrangements and contacted her housemates instead.'

'I'm getting the message that you're the one who's going to write the large cheque at the end of this story, George.'

'Well, the funeral won't be anything very grand, and anyway, I'm the one who's lucky enough to be able to afford it,' he said shortly. 'I've spent time with Mel and Lynne, who were her closest friends in the house they shared, and spoken to the other two housemates. And Conor. I've met Conor.'

There was a shift in his tone that indicated that his opinion of Conor was no better than her own. 'He was at Sam's party,' she said. 'I didn't speak to him much, but he was in the group under the trees with Sam and Kerri.'

'I was too involved with young children and ancient aunts to take notice of him then,' said George. 'But since I've been making the arrangements for the funeral – it'll be at the crematorium at eleven thirty on Thursday next week, by the way, if you'd like to be there – I've talked quite a bit to Mel and Lynne. They told me he's been hanging around at their place a lot since Kerri died, and talking wildly about Kerri and the animal rights campaigners, and insisting that none of it was his fault. To put it in their terms, they thought he was going mental. They told me about the folder of addresses found in Kerri's room, by the way. But I think that's something we might keep from Sam.'

'I've sorted that out: it was nothing to do with Kerri. I confronted Conor and persuaded him to admit that he's the one who was involved with the extremist wing of an animal rights

310

group, A-Skwod he called it, and that he passed on the names and addresses of the lab staff to the nutters.'

'If Conor had the list, how come it was found in Kerri's room?'

'He planted it. He admitted that, too.'

'Really? Did he say whether he and Kerri were in it together? I wouldn't be surprised: they were two of a kind, weren't they?'

'What do you mean?' asked Kate sharply.

'Young, idealistic, undereducated.'

'I don't think—'

'Seriously, Kate, no one would want it to end this way, but don't you think Sam's well out of it? She was hardly his type, was she?'

'Sam's the one to decide that, I'd have thought.'

'I can see we won't agree,' said George dismissively. 'But to get back to Conor, I think he got cold feet when he saw what was happening – especially the letter bomb, and then Kerri's death. It was no longer a joke – just a load of graffiti and a few threatening phone calls – it was serious. And there's no way he'd want to be associated with A-Skwod if they got caught. I suppose he thought he'd be in the clear if everyone believed that Kerri was the link. He's not finding it so easy to convince himself, though.'

'So he thinks they killed her, and Candra too?'

'Isn't it obvious?'

'Could be.'

George paused, having said all he intended about Kerri and Conor. 'And there's another thing,' he said eventually. 'I'm getting quite worried about Emma. She's simply taken on too much at the moment.'

'Emma always does.'

'But this time it's different. I've never seen her so stressed and, well, *angry*.'

'You think she's about to explode and do something outrageous?'

'I can't see it, myself,' said George.

'Nor me.'

'But something's going to happen, I'm sure.'

Next morning a second postcard came from Roz for Kate which put Kerri and Candra, and even Emma, out of her mind.

'Leaving Portugal shortly. Letter follows. Roz.'

'What on earth is this about?' she asked Jon.

'Your mother enjoys creating mysteries,' said Jon. 'And she enjoys winding you up, probably because you fall for it every time.'

'You could be right, I suppose. But—'

'There's nothing you can do until she gets in touch again. Just forget about it.'

But as Jon left for work, Kate was still staring at her mother's postcard, with its picture of blue Atlantic rollers breaking on a rocky black shore.

31

It was inevitable that one day Blake would turn up at Kate's house when Jon was at home.

First she heard the sound of the key in the door and Jon calling out, 'I'm home!' Scarcely had he told her that he had knocked off early to make up for some of the long evenings he'd worked recently when the bell rang and Kate opened the door to find Blake standing there.

Before she had a chance to respond, he was inside the house and making for the kitchen, saying, 'I've had a phone call from the man I told you about, Joe Greenham.'

'Sorry, you've lost me already,' she replied, following him.

'The man from the pharma who used to audit our results.'

'Oh, yes.'

'He was warning me, in fact, and I thought you'd like to hear about it.' He paused at the open kitchen door, looked back at Kate and asked, 'Any chance of a cup of tea?'

From inside the room Jon said, 'I don't see why not. The kettle boiled only a few minutes ago and Kate usually has chocolate biscuits hidden away for favoured guests.'

Blake stood in the kitchen, looking mildly uncomfortable, as Kate opened cupboard doors and found what she was looking for.

'Chocolate biscuits,' she said, putting the plate on the table. 'Any particular kind of tea, Blake?'

'Bog standard does me,' he replied. She hadn't noticed before that he had a northern accent, but perhaps he was putting it on for Jon's benefit.

'You two haven't met before, have you?' said Kate, into the pause.

'You must be Jon,' said Blake. 'I'm a friend of Sam Dolby's, Blake Parker.'

'Ah,' said Jon, still wondering why Blake looked so much at home in Kate's kitchen.

Kate joined them at the table and helped herself to a biscuit. 'Tell me about the warning from Joe Greenham,' she said.

'It was about your Susannah Browne,' said Blake.

'Susannah Browne?' asked Jon.

'Yes. To cut a long story short, Joe was ringing to warn me she wasn't to be trusted and that I should watch my back.'

'But I've know her for years. She's a friend of mine and I can't believe anyone would warn you against her, let alone describe her as untrustworthy. Who is this Joe Greenham?'

Jon will be suggesting pistols at dawn in a minute, thought Kate. 'Tea,' she said. 'Sugar, Blake?'

'No thanks. And Joe's someone I've known and trusted for years.'

'Did he have something specific in mind, or was it just a general beef about a colleague?' asked Kate.

'It was specific. You have to understand that it's nothing personal, Jon. I've only recently met Susie Browne, and I find her charming, but it's right out of character for Joe to ring me like this: we're not on close terms. We've talked in the past about work, but I don't know anything about him outside the office, and I've never heard him gossip about any of his colleagues at LDPharma. He certainly wouldn't phone me just to have a general moan about things.'

'Or to stick the knife in while Susie's back was turned?'

'No, not that, either.'

'Go on, then,' said Jon grudgingly.

'Since she's your friend, I'll miss out some of the more colourful epithets he applied to her, but his general message was that she's determined to make herself serious money, and nothing and no one will be allowed to get in her way. If she shafted me and the lab while she was doing so, "she really wouldn't give a fuck" – that's what the man said.'

'He was implying she'd do something illegal?' asked Kate.

'He didn't exclude that possibility.' Blake could be as pompous as Jon when he tried.

'And you mean money for herself, not just her company?'

'Of course.'

'I don't understand how she would get her hands on the money,' said Jon. 'I don't imagine the lab has much floating around.'

'Have you ever heard of stock options?' asked Blake.

'I've heard of them, but writers don't get paid that way, unfortunately,' said Kate.

'Well, LD's executives do, and if she makes the company look more profitable, so that their stock rises in value, she makes a lot of money. LD are happy and so is she. Not to mention *rich*.'

'Doesn't her husband work for LDPharma too?' asked Kate, remembering when she had asked Jon for basic information about the Brownes.

'Do you mean *Gary* Browne?' queried Blake.

'Yes.'

'I hadn't made the connection: Browne's a common enough name. But if it's the same man, then between them they know more about the lab's situation than I'd thought.'

'And they'd double their profit,' said Kate.

'They would.'

'Now we're getting to something like a proper motive,' exclaimed Kate. 'Money. *Lots* of money.'

'And Joe reckons Susie Browne would do anything to get her hands on it.'

'Are we really talking about the same person?' asked Jon. 'This doesn't sound like the woman I know.'

'Let me describe my Mrs Browne,' said Blake. 'She is beautiful, with a classic profile, platinum blond hair and a Freelander HSE Td4.'

'Five point seven Hemi V8 Overland,' said Jon.

'That's a Jeep,' said Blake.

Kate was about to switch off while the men argued about motors, but she had a good visual memory and she said, 'Just a minute,' as she closed her eyes to call the images back. 'As a matter of fact you're both right. Susie and Gary drove to Oxford in a Jeep. I don't know exactly what model it was, but it *was* a Jeep. And when I saw her in St Giles, the vehicle she was driving had "Land Rover" written across the front.'

'So? They're a two-car family,' said Jon.

'But Gary said that their other car is a Toyota. A small car for driving in town.'

'They must have sold the Jeep and bought the Land Rover in the last couple of weeks. So what?'

'The Jeep was brand new, or very nearly. And it had a specially fitted seat for Freddie. Why would they want to change it?'

'And for something inferior,' said Blake.

'I'm not sure I'd agree with that,' said Jon.

'Before you start on about torque and compression ratios' – both men looked scornful at her pretence at knowledge –

'can we get back to the fact that Susie Browne changed her car at about the time that Kerri Ashton was killed by a hit-and-run driver?'

That shut the two men up. They both sat and stared at her.

'That was quite a sideways jump, Kate,' said Blake. 'I'm not sure I follow your train of thought. We've all agreed Susie likes money, and earns a packet. Well, she can spend it on a third car if she wants, can't she?'

'Of course. But she wouldn't buy a Land Rover,' said Kate. 'She'd want something long and low and silver that made vroom-vroom noises when she hit the accelerator, especially if she was driving from London to Oxford without Freddie in the car. She'd have traded in the Toyota, not Gary's Jeep.'

'This is insane,' said Jon. 'Don't encourage her to fantasise like this, Blake. Her imagination's always on overdrive as it is.'

'How could we find out about the motor for sure?' mused Blake.

'Jon could ring Gary up and have a lads' chat about it,' said Kate. 'Go on, Jon. Take the phone into the other room and tell him you want to buy yourself a four-by-four, then ask him which make and model you should get. We won't embarrass you by listening in.'

'I thought we were going to buy a house, not a car,' said Jon.

'Try a bit of fantasising; use your imagination,' she replied. 'This is fiction, remember?'

'I don't like lying,' he muttered. 'But on the other hand, I'd like to know about that car of theirs. And I've got his mobile number here somewhere . . .' At which point Kate and Blake knew they'd won.

When Jon had left, phone in hand, Blake said, 'Have you changed your mind about the animal rights extremists? Didn't you and Sam Dolby believe they were responsible for Kerri's death, and Candra's, too?'

'We did, yes. But we kept coming up against the fact that the two deaths were in a different league from the other unpleasant things that were happening. We'd got used to demonstrations and threats, even the occasional letter bomb and the explosion at the lab, but driving your car at a vulnerable young woman? *Shooting* Candra, for God's sake? Doesn't that sound like different people?'

'Kerri's death could still have been an accident. Candra's could be related to something in her background we know nothing about. And why on earth would Susie want to kill Kerri? What would it have achieved? And then Candra – she'd barely met her.'

'You're more likely to know the answer to those questions than me, though I do have an idea or two. And you've already pointed out that Candra could be inflexible. I can't see Susie liking that.'

'Candra was *honest*,' said Blake.

'And no one's accused Susie of *that* yet.'

'You've taken a couple of unsupported opinions and a load of suppositions and turned them into an accusation of murder – double murder!'

'You didn't see Susie and Gary in action, Blake. The weekend they were staying with us, they really only came alive when they were talking about their expensive possessions. Well, that and their son, Freddie, I suppose.'

'Suppose they have a cast-iron alibi?'

'I bet it's a case of an evening at home listening out for a sleeping Freddie. They'd just be backing each other up. It would mean nothing.'

Before Blake could respond, Jon returned.

'Did you speak to him? What did he say?' asked Kate eagerly.

'He was rather uptight about it. I tried to get him talking about the Jeep, but he said he'd found it unsatisfactory, though he wouldn't be specific. And then he told me that it had been stolen and found a couple of days later, burned out in a field in Bedfordshire.'

'Convenient!'

'When I asked what he'd bought to replace it, he said it was "just a runaround". And when I pushed him, he said that yes, it was the Land Rover that Susie was using now.'

'Told you so!' said Kate.

'You're suggesting that one of them used the Jeep to run down Kerri?'

'My money's on Susie doing the driving,' said Kate. 'And then Gary took it off into a field and torched it to destroy any evidence.'

'You haven't convinced us yet, Kate. It's possible that's how Kerri was killed, but there's nothing to say Susie or Gary was responsible.'

'I'm sure between the three of us we could work it out,' said Kate. 'They must have made a mistake somewhere.'

'You're making assumptions about my friends that I can't accept.'

'You must have doubts about them by now,' said Kate.

'Do you mind if I smoke?' asked Blake, getting out his cigarettes. 'It helps me to think.'

Kate found the same saucer as before and placed in front of him. As Blake lit up, drew in the smoke and then exhaled, Jon sniffed assessingly.

'I see,' he said.

The other two looked at him enquiringly, but he didn't

explain. Instead he said, 'I reckon it's not too early to pour ourselves some of that excellent single malt that somehow managed to reproduce itself the other day. Let's get rid of this tea. You'd rather have whisky, Blake, wouldn't you?'

He poured the cold tea into the sink and brought out small tumblers.

'Whisky for you, Kate?'

'Yes, please.'

The mood was easing, she noticed. But they still had some tricky problems to sort out. Jon passed around the whisky and they lifted their glasses in unison and took an appreciative sip.

Eventually Blake said, 'Susie doesn't strike me as someone who makes mistakes.'

'Nor me,' said Jon. 'Though she might lose her temper and do something stupid, I suppose.'

'Like shooting Candra?' suggested Kate.

'That would have to be Gary,' said Blake.

'How can you say that when you've never met him?' asked Jon. 'We don't even know whether he owns a gun.'

'The police will have checked it out, surely?' asked Kate.

'Why should they? Not having your brilliant imagination, they won't have two law-abiding, solid citizens like the Brownes down as suspects. And anyway, Susie and Gary had little or no contact with Kerri, or Candra. What would make Susie set off like a maniac in her four-by-four to mow down Kerri, and Gary to rush off to shoot Candra?'

'Is it likely he has a gun?' asked Blake.

'I believe you can buy one quite easily if you know where to look,' said Kate.

'You've been reading too many redtops,' said Blake.

'Jon, could you bring the subject up, casually, with Gary?' asked Kate.

'First I question him about his Jeep, then I ask him if he owns a gun. If you're right about what they've done, he'll put me at the top of his hit list.'

'Even if you did ask him, I don't suppose he'd give you a straight answer,' said Blake.

After a few seconds' pause, Jon said, 'And in any case, we get back to the point that Susie hardly knew Kerri, and she can't have learnt enough over one Saturday night and Sunday lunchtime to give her a motive for murder.'

'I think she killed her by mistake,' said Kate.

'*What?* How can you make a mistake about a thing like that?'

'She did talk to Kerri for a long time, in fact. And she did a lot of listening, too. At the time I thought she was just being kind, taking notice of Kerri, drawing her out of her shell.'

'Maybe that's exactly what she was doing,' said Jon.

'There's something else,' said Blake. 'Something more that Joe Greenham told me.'

Jon looked up expectantly.

'He said that before coming up to Oxford she'd spent a long time in the office looking through the file on my research unit – not the other Oxford labs they have an interest in, but specifically *ours*. Now there weren't just scientific reports and analyses of our potential in the file; there was a section labelled "Intelligence" which was full of press cuttings and memos. "Intelligence" was an overstatement: they contained nothing much except gossip.'

'What gossip?' asked Jon.

'There was a lot about the way the animal rights people were targeting our lab, how they'd hindered our work, and how bad the publicity was, that sort of thing. And then there were memos saying that it looked as though there was someone in the lab who was actually working against us, passing on information to the activists. The conclusion was that this was one of the younger members of staff: Sam Dolby, Kerri Ashton or Conor Mawfey. I asked Joe who the hell was writing this stuff about us, but he wouldn't tell me, even if he knew.'

'So she'd done her homework before coming to Oxford,' said Kate.

'Yes. She would have done. She's that sort of person,' said Jon. It was possible that disenchantment with Susie was creeping in, noted Kate.

'There's more,' said Blake, cutting in. 'I said the Intelligence file was little more than gossip. Well, it told her that Sam wasn't a strong suspect – his family is well known in Oxford, he's serious about wanting to be a scientist and he was about to leave for China. Suspicion fell, according to the reports, on Kerri and Conor. One or the other. Just possibly both, in collusion. Now, if Susie believed that stuff, she also believed that whoever was responsible was going to do a lot of damage to our hopes of coming up with new drugs that could be exploited by LDPharma. Instead of boosting the value of her stock options, she'd see their price go down the plug. I believe she could have considered removing Kerri as a simple solution to a messy problem.'

'I just don't believe it,' said Jon. 'You're talking about a highly intelligent woman. As you said, she was doing her homework before coming to Oxford. She'd have made sure she had the right person before doing anything . . . final.'

'I notice you're not arguing that she's incapable of murder,' said Blake.

'I don't need to argue it. The idea's ridiculous.'

'If Susie had read the file carefully, as I'm sure she did, she would have seen just how close we are to announcing a breakthrough. I know that sounds like a media headline, but that's the way you have to talk up your results. To complete our work we need funding. To get funding we have to look like we're going to make money for the investors. And to do that, we have to produce credible results.'

'And what does any of that have to do with Kerri?' asked Kate.

'The demonstrators and direct-action crowd were drawing a lot of unwelcome attention to our unit. The explosion they caused at the lab held us up for several days. It also lowered morale and made everyone jittery. Then there were all the personal attacks. Who likes to live like that? If they could scare off some of the staff, then they could undermine our work. And why was the spotlight on *us*, rather than on some other group? Because, Susie had worked out, we had Kerri working with us. The attacks started soon after she joined.'

'When did Conor join you?' asked Kate.

'Good question. He actually joined a couple of months before Kerri. But he, as I'm sure you both know by now, *was* the animal rights mole, if you'll excuse the expression. I imagine he kept his head down for a while, until another two new people had joined the staff. It would have been too obvious if he'd encouraged his friends to attack us as soon as he arrived.'

'He didn't strike me as a particularly fanatical person,' said Kate. 'He's too indolent. And I'm not even sure how convinced he is that animals have rights.'

'I think he has a strong anarchic streak. He did it because he enjoyed it. It lessened the boredom of his life, I imagine.'

'But why would Susie have been so sure it was Kerri rather than Conor?' asked Kate.

'Because Kerri was Conor's friend, and she'd absorbed the

stuff he spouted about animal rights. She agreed with them in principle, of course, but she would never have condoned violence. But when she chatted away to Susie, she would have been parroting standard anti-vivisection propaganda.'

'But I don't see how Susie could ever kill Kerri,' said Jon. 'Really, she wouldn't kill anyone. It's a horrible thought.'

'How about Gary?' asked Blake. 'Maybe she told him what she'd found out and he was the one who went berserk and drove off into the night in his Jeep.'

'I had the impression that Susie was the brains and the driving force in that relationship,' said Kate.

'It's difficult to see how he can't have known what she was doing,' put in Blake. 'If Susie was driving the car, then he must have been at home, looking after the child.'

'Maybe she told Gary she was off to her pottery class,' suggested Kate.

'At midnight? In a storm-force wind and torrential rain? What do you think, Jon? Susie or Gary?'

'I can't see either of them doing such a dreadful thing,' Jon replied, but he sounded less convinced than he had before.

'Susie wanted the best of everything for herself and for her family,' said Kate. 'Remember the place in France they told us about? And then there are Freddie's music lessons, and I don't believe she'll want to send him to the local Sure Start nursery, will she? Or then on to the primary school down the road, let alone the inner-city comprehensive? You can bet that it will be only the best for young Freddie Browne. Eton and Oxford. They're old-fashioned enough to believe that would be the very best. And an education like that costs money. A lot of money.'

'They're both earning,' pointed out Jon.

'And spending,' rejoined Kate. 'Even if they bought it for

peanuts, refurbishing an entire village in Provence doesn't come cheap.'

'Bloody hell! Is that what she's doing?' asked Blake. Kate nodded.

'Don't you think someone should take a look at their car?' he said. 'The one they were driving when they came to Oxford for the weekend. Even if they set fire to it, there might still be evidence to link it to Kerri's death.'

'It must have been looked at when it was found, after they reported it stolen,' said Jon. 'And I imagine that nothing *was* discovered.'

'They wouldn't have been looking for signs of murder, after all,' said Blake. 'And I imagine it's been crushed to the size of a tin can by now.'

'If Susie killed Candra, too, it's possible that someone saw her – she's not someone you forget, is she?' said Kate. 'And there'd be Candra's blood on her clothes, and probably traces in whichever of their cars she drove that night.'

'Unless she's got rid of her clothes by now,' said Jon. 'She could have worn a tracksuit and disposed of it afterwards.'

'There would have been traces of her DNA on it as well as Candra's, wouldn't there?' said Blake.

'She's not stupid. She'll have incinerated it, composted it, maybe dropped it into a lake,' said Kate.

'It's not that easy to get rid of blood. I bet there'd be something she's overlooked,' said Jon.

'We need to get our skates on. Every day that passes makes it less likely there'll be any evidence to find.'

'How do you think you're going to get your hands on this evidence?' asked Jon.

'I thought the police might do that, once we'd told them all we know,' said Kate.

'They'll thank you politely for contacting them and put your "information" at the bottom of the heap of a thousand other wild theories with no basis in fact.'

'Oh, I'm not so sure—'

Blake interrupted her. 'How about inviting Susie round and then firing questions at her until she tells us the truth?' he asked. Then he added, 'As a matter of fact, I know she's driving back to London later this evening and won't be back for at least a week. There's something she has to attend to.'

'Then we need to get hold of her straight away,' said Kate. 'We can't let her go back to London until she's answered our questions.'

'More whisky?' asked Jon. The other two pushed their glasses towards him for a refill. 'I think you're both mad,' he said flatly.

'I'd like to ask her about the car,' continued Kate. 'When did she report it stolen, I wonder?'

'Where was she on the two nights in question?' asked Blake. 'And where was Gary? Do we have her mobile number, by the way?'

'I have it,' said Jon. 'Why?'

'I want to speak to her. I want her to come over and answer my questions. You two can back me up,' said Kate.

'No way,' said Jon.

'Not a good idea, Kate,' said Blake.

'But you just said you'd like an answer to those questions.'

'That's all very well,' said Jon.

'I don't think it's down to us,' said Blake.

'You two are just wimps!'

'We're being sensible. And how much of that whisky have you drunk?'

'Hardly any. I'm quite sober. I think I'll pop over to the lab.'

326

'She'll have left by now,' said Blake. 'I expect she's back at her hotel.'

'The Randolph? The Old Bank?'

'Neither of those,' said Blake.

'Then it'll be the new one they've opened where the prison used to be.'

Blake was silent.

Jon said, 'No, Kate!'

But Kate had picked up her keys and pulled on a jacket from the hook behind the door.

'Don't worry about me,' she said. 'I'm sure it's Gary who used a gun, not Susie. I'll be safe enough while he's at home, reading Freddie his bedtime story.'

'Please don't do it, Kate,' said Jon. But his words were drowned by the sound of the front door closing.

'I expect she'll be all right,' said Blake. He was slurring his words, and Jon unobtrusively moved the whisky bottle out of his reach.

'Why did you have to give away the name of her hotel?' he asked.

'I didn't! You can't accuse me of that! She guessed it, didn't she? It wasn't my fault.' Blake was reaching the truculent stage of drunkenness. 'It's a pity Susie wasn't at the lab, though. You can't get in there without a swipe card. Kate would have had to come home again without seeing her.'

'Pity you didn't send her in the wrong direction, then.'

'I couldn't tell a lie!'

Blake was slumped across the table, about to lay his head down on his arms. Then he'll fall asleep, thought Jon, and I'll won't be able to shift him till the morning.

'Don't you think we ought to go after her?' he asked.

'Wha'?'

'I'll make some coffee. You need to sober up and then we must follow her. After all, Kate's not going to persuade Susie to stroll quietly down to the police station and dictate her confession to a friendly policeman, is she?'

Blake raised his head. 'You don't think she's in danger, do you?'

'Not at the moment. What I'm afraid of is that she'll warn Susie that we're on to her, and then Susie and Gary will make quite sure that there's no evidence left for the police to find.'

It took Blake a few moments to absorb so many ideas, then he said, 'Good thinking. Where's that coffee, then?'

32

It wasn't far to walk from Kate's house to Susie's hotel, along Walton Street and down towards the station. By the time she reached the end of the road, the cool air was starting to counteract the glow from the whisky, and Kate was having a moment's hesitation over what she was intending to do and say when she saw Susie.

Susie's appearance – slim, expensively suited and high-heeled – didn't fill her with any trepidation. Yet if the three of them were right, this same elegant woman had committed two cold-blooded murders, all in a frenzy of greed. No, the word 'frenzy' could surely never apply to Susie.

There was a breeze blowing now, and it brought scurries of rain that dashed against Kate's face and made her wish she'd worn something more substantial than a linen jacket. The street lights reflecting off the greasy pavements gave her fellow-pedestrians an unnatural pallor.

Away from her kitchen and the comforting presence of Jon and Blake, the story she had elaborated about Susie seemed flimsy, at best. She had planned on barging into Susie's hotel room and demanding to know the truth about the night Kerri was killed. Where was Susie? What had she been doing? Where was the car she was driving that day? But with every step nearer to the hotel, she felt less certain of her ground.

Oh well, she thought, that had never stopped her plunging

into a tricky situation in the past. Forget about confronting Susie; she would be at her calm and reasonable best, just asking for information, not accusing the woman of murder – erm, *two* murders.

As she turned over the possibilities in her mind, she saw she was approaching the hotel. The conversion was elegant, but viewed from the outside, the crenellated grey-stone building was as grim as it had ever been as a jail. However, the atrium lights were shining brilliantly through the glass, beckoning her in.

'I wish to see Mrs Susannah Browne,' she told the receptionist. 'If you could tell her that Jon Kenrick's friend Kate Ivory is here.'

After a moment's conversation, the receptionist gave her the room number and told her to go up. 'Mrs Browne is expecting you,' she said.

I doubt it, thought Kate.

Thick metal doors clanging shut and bare brick walls were a constant reminder to the visitor that this building had once been a prison. Surely you wouldn't choose to stay here if you'd recently committed two murders?

Susie was standing in the open doorway when Kate reached her room. 'Come in, Kate,' she said, and Kate walked warily into a room decorated in black and cinnabar, with more exposed brickwork, and iron bars at the window. She stood just inside the door, looking around her, unwilling to hear the emphatic *clunk* as the door closed behind her.

'These are the original cells,' said Susie, in explanation. 'This one's been converted into a bedroom, and another's now the en suite.'

Susie had been packing; her open suitcase was half full of carefully folded clothes. A neat pile of underwear sat on the bed, waiting to be put away. On the table stood a carrier bag, bulging with presents for Freddie. A second bag, empty now of its toys, had been twisted into a knot. Susie's bedside reading, Kate saw, was a book on marketing strategies, which must have been even duller than the selection of Booker short-listed titles on her own bedside cabinet.

'You've just caught me,' said Susie. 'I'm driving back to London in ten minutes: I like to read Freddie a bedtime story.' She glanced at her watch and frowned. 'What was it you wanted, Kate? I need to get going if I'm to be home in time.'

'You'll miss the worst of the traffic if you leave in half an hour. You won't lose any time.'

'Really?' A touch of impatience coloured Susie's voice, but she sat down on one of the chairs and motioned to Kate to take the other. Kate's footsteps made no sound on the thick carpet as she crossed the room.

'I suppose the nanny's looking after Freddie at the moment?'

'Oh, no. Gary's with him. We spend as much time as possible with our son. Now, Kate, tell me what this is about.'

'I was hoping you could clear up an argument Jon and I were having about your car,' said Kate, watching Susie's face. There was a flash of something that might have been fear, but perhaps was merely annoyance. 'Tell me, when you came down to Oxford a couple of weeks ago, were you and Gary driving a Jeep, or was it a Land Rover?'

'What on earth are you on about?' Yes, Susie was annoyed, but there was a touch of uneasiness there, too. 'Did you really come here to ask such a stupid question? Couldn't you have phoned?'

Kate didn't reply, but waited for an answer. Impatiently, Susie said, 'I think it was the Jeep. The Overland.'

'And now you're driving a Land Rover, aren't you?'

'So what? We do have two cars, you know.'

'Yes. The Jeep and a Toyota. Gary told me. But I'm interested in why you had to get rid of the Jeep.'

'I don't see that it's any of your business.' Susie was frowning again.

'Indulge me,' said Kate. 'It's to settle an argument Jon and I were having, after all.'

'If you must know, we had a bit of an accident.'

Not the same story Gary had given Jon just an hour or so ago.

'How awful. What happened?'

'I don't like to talk about it, Kate,' she said. 'I was driving too fast, the weather was foul, I misjudged a corner and skidded into a tree.'

Almost convincing, thought Kate, though too well rehearsed for complete credibility.

'You weren't hurt, I hope?'

'No. I was lucky.'

Kate noticed she'd dropped the pretence of 'we'.

'Which night was that?' she asked.

'Why are you asking me all these questions?' Susie's voice was rising higher. Her slate-blue eyes shifted sideways to the bag containing Freddie's presents, and Kate saw again the empty plastic carrier twisted into a knot. And then she remembered where she had seen it before. Rising to her feet as casually as she could, she wandered towards the door. She didn't want Susie blocking her only exit if she could help it.

'It wasn't a tree you hit, though, was it, Susie?'

'Of course it was! What are you trying to say?'

'And you've been staying here in Oxford all week, haven't you?'

'What's it to you?'

'I find it odd that while you're in Oxford, two people are killed.'

'I didn't even know them!'

'Yes you did. You met and spoke to them and you reckoned they were standing in your way.'

'You're mad! Candra and Kerri were nothing to do with me!'

'You thought Kerri was responsible for bringing Blake's lab to the attention of the animal rights people, so you killed her. You were wrong about Kerri, you know. It wasn't her at all.'

'Yes it was. It must have been.'

'And then there was Candra. She wouldn't go along with your massaging of the results, would she?'

'I found her difficult to work with, certainly,' said Susie. 'She was very inflexible, but that doesn't mean I killed her. You're mad if you think that.'

'Her attitude was going to lose you a lot of money, though, wasn't it?'

'We're not exactly skint, you know.'

'But that's money for Freddie's future,' said Kate, watching Susie's face carefully. 'You weren't going to jeopardise that.'

'And anyway,' said Susie, 'I wasn't in Oxford the night Candra died. Ask anyone. I was at home in London with Freddie.'

'Oh,' said Kate, considering. 'In that case, it must have been—'

She had forgotten to watch the bathroom door, and now it had been pushed half open, a figure standing there.

'Hello, Gary,' she said. 'I thought you must be here.' She edged another inch or so towards the door.

'What made you think that?' he asked.

'You left your calling card on the table.' She indicated the knotted carrier bag.

'Silly of me.' He raised his right hand so that Kate could see the weapon he was carrying.

'I'd have thought you'd have got rid of that by now,' she said.

'You think it's the same one?'

He wasn't bothering to deny the suggestion he'd killed Candra. Kate felt herself stiffen with fear, and put all her effort into hiding the fact that she was scared. Why hadn't she noticed before how calculating he was. She was realising too late that Freddie was the only person who drew any real emotion from him. His only other enthusiasms were his possessions.

'I don't make mistakes,' Gary said.

'I imagine the gun's not traceable back to you, in any case,' she said.

'Of course not.' No, Gary wouldn't make a mistake like that.

'What are we going to do?' Susie wasn't nearly as calm as her husband. If there was a weak link here, it was definitely her rather than Gary. But Kate hadn't yet thought how to exploit the fact.

'So Susie killed Kerri and you killed Candra,' she said.

'Kerri's death was very nearly an accident,' said Gary.

'Really?'

'I was going to talk to her, that's all,' said Susie.

'But there she was, caught in your headlights, like a rabbit,' suggested Kate. 'And you couldn't resist putting your foot down.'

'No! It was a mistake. I meant to brake, really I did, but I hit the accelerator instead.' Even though the slate-blue eyes were round and innocent, Kate still didn't believe Susie had killed Kerri by accident, and she doubted anyone else would, either. 'I'm really sorry about it,' Susie continued. 'I've been feeling dreadful ever since it happened, but it wouldn't have done any good to come forward, would it? That wouldn't have brought Kerri back. It would just have made life difficult for Freddie.'

There was a short silence after this, broken by Gary.

'Well now, what are we going to do next?' He addressed the question to Susie, but Kate had the impression he'd made his mind up about it before coming out of the bathroom. She had edged within a foot of the door and now she measured the distance between herself and Gary: at least twelve feet, she guessed.

The handgun Gary was holding had a silencer attached to its barrel. If he pulled the trigger, the muffled sound of the shot was unlikely to bring anyone running to her rescue. However, the likelihood of his hitting her with a silenced weapon at that distance was remote, unless, of course, he was an expert shot. From the slight smile on Gary's face, he had probably followed her calculations and was wondering whether she was willing to take a chance.

She remembered that she had been so unwilling to lock herself into the former prison cell when she entered that she had failed to pull the door entirely shut. So she had a choice: turn her back on Gary, pull open the door, exit the room, slam the door shut – and run like hell. Risky, but possibly less risky than staying here while Gary decided how and when to kill her or otherwise persuade her to keep her mouth shut.

She was just shifting her weight to her left foot, ready to leave in a hurry, when the decision was taken away from her.

The door was pushed wide open and Jon appeared.

'Oh, dear,' said Gary. 'Now we'll have to construct a double accident. What a dangerous place Oxford is getting to be! And don't,' he added, dropping the facetious manner, 'think about trying to rush me. I'd kill at least one of you before you could get near the gun.'

And now Jon's blocking my exit, thought Kate. And I can't see him running for it if he had to leave me behind.

'Close the door, please, Jon,' said Gary.

Jon did as he was told, and this time Kate heard the heavy metallic *clunk* that meant it was really shut.

'I'd like you both to step away from the door, and move away from each other too,' continued Gary. 'It's going to take a little longer than I'd planned,' he said to Susie. 'Do you want to get back to London now? Freddie will be wondering where you are.'

'What about you?'

'I'll join you in an hour or two.'

It took Susie only a few seconds to put her remaining clothes in the suitcase, zip it shut, put on her coat and pick up the carrier of toys. She walked briskly between Kate and Jon and opened the door.

'Wha—' Susie's voice rose to a screech.

At the same time she came flying backwards into the room, dropping her case, scattering toys across the carpet. A denim-clad figure behind her had his arms clasped round her knees and was shoving her hard to the ground.

'Blake!' screamed Kate.

'Gary!' shrieked Susie from her ungainly position on the carpet.

There was a quiet *whump* and a sharp cry of pain from the tangle of bodies on the floor.

Shortly after that, Jon was in possession of the gun, Gary

was sitting on a chair, staring down the barrel, and Kate was sitting on top of Susie, pinning her to the floor. Jon used his spare hand to dial the police and request an ambulance.

Blake was sitting on the floor, leaning against the other chair, looking pale and surprised at the sight of his own blood soaking into the sleeve of his jacket.

As the howling of the ambulance siren faded into the drizzle, and the blue lights of the police car disappeared round the corner, Kate turned to Jon on the pavement outside the hotel.

'Just one thing,' she said.

'Hm?'

'Who do *you* think he was aiming at?'

'Ah,' he said.

'Exactly,' agreed Kate. '*I* think he meant to shoot Susie too.'

'Just Blake's bad luck he got in the way.'

'Susie's luck he's such a lousy shot.'

33

Next morning, unable to settle to any work, Kate was grateful when the phone rang to distract her from brooding about Susie Browne.

'I gather you've had a pretty hairy time recently,' said George Dolby.

'It's calming down again now.'

'Do you fancy a pub lunch? You could tell me all about it over a chicken pie and a glass of wine.'

'I'm catching up with some work, George. We'll have to put it off for a week or two.'

'Fair enough.' He sounded disappointed.

After she'd rung off, Kate wondered whether she'd made the right decision. What difference would a simple pub lunch make to her work? Or to her life, if it came to that.

Later she drove to the hospital to see how Blake was getting on. She found him still looking pale but sitting up in bed, his arm in a sling. Sitting next to him was a good-looking woman with a very worried expression on her face.

'This is Marianne,' he said, by way of introduction. 'My partner.'

'Isn't this dreadful!' said Marianne. 'He could have been killed!' She turned back to Blake. 'You could have been fucking killed, darling. What on earth were you doing, storming into a situation like that? The man had a fucking gun!'

'You're looking better than when I last saw you,' said Kate cheerfully. 'Have they told you when you can go home?'

'Not yet. But it'd better be soon. I'm dying for a cigarette.'

'But you've given up,' said Marianne tenderly.

'Have I?'

'Of course you have.'

Blake sent Kate a mute appeal over the top of Marianne's head, but she shook her head. She wasn't going to smuggle cigarettes into the hospital under Marianne's beady gaze. You wouldn't want to get on the wrong side of Marianne.

'This looks like the letter from Roz, at last,' said Jon the next morning, handing Kate her share of the post. 'Tell me about it this evening, I have to call into the police station again before going into the office.'

And so Kate was left on her own with a mug of strong coffee to read what her mother had written.

Dear Kate,

What I have to say may be a surprise to you.

You remember I told you a little while ago that I had married, while living in California, a man called António Soares da Silva. You may have wondered why I hadn't told you earlier, but there were good reasons, Kate.

António was a charming, amusing, good-looking and rich man. He is still all those things, but he has a lot more money now.

Oh my God! She's telling me she's fallen for him again, thought Kate in a panic.

What I didn't know at the time I married him was that his money came from the proceeds of crime. This was white-collar crime for the most part, but it hadn't always been like that. In short, he has people working for him who kill when he orders them to.

I won't go into all the details here, but when I read of the murder of my friends the Freeman family – Marcus, Ayesha and Jefferson – and particularly of the method that was used, I thought of António and I decided to get in touch with him again and find out if I was right.

Here in Porto we have met, and spent time together, and for the past week I have been staying at his house, well looked after by his servants and entertained by my charming former husband.

So they did get a divorce, thought Kate with relief. Or was her mother using the term 'former husband' loosely?

He is an honourable man, Kate. But his morality is not mine – nor yours. Last year he found out that the Freemans were encroaching on his territory, so to speak, when they extracted money from foolish old women (like your mother, I hear you thinking). And when he saw my name on a list of their victims he acted. As far as he is concerned, although we have been apart for a number of years, I am still his responsibility.

You will have guessed by now that he gave the order, and the Freemans were murdered.

If you were here now you would tell me to get on the next plane home, since there is probably no way António can be brought to justice. You may even believe that the Freemans deserved what was done to them.

341

I thought about going to the police with what I knew, but I doubt they'd take any notice. So I shall be returning to Oxford in the next few days, drawing a line under that particular period of my life.

And you and I will never talk about it.

With love,

Roz

When Jon came in that evening, he asked her about Roz's letter.

'Nothing much,' she said. 'She's had enough of being on holiday, I think. She says she'll return in the next few days. And then she'll be back to work, I imagine.'

'I thought she might have said more about her trip.'

'No.'

Jon caught the expression on her face and asked no more.

After a moment Kate took a deep breath and said, 'There was just one thing I'd like to clear up.'

'What's that?'

'Susie Browne. You still fancied her, didn't you?'

'Until I saw what she was really like.'

'So I wasn't imagining it. You did meet her while she was working in Oxford?'

'Just the once. Or maybe it was twice. It was nothing, I promise.'

They were both silent for a few minutes.

'Have we missed the news?' Jon asked, turning on the television.

'We might catch the local bulletin.'

Kate was leaving the room when from behind her she heard confused sounds of shouting coming from the television set, and she turned back to see what was happening.

'Another animal rights march through Oxford,' said Jon, lifting the remote to change the channel.

'No, wait a moment. I'd like to see this.'

'It's practically outside our door. That's St Giles, isn't it?'

'It must have been this afternoon, and I didn't notice.' She'd been thinking about Roz.

A thicket of banners and placards waved in front of the cameras, vying for media attention. Among the marchers Kate spotted a dishevelled forty-something woman, pushing her way through with her own, obviously home-made placard.

Remember Jenny, it read. *Speechless. Helpless. Dying.*

'It's Emma,' said Kate. 'Look, Jon, it's Emma.'

'What does she think she's doing? And who on earth is Jenny?'

'Jenny's her friend. And I believe that Emma's protesting in favour of animal testing, since it's the only hope that one day they'll find a cure for her disease. Though it will be too late for Jenny herself, obviously.'

As they watched, the cameras picked up Emma and followed her as she shoved her way to the head of the march. Microphones were pushed towards her face.

'Bastards!' she was shouting. 'Why don't you go home?' And she shook her placard, causing several marchers to step back nervously. By now she was face-to-face with the leader, and she lifted her placard high and brought it down on his head.

'Did she make it herself?' asked Jon. 'It was certainly sturdier than some of the others.'

Emma had disappeared from view, as had the leader of the march, and there was much confused shouting coming from the set. Then the cameras drew back as the police moved in to break up the fight.

'Do you think she's all right?' asked Kate.

'I imagine she's been arrested.'

'Oh, hell. I'll have to email Sam, I suppose.'

'There's nothing he can do. I should leave him in happy ignorance if I were you.'

'Who's looking after all the children, do you suppose? I should phone up and volunteer to help.'

'It all happened hours ago. Her husband will have bailed her out by now.'

'Is there any of that whisky left?'

'Enough for two glasses. You stay there, I'll go and get them.'

When they were sitting with their drinks Jon said, 'I thought it was time we talked again about getting ourselves a house and settling down.'

'Settling down?'

'House, garden, dog.'

'Children?' she asked.